The wo
enough c

G000245951

Miss Seeton Flies High

A MISS SEETON MYSTERY

Hamilton Crane

First published in 2018 by Farrago,
an imprint of Prelude Books Ltd
13 Carrington Road, Richmond, TW10 5AA, United Kingdom

www.farragobooks.com

ISBN: 978-1-78842-076-1

Have you read them all?

Treat yourself again to the first Miss Seeton novels—

Picture Miss Seeton
A night at the opera strikes a chord of danger when
Miss Seeton witnesses a murder . . . and paints a portrait
of the killer.

Miss Seeton Draws the Line
Miss Seeton is enlisted by Scotland Yard when her paintings
of a little girl turn the young subject into a model for murder.

Witch Miss Seeton
Double, double, toil and trouble sweep through the village
when Miss Seeton goes undercover . . . to investigate a local
witches' coven!

Turn to the end of this book for a full list of the series,
plus—on the last page—**exclusive access to
the Miss Seeton short story** that started it all.

Chapter One

Hidden from general view in a small wood halfway up a hill, two men lurked. Leaves rustled, birds sang, flying insects whirred and buzzed; only an occasional cough, or the rumble of traffic along the main road nearby, disturbed an otherwise unbroken silence. The pair had been waiting a long time. Conversation ran out quickly on a day as warm as this, when summer could still hold autumn at bay and the sun rode high above the horizon throughout most of the afternoon.

It glinted through the trees, and sent flickers of light from the binoculars resting on the dashboard of the car in which the two men sat. Muttering, the man in the passenger seat lifted the binoculars down and put them on his lap. "This is getting monotonous," he said.

His companion grunted, glancing at his bare left wrist. Normally he wore a watch, but he'd had to hide it in the pocket of his shirt because the links of his expanding metal bracelet caught the sun whenever he moved. His colleague had complained. "We could change seats," he'd offered, but the offer had been refused.

"Feels like hours," he said now.

"It is." The man in the passenger seat consulted his own, far cheaper watch with its non-reflective leather strap, and smirked for the shirt-pocketed model. "They said to get here well before, and that's what we've done."

The driver grunted again. He found his eyes closing, and blinked himself awake. "Time to stretch my legs," he said.

"Be careful opening that door. If he spots any movement—"

"He's got to get here first—but, okay, better check. Is there anyone in sight?"

The binoculars were raised, focused, turned from one side to the other, scanning the empty view perhaps a little more slowly than necessary. "Not a sausage—yes, there is, though." The passenger sat up; the driver snatched his hand from the door. "Lorry coming from the east—down the lane—turning into the lower road—can't see clearly because of the hedge, but it looks like crates of farm produce under a tarpaulin. Could that be him?"

"Anyone else in the cab with the driver?"

"The sky's reflecting too much to see properly, but I don't think so. Could always be someone hidden under the tarp, I suppose."

"If there is, and if that's a load of fruit, let's hope he's not bothered by wasps."

"Liven things up a bit, wouldn't it?"

For a third time, the driver grunted. Above the sturdy hedge the lorry was now clearly visible—and audible, as it clattered steadily and cheerfully along the lonely road.

"If that's not him," growled the passenger, "he'll scare him away. What a racket!"

"He'll be local, from one of the farms. They must have allowed for—hey!"

The cheerful clatter had become a sudden screech. Rubber burned on tarmac as the lorry swerved across the road and back, the driver trying his best to steer but obviously out of control. He swerved again. Brakes squealed. There came a jangling crash as the front of the cab hit a tree—crumpled—and the whole lorry tipped sideways into the ditch. The tarpaulin burst its securing ropes. Crates erupted messily across the road.

"That's torn it." The driver started the car. "He won't come now."

"Won't be able to, the road blocked like that." His companion was busy with dials, switches, and a microphone. "Hello, HQ, hello, HQ. Panda 123 calling. Do you read me?"

A tinny voice assured Panda 123 in brisk official tones that he was being read.

"Stakeout aborted, repeat, stakeout aborted. There's been an accident—overturned lorry blocking the road, driver still in the cab. We're on our way, but it looks as if we might need an ambulance—and a couple of patrol cars from Traffic to stop anyone else coming smash around the corner into this little lot ..."

"But whoever comes now," he added as the tinny voice acknowledged his message and began to issue instructions, "it certainly won't be chummy."

Two hundred miles away, on the eastern side of the country, at Rytham Hall in the county of Kent the women of the house had been baking.

Lady Colveden removed her oven gloves, dusted down her apron, and gazed from her daughter-in-law to the fruit cake sagging glumly on its wire rack. She sighed, and shook her head. "I wonder what we did wrong this time?"

Louise, half-French, half-Scottish and wholly practical, giggled. "Since I have come to live with you, dear Belle-Mère, the chickens of the house have started, so Nigel tells me, to lay many more eggs than they did before, and so many of them brown and of an intriguing flavour. Nothing is ever a waste, is it?"

"I suppose not, though at the rate we're going we may have to consider ducks or geese as well as hens." Her ladyship smiled. "We won't tell George, though."

"Or Mrs. Bloomer," nodded Louise. "It would be sad to disappoint her after so much kindness on her part in sharing her secrets."

Martha Bloomer, invaluable cleaner, cook and general factotum to a few select families in the village of Plummergen, had "took a real fancy to Nigel's bride" and resolved that once the historians and builders had finished work at Summerset Cottage, and the newlyweds could finally move into their new home (it being in fact several centuries old), young Mrs. Colveden would be able to keep house with the best. Some of the other ladies for whom Martha "did" were well set in their ways, but Louise, daughter of a French count or not, could still be taught, and Martha had made up her mind that she should be.

"If you've got the basics of sewing," said Martha sternly, "then you've a head start on some—" with a pointed look at her ladyship, barely able to do more than replace a button—"and that means I won't be wasting my time, as I might well be with others." Lady Colveden smiled ruefully. "But as two's little more bother than one, and you know I can't parley-vous, her ladyship can learn along of you and help out with explanations when needed."

The former Mademoiselle de Balivernes had surprised and pleased Mrs. Bloomer by the excellence of her scones, until recollection of the long-dead Scottish mother and the still living Scottish relations made Lady Colveden, to whose own efforts the term "excellence" hardly applied, suddenly laugh. "I should have realised when you called them *skons*," she said. "That's a very northern pronunciation. In the south we tend to think of them as *skones*, don't we, Martha?"

Martha shared in the general laughter, then said she would instruct both ladies in the art of making a rich fruit cake.

"She tried," said Lady Colveden, contemplating the sadly sagging shape now on the rack before her, "but at a guess there was some wrinkle—oh, a trick, a dodge—she didn't tell us, to pay us back for teasing her. Don't worry, my dear, Martha can take a joke with the best, and I'm sure next time everything will be fine. I never was much good at baking, as Nigel or George can tell you."

When in due course Sir George appeared for his afternoon break, he observed a large plateful of scones, some in rather better condition than others, and half a sponge cake left from the previous day. "Plenty of jam," he remarked. "Good. Far better indoors, this time of year. Wasps." He accepted a cup of tea, selected a scone and began happily buttering. "Nigel not in yet? Thought I heard a bit of a kerfuffle as I passed the sheep-run, but it didn't sound serious."

Louise looked only a little concerned for her husband's well-being. It had not taken her long to realise that life on a working farm had its frequent small excitements. "He is with Len Hosigg this afternoon," she said, half to herself, knowing that the young farm foreman would have raised any alarm he thought necessary.

"Not any more he isn't," announced a voice from the doorway. The baronet's handsome heir came in, grinning. "He's half dead with hunger, and in need of sugar. For shock."

"Nigel!"

"What happened?"

"Does it hurt?" burst from the other three in a startled chorus. Mr. Colveden's face was discoloured by a large purple bruise that was swelling into a fine example of the blackest of black eyes.

"A sheep kicked me." Nigel collapsed on a chair and regarded the teapot thirstily. "Thanks, Mother, just what I need. An extra lump of sugar, I think. A wasp at its most dozy buzzed straight at my head, so of course I ducked. Anyone would, but you just can't explain to a sheep. The poor old thing was as startled as I was—and there you are. Those hooves pack more of a punch than you'd expect."

"Ice." Lady Colveden rose to her feet. "If you don't try to stop that swelling you won't be able to see a thing tomorrow."

"Just so long as I can see tonight," said her son cheerfully. "Remember, Louise and I are joining the Young Farmers' trip to Ashford cinema for *Monty Python and the Holy Grail*. It's not been out long, but people say it's very funny, and we'll go for a drink afterwards. It's a coach party," he added, before his magistrate father could say anything. "Jack Crabbe will be driving and picking up as he goes, except that Louise and I will walk down to the garage because we're the only ones who live in this direction."

Lady Colveden, returning from the kitchen with a packet of frozen peas and a towel, passed both to her son and regarded her daughter-in-law thoughtfully. "Monty Python is very *English* humour, as I understand it," she observed. "I do hope it won't be too much for you, my dear."

"Nigel will translate," said Louise. "Or will try to," honesty made her add. "But it will in any case be pleasant for him to meet with his friends, and for me to meet them also."

"While the old folks put their feet up and spend a quiet evening at home," said Nigel, "leaving us young ones to roister through the night. Until closing time, anyway."

"Don't make too much noise coming in," warned his mother.

"Don't sleep too late in the morning," advised his father.

"We will be sure to set the alarm clock," promised his wife, and everyone smiled.

In the directors' office of a small factory on the outskirts of Glastonbury in Somerset, two men were waiting. There was a close physical resemblance between them, but while burly Bill Callender prowled up and down, consulting his watch at each turn and cross-checking it against the digital clock on the wall, his brother Crispin, two years younger, sat gracefully at his ease behind his desk, doodling on a pad of lined paper. The top sheet with his neat jottings had already been torn off and placed on a table to one side of the room. Every time the restless Bill saw it as he prowled, he sighed and looked pointedly at his watch.

"They really should be here by now," he grumbled. "Time's money, and we've a lot to discuss, and some of it's likely to be complicated."

"Octavia won't leave the shop until five," said Crispin. "We four can talk pretty much at any hour within reason, but the customers can't buy if the door's locked. Tavy's no fool."

"She has a business head on her shoulders," agreed Octavia's elder brother, grudgingly. "But Val works for herself, for pity's sake. She at least could have been here ages ago. She knows how important it is to start talking things over."

"Perhaps she felt it would look too much like us three older ones ganging up on Tavy if we had the chance to talk together first."

"If we wanted to gang up there's always the telephone. Nice and private. Ideal for hatching all sorts of plots behind her back—if we wanted to."

"Which we don't." Crispin nodded at him. "This family has spent more than half a century squabbling about one thing or another, right back to Great-granddad Ebenezer and his row with Granddad about setting up this business on his own. For goodness' sake, let's at least try to sort things out now without stirring up any more trouble."

"Any more trouble than needful," amended Bill, older and wiser. "They say you ought never to do business with friends or relations, and there's a deal of truth in that."

"We two get along all right." Crispin doodled a pair of doves with olive branches in their beaks. "Have done for years."

"Only because Dad was there to mediate when we disagreed, and to have the final word if we couldn't reach a compromise. Things were bound to change when he went, we all knew that, only we always thought there'd be plenty of time for the company to have grown so much there'd still be room for both of us—and even for the girls, if either of them wanted to change her mind and join us. But now ..."

"Now it's all been too quick for us to catch our breath." Crispin shuddered. "I still can't believe it—him dying like that ..."

"A freak accident, the coroner said. You know how he always joked about wanting to go out in a blaze of glory—"

"Don't!" Crispin's pencil stabbed dark, jagged lines across the paper. "Yes, I know he could see the funny side of being born on Bonfire Night, but ..."

Bill stopped prowling to clap him on the shoulder. Crispin rocked on his seat. "Graveyard humour's sometimes the best way to cope, Cris. He'd have laughed himself stupid at the way everyone told us to forget about a funeral in church, and cremation being the only answer—you can't say he wouldn't."

Crispin forced a grin. "Yes, and he'd have been thrilled to make the headlines, and he'd certainly have liked the publicity. Callender's Coats is a national name, these days. If only it hadn't happened the way it did."

The late Guy Callender, born on the fifth of November amid the sparkle and roar of England's annual firework celebration that Parliament was not blown up in 1605, had been "christened" by Peter, his exuberant father, with a splash of cider and a mouthful of jacket potato, roasted in the ashes of the Guy Fawkes bonfire. The newborn infant promptly spat out the potato but thoroughly savoured the cider, a fierce home brew that could strip the flesh from a joint of meat within weeks. Peter Callender's scrumpy was a man's drink, and Peter was resolved that his son should be as good a man as his father. Peter's own father Ebenezer had been all too strictly teetotal.

Guy grew up able to carry his liquor, and boasted a cast iron liver. Nobody could be sure how the accident that killed him had happened, but it was supposed that, early one chilly morning, wearing a nylon padded jacket, he had spilled petrol while fiddling with the lighting plant in a distant shed, and rubbed his hands thoughtlessly down his front to make them less slippery. It wasn't quite spontaneous combustion, but the static electricity thus generated had resulted in a sudden fireball from which, even had anyone else been with him, there would have been no time to save him.

"Yes, at least we could all agree on cremation." Crispin forced another grin. "And no arguments about the tombstone, thank goodness!" Grandfather Peter, founder of Callender's Coats, had been twice married, each time to a girl not Glastonbury born. Both wives predeceased him; both were laid to rest beneath their native turf rather than in their husband's parish. At Peter's own death in 1954 his two sons, half-brothers Guy and John, known as Janner, were unable to agree either on where he was to be buried, or the exact wording of his tombstone. In the end the matter was settled by the trustees appointed to handle Great-grandfather Ebenezer's will, which had been for so modest an estate surprisingly complex. The Callenders could be a quarrelsome family. Like Ebenezer and his only son Peter, disinherited when he went into business rather than work with his father on the farm, Peter's two sons refused to speak to each other after the tombstone disagreement—a family silence that endured for more than twenty years, until Peter's death meant that both sides had to meet under the same roof for his final obsequies. The Callender children might speak to their cousins, but all knew without saying that any close association would be frowned on by those of the older generation who remained.

"But now it looks as if we'll have to talk to them," said Crispin, roughing out a sharp-eyed legal head in a wig, surrounded by books and paper scrolls tied with ribbon. "Lawyers cost money, and with death duties we haven't much to spare."

"We haven't any to spare." Yet again Bill Callender produced the telling phrase. "Not unless Tavy's found a cult best-seller everyone's been flocking to buy from her shop, and has a fortune in the bank—"

"She hasn't," a cheerful female voice broke in. Octavia, afterthought child of Guy and his wife Eleanor, ten years younger than her sister Val, glided into the office in a floor-length caftan and sandals, her long hair floating free where it wasn't held out of her eyes by a headband of bright glass beads. She looked from one brother to the other. "Val not here yet?"

"As you see," said Bill. "And we told her, five-thirty at the latest."

Octavia, who wore no watch, glanced at the digital clock and smiled faintly. "I've often thought Val should change her name from Callender to Chronometer. I've never known her on time for anything." She drifted across to Crispin's desk, pulled out the visitor's chair and settled herself. "She's happy in her work, though, and says she makes enough to live on with a little left over, which I suppose in her eyes is what really counts."

"Nonsense," snapped Bill, as Crispin stabbed his pencil, breaking the point. "You've been building up that book-shop of yours year by year, haven't you? You're aiming for more than just a little left over, aren't you? It's only good business practice."

"Good for me, and for you two, but as for Val—could you honestly call her practical?" Octavia smiled as she put the question. "Was there ever a time, even when you three were children, that you boys weren't chivvying the poor thing to keep up with you? Not from what I've gathered, over the years. The ruthless business brain of the Callenders just seems to have passed her by—and as I said, she's happy enough."

"She is," conceded Crispin, "a bit of a dreamer."

"She'll need to buck up her ideas this afternoon," Bill said irritably. "Or this evening, if we have to wait much longer—but she's a shareholder, like the rest of us. She has to know and understand our plans—Dad's plans—for expanding the business, and agree with them—or not—which would mean a different discussion about buying her out—but either way, she should be here so we can at least start to talk about it."

"And here she is," murmured Crispin, who had caught a brisk footfall approaching the open door. "Hello, Val, better late than never."

All four Callenders had inherited their father's greenish-blue eyes, and his flyaway hair with a hint of russet, but Valentine was the only one to resemble their father in build. While Eleanor had been tall and a little angular, her husband Guy's farming ancestors had left their mark on his sturdy, almost barrel-shaped, frame. Val in her mid-thirties was short and plump; in middle age she would be tubby. "Muscles," she would chuckle, if anyone spoke of a diet. "Stamina. It helps to have staying power, with a job like mine." Val had for years been a spinner, dyer, and hand weaver, at first teaching herself from books, then at evening class. Only when she wasn't afraid of wasting his time did she venture to approach Glastonbury's noted expert, Job Haxey. Old Job had sniffed, watched her at work, and allowed that for a maiden self-taught she'd not done so bad. If she'd care to listen as he spoke, him not being of a bookish turn of mind, he might just share with her some of his lifetime's knowledge of the weaver's craft. She could even write his words of wisdom down so they'd not be lost to future generations.

Valentine took this for the compliment it was, and planned one day to turn her copious notes into a proper book—when she had the time. As she enjoyed her work, the book was a long time coming.

"Sorry I'm a bit late," she apologised with a wide smile, "but something funny happened with the latest batch of dye. It looked so interesting I had to wait and see how it turned out." She claimed a second visitor's chair, and flopped comfortably down in a flurry of skirts woven from yarn spun on her newly imported Ashford wheel. Made in New Zealand, with its revolutionary nylon-and-graphite flyer bearing it was worth every penny she'd paid, as she would inform anyone who teased her for such unbusinesslike extravagance.

"We won't waste any more time asking," warned Bill, as the other two displayed dangerous signs of interest in the dodgy batch of dye. "We want to get on."

"You'd better call the meeting to order," suggested Octavia, with a wink for the others that Bill saw, but thought it wiser to ignore. "Is there an agenda? I see what looks like notes on that table over there."

"Cris and I had a chat before you two came long, and roughed out a few ideas to be going on with, but it's hardly an agenda. This isn't so much an official meeting as a put-you-in-the-picture briefing." Bill picked up the sheet of paper with his younger brother's neat notes, rustled it, and began to speak without consulting it.

"We all know, or at least we should," with a frown for Valentine, who had taken a sheet of Crispin's doodles to fan herself, "that some of Dad's affairs are likely to be a while in the sorting out because his death was so unexpected. Sixty-five is no age, and the insurance people will argue every inch of the way. But that's not the point. The point is, in the weeks before the accident he'd been talking about the need to expand if we want to keep up with Morlands and Drapers. They both started out as small family firms, just like old Peter when he quarrelled with Ebenezer and set up on his own—and look at them now. World famous. Exporting Somerset sheepskin products all over the place. Mail order to select individuals. Made-to-measure gloves, coats, slippers. Dad said he knew he couldn't beat 'em, but he certainly wanted to join them and give 'em a run for their money."

"You mean we owe it to his memory to follow through with his plans?" Octavia gave one of her faint, knowing smiles. "It's a way of justifying an almighty family row, I grant you—and there's bound to be a row the moment we tell them we want to build—but waving the flag of filial piety might just avert the worst of the fallout. I suppose."

Val shifted on her chair. She dropped the paper fan to grasp a handful of her billowing skirt. "Some of this wool came from Uncle Janner's sheep," she said thoughtfully. "Young Jan let me have a couple of fleeces on the quiet, after the shearing. He won't like even to hear talk of building on our field—and I don't think we should build there, either." She looked at Octavia. "You joked about waving the flag of filial piety, but that's what that field of ours is, if you go back far enough. A compliment to the family—well, to old Ebenezer, anyway, and as such it ought to be respected."

"But Ebenezer was about the only other teetotaller the squire knew," objected Crispin. "Wearing a blue ribbon and both being churchwardens was good enough a century ago for the old fellow to put it in his will that Ebenezer should have it, but that was because there wasn't anyone else."

"He could have arranged for it to be sold and the proceeds given to charity, like the rest of the manor," persisted Val. "Only he didn't. Great-granddad was proud of being singled out that way, and even Granddad used to say it was a compliment because he remembered the squire from when he was a little boy. I don't think any of them would want the field built on for the sake of making money, when there must surely be more suitable land somewhere not too far away that isn't such good grazing."

"Which," said Bill heavily, "we wouldn't own. The field is ours, outright, or it will be once the paperwork is finished. We can't afford to buy, or even rent, anywhere else—all our capital's either tied up in the business or going towards death duties."

Crispin signalled his agreement with a nod and a murmur; Octavia was silent; but Val was unconvinced. "If it's money you're worried about, we could start by asking Janner for an independent rent review. The family's had the use of that field at a peppercorn rent since long before he and Dad quarrelled over Granddad's tombstone. I wouldn't want to see them turned off after all these years any more than have the land built on, but they should agree they've had a good run for their money and perhaps it ought to be referred to the National Farmers' Union, or somebody like that, to set a more realistic amount."

"They've had a run for *our* money," said Bill, as she drew breath. "The rent should never have been set so low in the first place, brother or no brother—but I take my hat off to you, Val. Maybe the family's ruthless business brain hasn't entirely passed you by. How did you come to think of that?"

She turned pink. "Young Jan wondered if there might be changes after Dad's accident, and mentioned something of the sort when he brought me round another fleece. He'd be willing to accept an independent rent assessment, I think, though he's not able to speak for his father and he's not sure Janner would agree anyway—but it could be worth a try. Anything, rather than build on good grazing land."

Octavia stirred. Being so much younger than her siblings and left a good deal to her own devices, she had a bookish, enquiring turn of mind and could, when she wished, look more deeply into things than many people outside the family might guess.

"According to *Farmers Weekly*," she said now, "if a landlord wants to increase the rent it can only be with the consent of the tenant—but if the tenant won't agree, the landlord can refer the matter to arbitration. And then it will take a couple of years for the increase to go through, assuming, of course, that there is an increase."

"There's bound to be an increase," said Bill, then shook himself. "No, this is all theory, for later, once we four can decide between us what we want to do, even if it means some of us having to buy some of the others out—Tavy? What is it?"

"There's more than one theory," said Octavia, who had been shaking her head as her brother spoke. "I've been thinking about all this since Dad died, and once you two started on the expansion idea I guessed you'd want Janner and his sheep off our field. There's certainly no more room for building here. And then I spotted something in the local paper ... So I checked in the library, and asked a few questions. How much later can we afford to leave it for us all to reach an agreement?"

The other three regarded her in some confusion.

"I mean," she went on, "that none of you seems to know anything of what's been under discussion in parliament—the new legislation that will come into force some time next year, if it's passed." She paused. "And if it's passed—well, if it becomes law in 1976, we might never be able to get Janner Callender's sheep off our field!"

Chapter Two

When Louise came to take her place at the breakfast table she smiled in a conspiratorial manner at her mother-in-law and, for the first time in her married life, greeted Sir George with a fingertip kiss on his bald head as she passed him. Ignoring his start of surprise Nigel's wife sat down, took an illustrated magazine from her pocket, opened it, and began to flick through the pages.

"*Paris Match,*" cried Lady Colveden, who'd wondered why her daughter-in-law had been wearing a jacket so early in the day. "Is that the latest number? Where did you find it?"

Louise lowered her magazine, but kept it open in her hands. Sir George, who had been pondering the unwonted caress, was stirred from his reverie by his wife's exclamation and now gazed with quickening interest at his daughter-in-law. "Close to the cinema there was a shop selling tobacco and sweets—and journals," explained young Mrs. Colveden. "It was a small moment only for me to enter, while everyone else formed the queue, to enquire if by chance they might have such a paper as *Paris Match*, and they had. So I bought it."

Sir George hesitated, then beamed at her, while his wife and his son exchanged swift, knowing looks. "Missing your native lingo, m'dear? A little homesick? *Paris Match*, eh? You'll enjoy that." With a deep, contented sigh he reached back to the sideboard, where the temptation of *Farmers Weekly* waited for him to succumb. He turned at once to the Letters page to see if his views on pigs had met with editorial approval. Oh, well. Maybe next week.

Nigel mopped a dramatic brow, patted his wife's hand, and took up his knife and fork. "We breathe again," he said through eggs and bacon. "Normal service has at last been resumed. Isn't she wonderful, Mother?"

"Thank you very much, my dear," said her ladyship in heartfelt tones. Sir George had suffered torments of courtesy ever since the young couple, returned from their honeymoon, had because of builders been unable to move into their new home as planned. Nigel might happily tease his mother about non-paying Paying Guests, but it had been his father who paid the price, good manners forbidding the baronet's habitual disappearance behind his newspaper while there were visitors in the house.

Louise, folding away *Paris Match* and accepting coffee, smiled back at her.

"Did you have a good time with the Young Farmers?" her ladyship went on, passing toast and butter. "And how was the film?"

Nigel speared more egg and forked it to his mouth. "Louise is too polite to say so, but I think it was all a bit much for her. The rest of us enjoyed it well enough."

"You are accustomed to such humour," said his bride, "while I am not, and it is too often not possible to translate."

"You don't need translation for a pair of coconuts and an imaginary horse. You laughed at that bit, didn't you?"

"For such jokes one does not require language," said Louise. "One has but to observe. The illustrations—animations, yes?—they too were clever, although I think perhaps some mistakes were made in the words, for the evil black monster was of a decided green. But for me it was pleasant to see the castles of Scotland. They reminded me of my dear mother's home, where I have so often stayed. Yet some of the voices—the accents—I found not easy to comprehend, even the wizard throwing fire with great horns upon his head, who was trying to sound Scottish."

"Tim the Enchanter," supplied Nigel with a grin. "Reminded me of Tim Foxon—you've met him, Louise, detective from Ashford, nice chap, wears the oddest clothes—I thought you'd know who I mean—anyway," he explained to his mother, "this chap with the horns had long black robes, and a livelier contrast to Foxon's colour sense you've yet to see." His grin widened as he began to laugh. "And those great curling horns made me think of the sheep that kicked me, even though our Romneys don't look a bit like that."

He went on laughing, and Louise watched him fondly, though puzzled. "It is so English, is it not," she said to Lady Colveden, "to make a joke of almost anything? Poor Nigel can this morning barely see from his swollen eye, yet still he laughs."

"Stiff upper lip, m'dear," offered Sir George from behind *Farmers Weekly*.

"Humour is hard to explain, because everyone's sense of the ridiculous can be so different." Lady Colveden smiled. "We watched the television news last night while you Young Farmers were Monty Pythoning in Ashford, and even your father was tickled by the Traffic Jam item at the end, because of Nigel's wasp." Nigel, munching toast spread thick with marmalade, raised his eyebrows in query. "It seems," went on his mother, "that an unfortunate lorry driver taking a load of fresh plums to market had a wasp fly in and buzz at him just the way yours did, Nigel. He ducked out of the way too, and ended up in a ditch with plums all over the road."

She looked hopefully at Louise, who frowned, then smiled. "But of course, a traffic jam," she said. "Was the poor driver much injured?"

"He knocked himself out on the dashboard, they said, but by a stroke of luck a police car happened to be passing and stopped to help. Of course," her ladyship added, "with the plums smashing everywhere like that they couldn't have gone past anyway. I suppose they could have turned round and taken another route to wherever they were going ..."

"Middle of nowhere," supplied Sir George.

"On the way to somewhere," said his wife. "So they radioed for an ambulance, and he was taken to hospital and kept overnight for observation, because bangs on the head can be nasty. Otherwise there was nothing broken, and the television people were happy to have some fun with it all."

"I think," decided Nigel after a pause, "Monty Python was funnier."

It was tacitly decided between the four Colvedens that everyone should find amusing whatever took his or her fancy.

In the post office, tempers were running a little high. Postmaster Stillman had been forced to dart to and from his official cubicle to deal with ordinary customers, while his wife Elsie had to alternate general dusting and tidying with serving groceries at the other counter. Service was slower than usual; more erratic. The question had to be asked of her employers: where was Emmy Putts?

"Late for work," said Mrs. Stillman. "And no message to say why."

"They haven't the phone laid on," her husband reminded her peaceably.

"And it's her mother's day for the biscuit factory," said Mrs. Spice. "Clarrie will've caught the bus to Brettenden long before young Emmeline was out of bed."

"She would've checked the girl was awake, surely, before she left the house?" Mrs. Henderson felt that maternal instincts must always win through.

"Emmy Putts is old enough to take care of herself," countered Mrs. Skinner, who seldom missed the chance to disagree with Mrs. Henderson. Some years back there had been confusion and consequent Words Spoken over the church flower rota. The one thing on which the two ladies could now agree was that they never would agree on anything. "A great girl like Emmy, earning her way in the world ..."

The bell above the shop door jangled, and the subject under discussion came in looking flustered, apologetic, and amused at the same time. It was rare to see Emmy Putts in an animated state. "You're late," said Mrs. Stillman, handing her a feather duster.

"Take your coat off first," suggested Mr. Stillman, retreating behind his official grille.

"What happened?" demanded Mrs. Spice, pertinently.

"Sorry," said Emmy, as Mrs. Stillman wagged an admonitory finger. "Bin talking to Maureen, and we didn't realise the time."

"You're not paid to talk to Maureen on our time, Emmeline Putts," said Mrs. Stillman. "What could she have had to tell you that was so important you'd be late for work?"

"About her Wayne," said Emmy, flicking feathers along a topmost shelf. "Ever so cross with him, she is. Dead furious."

The post office rustled in shock. Maureen, who waitressed at the George and Dragon at the far end of The Street—as Plummergen's main thoroughfare is known—and her Wayne, with his Kawasaki motorbike and black leathers, had been going steady for so long that if either of them passed within a mile of a jeweller's shop the village had them walking down the aisle within six weeks. A split between this young couple seemed impossible.

"Why?" demanded Mrs. Spice. "What's he done?"

Emmy giggled. Decidedly, the girl was less dozy than usual. Had she hopes of Wayne if Maureen had indeed "chucked" him, as youthful parlance phrased it? "Took her to the pictures," was all she could say, at first.

Visions of back-seat frolics going too far floated before the eyes of all. Would the banns be called on Sunday? Would the bride, in honesty, wear a colour other than white?

"No harm in that," said Mrs. Skinner, probing.

"There can be," said Mrs. Henderson, darkly.

"Wayne," said Emmy, "heard tell the Young Farmers was organising a trip to the Regent in Brettenden, to see a dead funny new film about King Arthur, and he told Maureen they'd go too." Once more she was assailed by giggles. She passed the feather duster idly along a row of tins, savouring her audience's attention as she worked.

"Well?" said Mrs. Stillman at last.

"Only he got it wrong." Mrs. Stillman's tone told Emmy she'd better not spin out her tale too far. "It was the

28

Phoenix in Ashford the Young Farmers was going to, not the Regent. *They* were showing another film about King Arthur, an old one, *Camelot*—and they were stuck right in the middle of the back row so they couldn't get out when they saw it was all acting and scenery and songs—lots of 'em. And," she was overcome again with mirth, "it was more'n three hours long!"

Even the Stillmans had to join in the outburst of laughter that filled the post office, and Emmy smirked with pleasure. Her expression then grew thoughtful.

"All about King Arthur," she said, "and lovely costumes, Maureen said. Didn't King Arthur have a queen called Guinevere?"

The post office remembered that Emmy Putts, whose long blonde wig (in which she had twice been crowned Miss Plummergen) had become sadly scruffy, had recently bought a long, dark, luxurious replacement.

And Plummergen's Amateur Dramatic Society had yet to choose this winter's annual production ...

On a desk in an office on the umpteenth floor of New Scotland Yard, the telephone rang. The tall, rugged, middle-aged man behind the desk sighed, kept his head resolutely bent over the file he was studying, and murmured only one short word.

"Bob."

Detective Sergeant Ranger had endured the mutterings of his superior officer for over ten minutes now, and knew that an interruption at this stage was the last thing the Oracle—Chief Superintendent Delphick, in a formal way—wanted. The mutters had been at first intense, then calmer. Bob had been waiting for the sigh of triumph as the file's complexities were finally unravelled, mostly because he had his own copy before him and couldn't make any sense of it at all. He'd like to know what was meant to be going on.

He picked up the telephone extension, gave the number, and heard a voice bark:

"That you, Ranger? Is he in hiding, or is he there with you?"

Rather than the Oracle, it was now Bob who sighed. "Well, sir, he's rather tied up at present, but if you could wait I'll get him to—oh." The bark at the other end of the line had, apparently, cut the connection. Bob jiggled the cradle up and down a few times, then gently replaced the receiver.

Still the Oracle did not look up from his studies. "Say nothing," he warned his loyal sidekick. "If my concentration isn't broken, I might just make sense of all this before he comes through that door."

It was not to be. As the last page but two was turned over, there came a peremptory thump on the door followed at once by a crash as it was thrown open. A small, wiry, black-haired tornado with a handlebar moustache swept into the room, closed the door, and strode over to the Oracle's desk with barely a nod of acknowledgement for Bob at his own discreet desk in the corner.

"No time to run away," remarked the tornado, dropping into the visitor's chair and giving Delphick a sharp look. "Good. That's what I hoped."

Delphick regarded Detective Superintendent Kebby with mild irritation. "I take it this is not a social visit, but I wish you'd left it another ten minutes." With a sigh—not of relief for a job concluded, but of resignation that he'd have to start all over again—he slipped his notes and jottings into the file, and firmly closed it. "What can we do for you?"

Superintendent Kebby twirled his moustache. "I'll do my best to put you in the picture— and that's more apposite than it might sound," he began. Bob in his corner, Delphick at his desk, both felt the emphasis and instinctively braced themselves. Whatever tale it was the superintendent had to tell, they both suspected how it was likely to end.

"You've heard of Garth's, the building and property firm? Caleb Garth started out as an odd-job man in some middle-of-absolutely-nowhere village." Jasper Kebby, city born and bred, mistrusted the wide open spaces. "Ended up a tycoon. He was good at his work, able to learn, picked the best people to employ as the business grew. Now he probably couldn't tell you himself how much he's worth, and he wouldn't know which of his accountants to ask because he's got so many to choose from."

"Garth's," Delphick said as Kebby drew breath. "Yes. There's a playboy son who's always in the news for misbehaving, and another who joined the firm at the bottom to work his way up, presumably to the very top in years to come. I believe there's a sister, too."

"It's the playboy I'm interested in. Christy. He's been kidnapped."

"That," said Delphick after a pause, "has *not* been in the news. How long ago?"

"Start of last week. A ransom note was sent to the family, but Ma and Pa Garth are off cruising somewhere on one of their yachts and Letty, that's the daughter, didn't like to open what looked like their private correspondence until a follow-up note arrived addressed to her, telling her to check in the other envelope. So she did."

"And?"

"And she consulted with brother Ben, who authorised the payment. Routine stuff—used notes, anonymous bag left somewhere quiet—and they waited for Christy to come home. But he didn't. And when a follow-up demand for more cash arrived, they decided to ignore the don't-contact-the-cops advice and got in touch with the Yard."

"And?"

"And it all went wrong—and that *did* get in the papers. Remember the Traffic Jam?"

Delphick frowned. "Evesham way, wasn't it? Fruit-growing country, certainly. A lorry-load of squashed plums thoroughly blocked a minor road when the driver came into contact with a wayward wasp, to be pulled from his overturned cab by—ah. Hmm. I see."

Kebby nodded. "Oh yes, it's only to be expected that a police patrol car should just happen to be passing by on an unclassified road right out in the depths of the country, isn't it? But we can't blame our two lads for acting as they did. If that lorry had caught fire there might have been far worse injuries for the driver than concussion—and of course they had to let the traffic people know what had happened—but the resultant kerfuffle scared chummy away, and we've not heard a dicky-bird since."

"And?" prompted the Oracle, who guessed what was coming. So, from the muted choking that emerged from his corner, did Detective Sergeant Bob Ranger.

"And the only clue to the poor chap's whereabouts is some vague idea the brother and sister have that he was heading west. Which sort of ties in with the Evesham area, but could be a complete red herring. We've no idea what to try next."

"You could start," Delphick said, "by handing me the envelope of photographs from your inside pocket."

Kebby looked at him. "Oh yes, you're the Oracle all right. Ten out of ten." He reached into his jacket and withdrew a stout brown envelope. "But if your Miss Seeton can come up with the goods, it'll be twenty out of ten for her!"

Picture Miss Seeton. Five foot nothing in her sensible shoes, seven stone fully clothed and wringing wet. An English spinster-of-a-certain-age with greying hair, a capacious handbag, skirts below the knee, lisle stockings because nylon ladders so easily and silk is expensive. Apart from her somewhat outré taste in hats Miss Seeton, the casual observer would say, is a typical product of her class and generation, backbone of England's green and pleasant land throughout which her sisters can be numbered in their hundreds, thousands, millions.

The casual observer would be wrong. No other spinster gentlewoman, homeward bound from the opera, would interrupt a vicious killer mid-murder by poking him in the back with her umbrella as a rebuke for his bad manners. Miss Seeton afterwards conceded that his female companion had indeed addressed him in words that sounded, well, rude, though fortunately she herself spoke very little French—yet even foreigners ought to know how to behave. To hit (as she at the time supposed he had) anyone, particularly a member of the opposite sex, was undoubtedly an even greater discourtesy.

Scotland Yard, in the persons of the then-Detective Superintendent Delphick and his sergeant, had begun investigation of the murder by asking Miss Seeton, whose official statement identified her as a teacher of art, if she could produce a likeness of the rude young man who had run away after knocking her down—not because, as Miss Seeton believed, he had been startled by the prod of her umbrella, but because his French associate now lay with his knife thrust firmly into her heart, and he had no time to dispose of the only witness to his crime before further help and witnesses arrived. Miss Seeton, unable to imagine that anyone could wish her harm, sketched an immediately identifiable likeness of a wild-eyed tearaway behind bars—bars behind which, after escapades that in the following weeks included murder, suicide, drowning, gas, shooting, car crashes, abduction and embezzlement, César Lebel was firmly and finally imprisoned.

Six months later, not only did Miss Seeton's attempts to draw a neighbour's young daughter suggest that the girl was likely to be the next victim of a serial child killer, but (after the girl's death) she produced further drawings identifying the killer beyond all doubt. By the time of the third occasion on which her quick, inspired drawings had helped the police to thwart the worst machinations of a pair of villains working a huge swindle on the credulous populace through the skilful exploitation of witchcraft, Satanism, and bogus philosophy, Miss Emily Dorothea Seeton had been recruited into the force as a special art consultant, and paid an annual retainer for her services by Scotland Yard. Grateful though MissEss (as the Yard's erratic computer insists on addressing her) might be for that generous retainer, she has never really understood why the police believe what she calls her scribbles to be of such importance. She is always a little ashamed of her scribbles, which come upon her without warning and therefore suggest a sad lack of self-discipline. As a teacher she always taught her pupils to restrict themselves to drawing only what they could see, which meant only what was there. She is uneasy at the idea that it is because of what she can sometimes see that is *not* there—but, if the ultimate truth could only be shown, *would* be there—that the police find her work invaluable. She has managed to persuade herself that all she does for them is supply IdentiKit drawings when, for reasons she feels she has no need to understand, photographs would be unsuitable.

The police officer who best understands Miss Seeton is the now Chief Superintendent Delphick. From the start there was an empathy between them that even Bob Ranger (who later adopted her as an honorary aunt, and recruited her as godmother to his firstborn, Gideon) could never entirely grasp. Miss Seeton had first seen the enormous Bob himself as a footballer (which in his spare time he was) and Delphick as a grey day on heathland—not bleak, but a little chilly; detached and impersonal, to a lesser degree echoing that detachment and otherness Miss Seeton had for much of her life felt towards the rest of the world. Miss Seeton might sometimes be rendered uneasy by her sense of detachment; Delphick cared little for his, and relished hers for the invaluable insights she could so often provide.

And now it seemed she was to be asked for her views on a kidnap.

Chief Superintendent Delphick, contemplating in thoughtful silence the glass box on his office wall that displayed Miss Seeton's celebrated, but fatally damaged, umbrella from their first professional encounter, contemplated also the phenomenon that was Miss Seeton. He knew her fairly well; understood her a little.

Superintendent Kebby did not know her at all.

The Oracle wondered ...

Chapter Three

It was one of Martha Bloomer's days when she "did" at Sweetbriars, the Plummergen cottage formerly owned by Miss Seeton's godmother and first cousin once removed, Flora Bannet. Old Mrs. Bannet, achieving the grand age of ninety-eight before dying, had by just two years missed her telegram of congratulation from the Queen. Miss Seeton had never seen one, and regretted that probably now she never would, but was deeply touched when her elderly cousin bequeathed to her only close relative her cottage, her cleaning lady, and the services of her cleaning lady's husband Stan.

Mrs. Bloomer had come to regard the elderly widow and her goddaughter as almost part of her own large family, a lively Cockney hubbub whose first acquaintance with Kent had been coming down from London each pre-war autumn to pick hops. Martha met, over the years befriended, and eventually married village-born farmhand Stan, settling not far from Sweetbriars in a one-storey cottage with a correspondingly small garden. An arrangement was before long reached whereby Mrs. Bannet supplied the funds, Stan the expertise and energy, for (at first) the building of a fowl-house and the keeping of hens, the surplus of whose eggs could be sold in village shops to the Bloomers' profit, in lieu of wages. Very soon vegetables, fruit and flowers from the cottage garden joined the hens beneath Stan's knowledgeable sway. When Miss Seeton came into her inheritance she was more than willing to continue the arrangement.

Martha, her habitual apron swapped for a voluminous pinafore, had arrived early for work and was trying to chivvy her employer out of the house so that she could make a good start on shifting furniture. "You'll only be under my feet if you stay, dear, and when I need help with rolling up the rugs I'll let you know, but help carry them you will not, fit as your yoga keeps you, because it's for tying yourself in knots, isn't it, not for giving you muscles like a freak in a fairground. Besides, Stan said he'd pop in at dinner-time to help me take them all out the back for a good beating, and again before supper to help me bring them all in again so as to have everything nicely settled before winter, with the ground so damp as it always gets this close to the canal." The large garden to the rear of Sweetbriars slopes down to the Royal Military Canal, originally constructed to thwart a Napoleonic invasion and now one hundred and seventy years old.

"Very well, Martha dear, if you are sure I can be of no assistance." Miss Seeton, ever obedient to her domestic mentor's advice, retreated hurriedly from her own sitting-room as Martha seized a wing chair by its high back and began tipping it to and fro in a meaningful manner. "It is a little early," ventured Miss Seeton from the hall, "but is there anything you would like from the shops? I had planned to buy stamps from the post office a little later—but of course," she added, for Martha's feelings must not be hurt, "it will be pleasant on so fine a day to stroll about the village enjoying the fresh air until Mr. Stillman opens."

"Stay here much longer," retorted Mrs. Bloomer, "and what you'll enjoy is dust, not fresh air. Hoover and sweep these rugs as I may, there's no denying a good go outside in spring and autumn with a carpet-beater's best of all, though I sometimes think we could do with one of them shampooers too, except I've never understood how you can be sure of it drying properly indoors." She paused. "'Specially when tea leaves work almost as well." Miss Seeton, in an unwonted hurry, had recently come home from the shops with tea bags, by mistake. Her house-proud henchwoman now seized every opportunity to remind her charge that Mrs. Bannet's tea caddy had served the house well for years, loose leaves being far better than any nasty paper, and if Miss Emily didn't believe her she had only to try nibbling on a paper hankie and she'd soon know what she meant.

Miss Seeton had been quick to apologise, and Martha as quickly appropriated the tea bags for Stan to use as mulch on some experimental cuttings being nurtured under glass. Stan, except in the depths of winter when it was too dark, too cold, or too wet for working out of doors, was no great television watcher. He left Martha to tell him of anything that might interest him, and when she mentioned pink laburnum—there was a tree in Cambridge, they'd grafted Golden Rain on to purple broom, or maybe the other way round, she couldn't remember—he thought the matter over and decided this was a challenge to which his reputation as Plummergen's best gardener really ought to rise. The word "chimera" was unknown to Stan Bloomer, who wasn't that much of a reader, either; he might otherwise years before have learned of the Victorian passion for the pink laburnum hybrid developed by Monsieur Adam in 1825 to produce separate racemes of yellow, purple, and pink-with-yellow blooms on separate stems, and proudly known as *Laburnum Adamii.*

"My duster's a little bald," conceded Martha after a few moments of unseen furniture-bumping, "and I dare say after today it'll probably have had it, so a new one would be nice—only not one of the fancy sort with nylon bristles, dear, proper feathers or nothing and I know Emmy Putts uses them so try the post office first, if you're going there anyway—and talking of the post, here's Bert," as a clatter outside heralded the arrival of Plummergen's genial postman at the southern end of The Street. "Hang on a minute, dear, in case he's brought anything for you."

Miss Seeton gave the loyal retainer no time to brush her hands free of grime and remove her housecoat, but opened the front door herself, as she heard the tread of official feet coming up the path.

"Good morning, Bert," she greeted the cheerful redhead, like Martha a Cockney but, unlike Mrs. Bloomer, resident six miles away in Brettenden. "And such a beautiful morning!"

"True enough, ducks, and we'll hope it stays that way. Here's your letters—one from Scotland Yard, still calling you MissEss on the envelope. Wouldn't you think that computer of theirs oughter know by now who you are?"

Miss Seeton, with a smile accepting a small bundle of correspondence, thanked Bert and explained that no doubt it was to avoid confusion, everything these days apparently needing initials like OHMS for anything sent On Her

Majesty's Service, such as the income tax, or GPO for the General Post Office, and while MP always meant Member of Parliament, MS could mean manuscript as well as Mine Sweeper, so Admiral Leighton had once told her, although it seemed most unlikely that anyone would suppose she, who led so quiet a life—Miss Seeton honestly believes this—would know how to sweep mines and, indeed, if any sweeping of the other sort was to be done then dear Martha must know more about it than anyone else in the village.

"Unless it's chimneys," called Bert over his shoulder as he went back down the path. "She'd look a sight in a top hat and weskit, Martha Bloomer would!"

"Cheek," observed Martha, emerging from behind Miss Seeton to brandish her feather duster in his direction. "Now, dear, as he's brought your letters I know you'll be wanting to read them, but just you take them into the kitchen because then I'll be sure where you are, and you won't bother me."

"Oh, dear, I'm so sorry. Of course. I wasn't thinking." Miss Seeton, who had begun instinctively to head for the sitting room and her paper-knife, now began moving down the hall passage towards the kitchen, and to the cutlery drawer for a paper-knife substitute. She took from the drawer the metal skewer that had secured one of butcher Mr. Stacey's finest rolled joints of prime beef, cooked (by Martha, who worried about waste) for a small family luncheon party hosted by Miss Seeton for Bob and Anne Ranger, and Anne's parents Dr. and Mrs. Knight, to celebrate the registration of young Gideon Henry's birth once his names had finally been selected.

"Good gracious." Miss Seeton turned pink with surprise and pleasure. "After almost twenty years." While the envelope addressed by the Scotland Yard computer had held a cheque, as she'd expected, for the IdentiKit drawings she had not long ago supplied, the other official-looking letter announced that Miss Emily Dorothea Seeton had won a prize with her small holding of Premium Bonds. Back in 1957, Miss Seeton had weighed the arguments carefully, then decided at last that it didn't really count as gambling if the government was behind the scheme. She hadn't been able to afford to buy many but, hearing the girls at Mrs. Benn's school talk of the one- or two- or ten-pound bonds given them for birthday or Christmas presents, she had in the end risked a modest sum that, disappointingly, had never until now reaped any financial reward.

But now ...

"Martha, dear." Miss Seeton trotted back along the passage to interrupt Martha as she shifted furniture. "Such a surprise. I have won a little something with my Premium Bonds, and you shall have that special carpet machine if you would like it, for shampooing."

"Well, I never." Martha paused in her labours to beam with delight at her employer and friend. "Congratulations, dear! My Stan once thought he'd won on the football pools, but so many other folk had the same numbers we ended up with barely enough for a new wheelbarrow, though better than nothing, bless him. All excited at first, he was, not that Stan gets worked up easy about things and what I told him then was, money's useful but it isn't the most important thing by any means, and if you've got your health and strength you're a lot better off than many. But a shampooer, now. I'd have to think about that, unless they come with a fan heater built in. The shop would know."

"Indeed they would," agreed Miss Seeton. "And should you perhaps wish for another vacuum cleaner, it would save having to carry it up and down the stairs—the old one, that is, from the cupboard under them. Of course one cannot approve of waste, and it does still work, but the more up-to-date models weigh rather less, to judge from their appearance in shop displays." Not for worlds would Miss Seeton hurt Martha's feelings by reminding her that neither of them was growing any younger. "And it is, I think," she added to salve her conscience, "a little noisier than it once was, which could suggest—though I know nothing of motors or electricity—that it might in any case before too long require replacement."

"A nice little cylinder would fit away tidy in a wardrobe. Or under the spare bed, in its box. It would still look neat. But—"

Martha was interrupted by the telephone's shrill ring. "I'd best let you get that, dear." She remembered that it wouldn't be long before Stan arrived to carry carpets, and talk of upstairs had reminded her that she'd not finished downstairs yet.

"Good morning, Lady Colveden." Miss Seeton spoke brightly into the mouthpiece, and for some minutes thereafter just listened. "Why, yes, something," she said at last. "And naturally I would be happy to help, but I know very little beyond the stories, and certainly have no idea of the scenery." Lady Colveden's voice came tinnily along the wires. Miss Seeton listened some more.

"Perhaps," she suggested after further details of the proposed *Camelot* production had been supplied, "as Mr. Jessyp is always so interested in history, he might be able to lend me some books, should he have any with suitable illustrations, even if King Arthur did not really exist, for he is just as real to us all as the Loch Ness Monster, and I understand there are even photographs of that." Then she frowned. "Or should one more properly say photographs 'of her'? Nessie," she enlarged, recalling her recent holiday in the Scottish Highlands. "Of course he will be busy at the school just now, but I could telephone at morning break to discuss the matter with him. He is happy to lend books to those who promise to take care of them, as naturally I always do."

Lady Colveden, knowing Miss Seeton so well, was easily able to disentangle King Arthur, the Monster, and the headmaster. She expressed due gratitude for Miss Seeton's assistance; and the two friends said goodbye.

Miss Seeton then went out to the shops, her mind a happy confusion of King Arthur's knights on horseback, their lances couched, their plumed helmets proud, and the feather duster Martha had asked her to buy. To celebrate her Premium Bond win she brought back not one, but two, dusters on their slender bamboo sticks, and Martha scolded her gently for extravagance before the happy circumstances returned to mind.

At the hour when she knew Plummergen's Junior Mixed Infants would be enjoying their morning playtime under Miss Maynard's kindly supervision, Miss Seeton telephoned the school office and began to put her Arthurian Background Books request to Mr. Jessyp, who laughed. "They didn't waste much time roping you in," he said cheerfully.

"As you know, Mr. Jessyp, I am always ready to help in a good cause, and with so ... so ambitious a project," said Miss Seeton, trying to express her unvoiced doubts with as much tact as she could, "I do feel that the earlier one makes a start, the better, if the performance is to be instead of a Christmas pantomime."

Martin Jessyp seized with relief on her words. Miss Seeton, now some years retired, would still help out at the village school if asked. Mr. Jessyp had the highest opinion of any qualified teacher's common sense.

"I'm glad you said that, Miss Seeton. I've been thinking it over and, really, for a place as small as Plummergen I'd say 'over-ambitious' more accurately hits the mark. For one thing, we haven't enough people who can really sing—though the film is no shining example—and it's undeniably long. To suit a village audience we'd have to make pretty drastic cuts to bring it down to an hour and a half, two hours at the most, and I doubt if the writers would be happy to let us chop it about quite so much."

Miss Seeton replied that—although of course she could not speak from personal experience, being merely one who taught as opposed to one who created—as she had always understood it, creative persons tended to be protective of their work.

"Yes," went on the headmaster, "and when it's such good work they'd expect a lot more money than we could rustle up, for the performance rights."

Miss Seeton's unexpected windfall flashed into her mind. She wondered guiltily if perhaps she should offer—

"So I think," went on Mr. Jessyp, "we'd be better off with an original Arthurian script based, like *Camelot*, on Malory and T.H. White but without in any way risking copyright infringement. That way, we'd have nothing beyond the usual routine expenses. Especially," with another laugh, "as you have—aha—been volunteered, Miss Seeton, to design the scenery."

"Of which," said Miss Seeton, willing conscript to her dear village's concerns, "I know very little, except that there must be a castle, of course. With pinnacles, and flags, and turrets. The river winds *down to tower'd Camelot*, as Tennyson tells us—a lake for throwing Excalibur away at the end—and should there be need of a forest through which the knights of the Round Table may ride in order to encounter dragons, and maidens in distress, there might be something suitable from when the Padders acted *Babes In The Wood,* which would leave me more time to spend on other details." An idea for making far better use of her good fortune than subsidising the performance rights of a three-and-a-half-hour musical had occurred to Miss Seeton.

"Tintagel, of course," she said happily, thinking of Cornish sands and sunshine.

Martin Jessyp tutted in pedagogic fashion. "That's not Camelot, Miss Seeton, that's merely where Arthur was born. All that towers at Tintagel is the cliffs, and while the scenery is admittedly dramatic, it's hardly Christmassy. What people want to see at Christmas is bright costumes, pageantry, spectacle—but I'm sorry, the bell is about to ring." Miss Seeton in her turn began to apologise, but he courteously interrupted. "May I suggest that I look out one or two background books, with suitable illustrations, for you a little later? During the lunch break, if I've time. Nigel Colveden can drop them off at Sweetbriars for you this afternoon, once he and young Len have delivered the straw bales Sir George promised for the children to construct a small labyrinth. Miss

Maynard wants to encourage the development of their spatial awareness, and the application of mathematics to real life."

Down the telephone wires Miss Seeton heard the distant clangour of the hand-bell generations of Plummergen's Junior Mixed Infants had in strict and fair-shares turn been permitted to ring as a signal that playtime was over and they must resume their classroom activities. She hurriedly thanked Mr. Jessyp for his kindness, hoped he would not put himself to too much trouble, and rang off. Then she went to ask Martha if she might just slip out to the shops again and be permitted to buy a cake from Mrs. Wyght's bakery across the road, because it seemed likely that dear Nigel Colveden would be dropping in for tea.

"Ah," said Martha, with a grin that went unnoticed.

"And maybe some chocolate biscuits," Miss Seeton added wistfully. Mrs. Bloomer, whose cakes were renowned in Plummergen and beyond, at once forgave Miss Emily her support for commercial baking. Dark chocolate thins were an indulgence her employer seldom allowed herself.

When Nigel appeared on the front doorstep he had a carrier bag of books, and a most colourful and startling appearance. "Good gracious," said Miss Seeton faintly. "Nigel, what can have happened to you? Does it hurt? Do come in."

Nigel grinned as he dusted his shoes on the mat. "Hasn't Martha told you? I know it's one of her days with you. She laughed quite as much as the rest of the family when she heard I'd been kicked by a sheep."

Miss Seeton regarded him doubtfully. She knew Nigel's sense of humour.

"Honest Injun," he assured his hostess as he followed her into the sitting room, restored now to its usual neatness. He set the books down and headed thankfully towards a chair, rubbing his back as he went. "Martha's been busy beating all your carpets, I know, but she should just try shifting bales of straw. Ugh!"

"And with only one eye," said Miss Seeton faintly. That purple, black and orange swelling held swirls of vivid red and yellow in its depths. Psychedelic, she believed was the term. "Do sit down, Nigel, and I will make the tea. It will help to restore you."

"Thanks, I could do with a cup or two, or even three if you can spare them. Tea and sympathy—but does anyone offer them besides you, Miss Seeton? And Louise," he added quickly. "Louise, of course, but even she giggled once she was sure I was okay really."

Nigel was so obviously preparing to make a lengthy and humorous anecdote out of his experience that Miss Seeton happily played along with her guest as he drifted behind her into the kitchen.

"But how could you be kicked in the eye by a sheep, Nigel? You are over six feet tall."

"September," said Nigel. Miss Seeton studied him thoughtfully. "Annual sheep-cull," he went on. "And dozy wasps."

Miss Seeton believed that part, at least. The growing sluggishness of wasps as autumn drew near meant that one must keep a closer watch than usual on fruits in the garden and jam in the jar, for fear of stings, and be wary about window sills and curtains.

"Vinegar for wasps," she murmured.

Nigel grinned. "Bicarbonate for bees—though it wasn't a bee that did this, any more than it was Louise, in case you wondered." Miss Seeton looked startled. "Oh, yes, after they've finished laughing quite a few of my nearest and dearest have suggested my wife has found me out and taught me a stern lesson."

"I'm sure there is nothing for dear Louise to find," said the loyal Miss Seeton. "Indeed, if there were, not that I can believe for a moment there would be, but if there were, it would be in your past, which is, after all, another country ..." With dismay she remembered where this quotation led, but Nigel knew nothing of dead wenches and merely nodded.

"Louise is wonderful," he said with pride. "Did Mother tell you how the breakfast newspaper problem was solved?" Lady Colveden had; Miss Seeton was duly complimentary.

They carried the tea-things through to the sitting room and Nigel, with little encouragement, accepted his first cup and continued his thrilling narration.

"Every year we check the ewes to see if they'll be up to producing good lambs next spring. And if they aren't, that's them for the chop," began the young farmer briskly. "We cull about a quarter of the flock each time, and Mr. Stacey has first pick of the bunch before they're sold on the open meat market." Miss Seeton nodded. She knew the basic facts of living and working in the country.

"But how," she prompted, "do you decide which sheep to cull?"

"Teeth." Nigel used his own fine specimens to bite into Mrs. Wyght's plum cake. "The older the sheep, the fewer the teeth, or at least the poorer the condition of their snappers. Did you know sheep have no upper front teeth? Just molars and so on, for chewing. Lambs are born with enough to start with, and the adult teeth come along gradually, two a time. A sheep isn't full-mouthed until she's around four years old, then after a few more years she starts to lose them the same two-by-two way. Once all the incisors are gone or damaged she can't bite or eat properly, she can only chew. So in general, when a ewe is too broken-mouthed, off she goes to the butcher." He grinned. "Unless she's a good breeder."

Miss Seeton poured another cup of tea, cut a second slice of cake, and continued to look and listen with interest. Enthusiasm always pleased her, expertise even more so.

"A good breeding ewe is worth keeping, Miss Seeton. Always drops healthy lambs, looks after them properly—you'd be surprised how many don't—gives good fleece as well as good flesh. You know the sort of thing." Nigel gave her no time to admit or deny such knowledge. "Before we run the flock through the sheep-dip, we grab 'em one by one and tip them on their backs to give their hooves a thorough check, and the same goes for their lower incisors—well, their only incisors, if we're being accurate." The teacher in Miss Seeton approved of accuracy, but Nigel took her nod of approval as one of shared knowledge, and pressed on. "In the not-so-distant past a farmer might even pay a vet to fit his best breeders with dentures so they wouldn't find it so difficult to eat, but these days most people will take extra care to chop the feed into small enough pieces that nobody needs to pay for false teeth at all, which is just as well because they come pretty expensive."

False teeth for sheep. Miss Seeton favoured Nigel with her best teacherly gaze. The Colveden sense of humour. She smiled, politely.

"Honour bright, Miss Seeton. There was something in *Farmers Weekly* only the other day." Nigel grinned once more at her expression. "Louise didn't believe me, either, until I showed her the ad proving it was far cheaper to buy one particular machine for shredding hay and root crops than to hunt high and low for a vet who still specialised in dentistry."

Miss Seeton hesitated, then frowned. "I am still a little unclear, Nigel, as to how looking at the teeth of a sheep would lead one to kick you. Surely it is a painless procedure? Or," with memories of a troublesome wisdom tooth, "do you have to give an injection?"

"If a wasp flies straight at your face, and you duck down out of its way, if you're holding a sheep—and they hate being on their backs—it will wriggle, at the very least, and the one I was holding did more than wriggle. Hence," concluded Nigel as a third slice of cake was put on his plate, "this magnificent shiner."

Miss Seeton recalled the recent amusing television item about the lorry-driver and the Traffic Jam. She had not until now realised the extreme threat posed by wasps to general life and limb. Farming must be rather more dangerous than she had ever realised.

Nigel drank tea, and chuckled. "Dangerous for some of the animals, too. Did you know there's a breed of pig so obese it can barely walk? And it needs a pillow?" Once more a doubtful gaze met him across the table. "To stop it suffocating," he explained. "Thick wooden sausages to hold up its head, poor thing—the Dorset Gold Tip, it's called."

Miss Seeton once more gave her young friend the benefit of the doubt. "A charming name," she murmured non-committally.

"Names can be fun," agreed Nigel. "We learned lots at college about various breeds of sheep, and of course you wouldn't expect us to have anything here but Romneys or Romney crosses, but I always had a secret hankering after a Lonk or two, just because of the name. Or even a Beulah Speckled-face."

"Lonk," echoed Miss Seeton. "Beulah Speckled-face. Nigel, really?"

"Really. But they're upland breeds, and because much of our land is barely six inches above sea level it wouldn't suit them. Besides, Romney Marsh farms ought to farm Romney sheep. It wouldn't be right not to, when people have spent generations breeding them to suit our unusual—no, unique—conditions."

Nigel in full farming flow was an entirely different person from the light-hearted young man Miss Seeton had known for so long. She heard further gems of agricultural wisdom ("Catch any shepherd culling a sheep that's blind, no matter how old she is!") and was listening, enthralled, to a lecture on the habits of spiders in autumn, when the telephone rang and she had to tear herself away, urging the last piece of cake on her guest while she left him alone.

"Why, Chief Superintendent, what a delightful surprise," he heard her say.

Chapter Four

Plummergen opinion on Miss Seeton has ever been mixed. There are many who regard her as nothing but an asset to the village. Others see her ostensible dealings with the police as camouflage for something—upon the exact nature of which nobody can agree—rather more sinister, probably criminal in intent, surely indicative of corruption (at least) at the highest level, and definitely nothing whatsoever to do with sketching, painting, or drawing.

"Such a feeble excuse," scoffed Miss Nuttel.

"Unbelievable," agreed Mrs. Blaine, "even if she really did teach art before she retired."

"If," echoed Miss Nuttel. "No proving it after so long, of course."

Mrs. Blaine uttered a regretful sigh before returning to her theme. "It's obvious that photographs would be far more helpful to the authorities than anything man-made—"

"Or woman-made, Bunny."

Mrs. Blaine tittered. "Too clever of you, Eric—but aren't I right? A photo always looks exactly like what it's of, which simply has to be a better clue that any drawing, because with a drawing you can't be sure. Suppose your hand were to shake? Besides, with an india-rubber it can too easily be altered. A photograph is a fact."

"Say anything to cover their real reason for meeting her," said Miss Nuttel. "Think we'll swallow it, of course. Messages in code," she concluded, inspired.

Chief Superintendent Delphick had long ago realised that nothing he or his colleagues—not even Sergeant Ranger, adopted son of Plummergen through his marriage to the doctor's daughter—might say would ever wholly eradicate the doubts of the suspicious. While doing his best to rouse as little comment, and stir up as little trouble as possible each time he had cause to consult the Yard's retained consultant, the Oracle's lurking unease was always soothed by the reassuring knowledge that Miss Seeton herself never knew what people said of her, and that even if she did, any true-blue English gentlewoman must disapprove of, and ignore as vulgar, any public discussion of her very private life.

For this particular consultation Delphick had travelled by train, and by taxi, alone.

Bob voiced regret at missing the chance to see his adopted aunt, and perhaps his in-laws if there was time, but Delphick reminded him that should both of them go to Plummergen it would have far too official an appearance.

"We're trying to keep the lid on this kidnap, remember," he warned. "Plummergen will always add two and two and make fifty with no effort whatever."

Bob seized the darts metaphor, and hurried on with it. "Only sometimes the bull's-eye they hit is the wrong one, sir."

"Too often, it is, but there's always the risk that for once it will be correct. Miss Seeton is a friend, remember, as well as a colleague. Isn't her birthday some time around now?"

"September the eleventh," supplied Bob at once. "Martha made a cake."

"Courtesy requires that I deliver her card in person rather than entrust it to the post, as an apology for my forgetfulness."

"Take a box of chocolates too," suggested the adopted nephew promptly. "She's not that keen on the milk, so you could bring them back with you to swap for plain."

"How your mind seems to run on food, Sergeant Ranger. Can it be that your enthusiasm for joining me in this flying visit is prompted by thoughts of gingerbread?"

Miss Seeton, knowing that Mr. Delphick was less keen on gingerbread than was dear Bob, had begged a Victoria sponge from Martha as more suitable than rich fruit cake for a morning visitor. Delphick expressed pleasure at this kindly thought, and commended the jam upon being told that it was from Miss Seeton's own fruit, last year's crop, and Martha had made that, too.

"Which she enjoys so much," explained Miss Seeton, "partly on account of waste—she wishes to avoid it, of course—and also because it does taste better than much of what can be bought in the shops, not at all from any need to make financial savings." She smiled. "Indeed, Mr. Delphick, at present I feel almost rolling in wealth."

"I've never won tuppence with my Premium Bonds," lamented the chief superintendent, as she finished explaining. "Congratulations, Miss Seeton. I hope this doesn't mean you will allow your contract with Scotland Yard to lapse. Your services to the forces of law and order would be a sad loss."

Miss Seeton, turning pink, assured him that she knew her duty, and her contract would be honoured for so long as the police might ask it of her.

"I had, however," she went on, "thought of spending a few days in the West Country. Plummergen Amateur Dramatic Society is considering a Christmas play about King Arthur, and they have asked me to design the scenery, which will take time as I know so little about it, although the stories are of course familiar. One does like to be accurate, and Mr. Jessyp assures me there is no need to go as far west as Cornwall, for Tintagel is merely where he was born and Somerset is far more suitable. Glastonbury, you see. The Isle of Avalon."

Delphick had stiffened at the unexpected coincidence of this West Country connection, and swiftly changed his mind about asking her to look, immediately after their tea and cake, at the photographs of Christy Garth hidden in the birthday parcel. On first arriving at Sweetbriars he had warned that the milk chocolate selection was a deliberate mistake, and that her proper present would arrive in the post later. Miss Seeton, blushing discreetly, had assured him no present was necessary; and thanked him, with a little chuckle, when he said that Sergeant Ranger would never forgive him if he paid insufficient attention to young Gideon's fellow godparent.

The West Country. He had often felt Miss Seeton might be psychic. He pressed now for further details of her proposed break, and her reasons for taking it.

"Mr. Jessyp is to write the script," she enlarged, after *Camelot* and the confusion over Monty Python and the ambitions of Emmy Putts had been explained. "It is so much cheaper than rights, he tells me, and so few Padders apparently can sing." Delphick's brain spelled through this statement twice, in the end making sense of her homonyms. "He has kept back his Malory," she added, "but he sent several books, with illustrations, and I have my own Tennyson, or rather, Cousin Flora's. So very kind of him. But of course it is to the benefit of the whole village, and there are few photographs except in Geoffrey Ashe. An excellent book and most interesting, from the little I have so far had time to study. One can trust it because it is all really there, you see."

Delphick picked up *The Quest for Arthur's Britain* and searched the index for Camelot. He smiled. "Now I understand why you're going to Somerset. Glastonbury, where he sailed in that mysterious barge to be healed of his fatal wound. South Cadbury, where in real life he would have lived in the hill fort that became the Camelot of legend. The scenery, as far as one can judge from photographs, might be called almost inspirational."

"It would be possible," conceded Miss Seeton, "to invent some appropriate background, or even—" she twinkled at him—"to *appropriate* a castle or other scenery from a different part of the country, but I feel strongly, knowing as I do that the real places are there to be seen, that I should. Don't you? See them. It is of course unlikely that an audience would notice, and indeed one hopes their concentration would be on the performance rather than the background, but one does like to be accurate. Which going to the West Country is sure to help me to be."

Delphick wondered secretly whether library books might save his hostess some degree of inconvenience and expenditure. Not for the first time in their acquaintance, Miss Seeton seemed to forestall him. "I had thought," she went on, "about the library. There is, you may know, such a thing as an inter-library loan, books on Somerset being few in Kent, even if King Arthur himself is known throughout the country. Only, with the weather at this time of year being so variable, and just now so temperate, a short holiday would be a pleasure as well as an obligation. And inter-library loans take time."

"Talking of time—" regretfully, Delphick interrupted her train of thought—"I should like, before my return to the Yard, to have your opinion—your impression—of the young man in these photographs, Miss Seeton."

Miss Seeton was all apology. The chief superintendent had explained yesterday the professional reason for today's visit. She had duly set out sketchbook and pencils on a side table—and then she had distracted him with tea and cake ...

"After a train journey from London to Brettenden, and the excitement of Mr. Baxter's taxi, I was very glad of the rest and the refreshment, Miss Seeton." These days Mr. Baxter plied his trade more or less on a whim, depending on how much he had recently won (or lost) on the horses. It was an unlucky passenger who found him at the front of the Brettenden taxi-rank. His previously asthmatic car had developed near-terminal bronchitis. While the route to Plummergen was safely downhill, the Oracle resolved that any future visit by train would see either Headcorn or Ashford as the railway station of choice. A telephone booking with Jack Crabbe of Plummergen's garage would arouse too much village speculation for his liking, well though he knew how Jack himself could be discreet.

Discretion. Yes. As he reassured his hostess, he was taking the envelope of photos from the swirl of wrapping paper. An English gentlewoman could be trusted, he knew.

"This poor chap," he said, "has gone missing. It isn't generally known, and we don't wish it to be, but it seems he could have been kidnapped."

"Oh, dear." Miss Seeton was shocked. "How very distressing for his poor family, and how extremely unpleasant for him. Oh." She contemplated the first photograph. "Dear me, I may be wrong. He gives the distinct impression of reckless youth, does he not? Adventurous, as of course the young should be, enquiring, experimenting, taking risks—but he seems to be one who is over-adventurous. Being young, he would pay little heed to the future." She recalled some of her fellow students at art college, so many years ago. "Such persons rarely do. Yet one would not call them heedless or irresponsible, exactly ..." She shuffled through the other photos. "More, living for the moment," she concluded. "He might even, for a short while, find the whole experience something of a joke."

"Spot on, Miss Seeton. I doubt if his picture ever appears in your paper, but the tabloid press all too frequently snaps him being thrown out of nightclubs or involving himself in other disreputable antics. I'd say 'irresponsible' is a generous description. Far too much money for his own good, lacking the brains to make sensible use of it—or of his time. He drinks, he drugs, he gets into fights at the slightest provocation, and of course he drives too fast under the influence, though mercifully he hasn't yet done any serious damage to anyone." He smiled grimly. "No doubt it's only a matter of time, the young idiot. And it goes without saying that he womanises, which explains quite a few of the fights. Some of these snaps are mug-shots, as you probably guessed. I can't recall how many times he's been arrested, but it's well into double figures."

Miss Seeton sighed. "A spoiled child," she suggested, regretting the waste.

"In the sense of being damaged, yes. He's the eldest of three, and while he was growing up his parents concentrated so hard on establishing the business they tended to neglect him. Once they were established, they appear to have over-compensated for their earlier neglect and he was smart enough to take advantage. His younger brother and sister aren't, apparently, in the same league of wild child craziness—the brother has joined the business, the sister does a lot of charity work."

"One must hope the good example of his siblings will bring him to his senses," said the retired teacher, almost sternly. "It should, of course, be for the older ones to set an example to the younger, but there are always exceptions and this kidnapping may be just the shock required to make him think for once about the sort of life he has hitherto led." She looked again at the half-dozen photographs on the table. "But do tell me, in what way can I assist you, Chief Superintendent?"

Delphick hesitated. He had, in the anticipation of one of her special drawings, asked Miss Seeton for her impression of Christy Garth; but she had without prompting sketched the young tearaway very neatly in words. "None of these photos is more than a rigid likeness," he said slowly. "Static. I'd like some sort of handle on the young man as he really is—the chance for a guess at what he might have been doing when the whole affair began. All we've been told is that he was heading west, which covers a lot of this country and might even refer to a trip across the Atlantic, although Superintendent Kebby, who's in charge of the case—oh, I am merely the humble messenger," he added as she looked surprised. "Superintendent Kebby has checked every airline booking and ocean-going liner in the past month, and the young man appears to have made no plans to go abroad, whether bound for the west or, indeed, the east."

Again Miss Seeton looked surprised.

"Kebby wondered, you see, if he might have crossed to the continent in order to start for North America from a European air- or sea-port. However, the most diligent search found no bookings registered anywhere in his name."

Miss Seeton noted the chief superintendent's caution. If the matter was to be kept secret, of course he must not let slip the identity of the unfortunate young man whose face—sullen, sneering, reckless—gazed up at her in glossy black and white. She gazed back at that face for several long moments.

"His family's wealth seems to have bought him little happiness," she said at last, and indicated two photographs rather more blurred than the others. "These, I suspect, are not ... official pictures." She was unable to speak of *mug-shots* with Mr. Delphick's assurance. "Perhaps from one of the tabloid newspapers to which you referred?" Delphick, smiling, nodded. She sighed. "He does not give the impression of having gained any pleasure from his way of life, no matter how much money he may have spent in its pursuit. One always supposes that playboys must relish the excesses of a lifestyle with few worries, but this young man seems, if it is not too fanciful, almost crushed under a burden of discontent and, indeed, of boredom." She sighed again. "How wise of his brother and sister to have found some gainful occupation. And how fortunate. And how very sad for his parents."

"Poor little rich boy, you mean?"

Miss Seeton agreed, adding quickly that while she felt some sympathy for this young man it must be limited, because people had to take responsibility for their actions and the impression these photographs gave was that he was both irresponsible and thoroughly spoiled, when he was certainly old enough to know better. As for his parents, so were they—old enough, she meant—and it was a matter for their consciences as to how far neglect of their eldest child might have contributed to his problems. Although, of course, one could hardly blame him for having been kidnapped. "Unless he was foolish enough to put himself in the way of temptation—of tempting someone else, that is, to take advantage of his weakness. You say he drinks, and takes drugs?"

"He does. On an almost heroic scale, some would say."

Miss Seeton contemplated the surly face of Christy Garth. "A sad waste. When one thinks of the artists—writers—musicians who have at least created something worthwhile from their excesses ..."

"For others apart from themselves to enjoy? Yes, indeed. We may, thanks to that untimely person from Porlock, have only half the poem, but think how many people admire what there is of *Kubla Khan*."

She nodded. "As I used to tell my pupils, to experience and to keep it entirely to one's self is—well, selfish, when there can be so much pleasure in sharing and even, perhaps, encouraging others to see not only the same, but something extra. This young man seems to have won no pleasure at all from his experiences. Although," a sense of fairness made her add, "he may have no particular creative instinct, which could explain it."

Delphick smiled. "Not everyone has your talent, Miss Seeton." He rose to his feet, and collected her sketchbook and pencils. "A talent I now ask you to use on behalf of this young man, by giving me—and Superintendent Kebby—some idea of what he might have been planning to do, and where he was planning to go. I'll tidy the tea-things into the kitchen to clear some space for you."

He ignored her faint protest, set down the drawing materials and whisked plates, cups and tea-pot from the table even as her hand instinctively moved to bring the tools of her profession within reach. He watched her push the mug-shots, posed and stiff, aside, leaving the two newspaper photographs as the focus of her attention. He heard her sigh, saw her sadly shake her head—that wasted life still worrying her, of course ...

"Please don't." He had stood silently watching, and guessed what she meant to do.

Miss Seeton turned a guilty face towards him. The hand that had been prepared to rip her finished sketch from the block and crumple it, or perhaps tear it in pieces, wavered and fell. She blushed. "I'm so sorry," she murmured. "I quite forgot."

Delphick smiled kindly at her. She always "forgot", hoping he would not notice until it was too late. He knew that Miss Seeton's disapproval of those cartoons, doodles, sketches she produced by instinct rather than by painstaking skill was marked, and tempered always by embarrassment. She felt that one should draw only what was there—unless, of course, one had sufficient talent, which she freely acknowledged she had not—and most certainly

62

no genius, which could excuse almost anything—and it was only by stern reminders that she was under contract to Scotland Yard, who had first refusal on any, repeat any, of her work, that Delphick managed to prevent her concealing, or even destroying, what she had drawn when that drawing was what he particularly wished to see.

Now he drew close, to look over her shoulder. "I wonder what has you so bothered this time—oh. Yes. Somewhat unexpected, I agree."

Certainly it was a face that he saw on the paper; but not a human face. White and woolly, capering wildly at the forefront of a group of its fellows static in wraps of some heavy fabric—canvas, perhaps—a single sheep grinned at him, displaying enormous teeth—no, not teeth, dentures. The entire flock, canvas-wrapped though it was, wore the same over-exuberant smile and shared the same bright-eyed, almost manic, expression. Could they but burst their bonds those sheep, Delphick suspected, would not remain meekly in their field but would run riot through the countryside.

"I'm so sorry," said Miss Seeton again. "It doesn't look in the least like that young man, does it." This was no question, but an apology. "It—it's Nigel Colveden, you see." This made Delphick blink. Miss Seeton hurried to explain. "Such amusing stories of farming life yesterday—how he was nearly stung by a wasp when holding a sheep, and it kicked him—the sheep, not the wasp—and he knows a great deal about them, as you would expect, but I didn't. For instance, I had no idea that spiders can float on silken threads several thousand feet into the air—ballooning, he called it, which the young ones do in autumn. He said I should watch early in the morning as the sun rises and the air warms, for hedges or trees covered in gossamer, which is a preliminary to the phenomenon, and especially should there be a breeze. It all sounds most interesting."

"As interesting as these sheep in false teeth?" Delphick knew Nigel's sense of humour, and knew also that Miss Seeton, despite her long experience as a teacher, tended to believe the best of people.

"Oh, I know. One of Nigel's little jokes, I thought at first just as I am sure you did, but he explained that farmers would sometimes have them fitted to a good breeding ewe rather than cull her when she could no longer graze, until they thought of cutting food into smaller pieces. Which one would have considered no more than common sense." Miss Seeton, apart from an extracted wisdom tooth, was blessed with excellent teeth. "I believe one minces or mashes adult, as it were, food for toothless human babies—though possibly they lacked the proper equipment for sheep, in earlier days."

Delphick, avoiding entanglement in a discussion of ovine masticatory habits, made a mental note that false teeth might, in some way, have played a part in the disappearance of Christy Garth. Perhaps an emergency appointment with an opportunist dental practitioner had ended with the young man's being fed knock-out drops. Perhaps ...

Idly, he turned the page to admire Miss Seeton's previous sketch. He caught his breath—turned the sound into a hasty chuckle. "Traffic Jam," he said, looking at the sprightly glass jars, all but one labelled *Plum* and all topped with frill-edged gingham secured with ribbon, crowded along and filling, in both directions, a narrow country lane. She'd obviously seen the same television news item so many others had seen—but how many others would have known-without-knowing, as she seemed to have known, the significance of that unfortunate accident in the kidnap of Christy Garth?

"A little foolish word-play," said Miss Seeton. "Some puns are needlessly tortuous, but this seemed so quick and amusing, although one has to feel sorry for the driver and thank goodness it was no worse than concussion. At this time of year, while bees are productive and busy, wasps can be most inconvenient creatures, can they not?"

Which, Delphick guessed, explained the single jar of honey. "They can indeed." He leafed further back through the sketchbook, finding no more than routine studies of trees, buildings, a few garden birds, and one lifelike portrait of Martha Bloomer brandishing a carpet beater while Stan propped a patterned rug over a set of wooden steps. "Spring cleaning? In September?"

Miss Seeton twinkled at him. "Dear Martha will be so glad when I take my little trip into Somerset. I won't say that she has already packed my case, but once I am out of the way she can dust, and sweep, and move furniture and beat carpets to her heart's content—except the other way around, of course, for there is no sense in dusting before you disturb everything—and then she will feel the house is ready for the onset of winter, though since the central heating there is far less dust than used to come from Cousin Flora's open fires. Indeed I would be happy with just spring, though I would never tell her so. Martha, you see, positively enjoys cleaning. She wishes for a carpet shampooer, after my little Premium Bond win, although I myself would much prefer to take a holiday than shampoo a carpet."

"Martha," Delphick said, "is one in a million, Miss Seeton." As, in her own invaluable way, was Miss Seeton herself.

Back at the Yard, the chief superintendent advised Superintendent Kebby of his return and invited him to his office to inspect the sketches produced by Miss Seeton's pencil. "I told her I'd like this one too," the Oracle tapped the Traffic Jam cartoon, "because it made me laugh, which it did—but in my opinion it's something more than the 'foolish word-play' she herself called it. She drew it as a direct result of the television news item a day or so before."

A twirl of the superintendent's moustache, a frown as he contemplated the crowded ranks of gingham-topped jars. "The day the second pick-up went wrong," he said at last. "That woman psychic, Oracle?"

"Something very like, although I suspect she wouldn't care for the term herself. She'd think it far too eccentric and other-worldly for the way she sees herself as a typical English spinster—Sergeant Ranger," as Bob in his silent corner failed to suppress a gurgle of mirth, "please go outside if you mean to choke to death. The superintendent and I need to concentrate, and we don't wish to be disturbed."

"Sorry, sir," murmured his unrepentant sergeant. Kebby turned and gave him a wink, a wry grin, and a sideways jerk of the head. Bob, glancing towards Delphick and receiving his nod, took this as an invitation to join the picture-fanciers.

"Traffic Jam," he said. "Evesham's to the west of London, of course, and didn't you say, sir, the family thought young Garth might be heading west?"

"Yes, and it looks as if your MissEss agrees." Kebby looked from one of Miss Seeton's friends to the other. "When she dashes these sketches off like that, that's when you sit up and take notice, you say?"

"It is," Delphick agreed, "which is why I found an excuse to appropriate this one even though it wasn't my original purpose in going down to Kent. This one—" with a flourish, he produced the Dancing Sheep drawing—"is what she drew after studying the photos of the young man who's gone missing."

"Sheep in strait-jackets," muttered Superintendent Kebby. "Firmly bandaged, at any rate—and grinning like crazy. Translation, please."

"Miss Seeton attributed the false teeth to some humorous stories recently told her by a young farmer friend," began Delphick. "Studying the photos of Garth, she said he gave the impression of severe discontent at, she assumed, a life wasted and unproductive when his siblings were both useful and happy. No doubt she would, if pressed, argue that the wide smiles produced by the dentures were her attempt to induce a more cheerful frame of mind in the unfortunate youth, and the fact that the smiles belong to sheep is entirely due to Nigel Colveden's anecdotes."

Bob stirred. Delphick shook his head. "Yes, I wondered, too, but apparently it's not so. Nigel takes farming very seriously and wouldn't joke about it, Miss Seeton says. A teacher can usually tell if the wool—I beg your pardon—is being pulled over her eyes."

"Baa," said Kebby, and the others grinned. "All right, then. Might this mean Garth is being held in some part of the country that specialises in sheep? Maybe even near Romney Marsh, where your MissEss lives? Good grief, he could be tied up in the cellar of the house next door! You sure you heard nobody yelling for help?"

"Kent is hardly to the west of anywhere," Delphick reminded him, "with the obvious exception of France— which, after your thorough record-checking, I think we may regard as no more than a distraction."

"The Traffic Jam business does suggest the westward idea could be worth pursuing." Kebby tugged at his moustache. "Where in the west do they grow sheep?" Jasper Kebby was a resolutely urban man.

"Wales," said Delphick at once. He, too, had been checking facts, though in the office encyclopaedia rather than at air- and sea-ports. "Shropshire, Herefordshire ..." He saw Kebby stiffen. "Yes, the Traffic Jam, where the ransom pickup went wrong. Worcestershire is the adjoining county, and Evesham is in Worcestershire—there could well be a connection. But we should not forget to add Wiltshire, Dorset ... and Somerset, to the list of westerly sheep-farming areas." He glanced at Bob. "Miss Seeton tells me she plans a short break in Somerset before long."

"Yes, sir. She's been roped in as scenery designer for the Christmas play," he explained to Superintendent Kebby, who had looked startled at the coincidence. "She prefers to be as accurate as she can, sir, and—"

"Accurate?" Kebby's eyes flashed. "A field of sheep wearing false teeth and bandages, and you tell me the woman likes to be accurate?"

Bob hesitated. Delphick came to his rescue. "It is when Miss Seeton is ... less than accurate that her drawings are of such importance. Wasn't that why you asked me to consult her in the first place?"

Again the handlebar moustache was tugged before Kebby grinned. "It's a fair cop. And that Traffic Jam doodle's a hoot. She could make her fortune designing saucy seaside postcards. So, what's your interpretation of our woolly friends in dentures?"

"False teeth," amended the Oracle, after a pause. "Could the inference be that the disappearance itself is false? A kidnap faked by Garth to extract money from his brother and sister when, perhaps, his parents had already refused to give him an increased allowance? You said both the parents were away, and that's the reason the daughter—Letty? thank you—left it rather longer, perhaps, than the kidnappers would have liked to discover the original ransom demand. Was anything said about money, apart from the obvious, when you spoke to the brother and sister?"

Kebby was frowning. "Now you come to mention it, I'm not sure the subject came under discussion at all. They were upset, worried—more concerned for their brother's safety than about giving us the gory details of his spendthrift habits."

Delphick nodded. "This is your case, Superintendent Kebby, but since you have asked for my—for Miss Seeton's—help, I would strongly suggest that you take the advice hinted at in her sketches as a starting-point for further investigation. Discreet enquiries in westerly areas noted for their sheep. You can find an excuse, I'm sure—something to do with drugs, perhaps, which may turn out to be less of a cover story than you might suppose. Garth's habit is hardly a secret."

"Starting in Evesham," said Kebby. "I'll talk to someone in charge down there. No use complete strangers turning up to ask questions—the locals would clam up the moment they set eyes on anyone from the Smoke."

"You could take an interpreter with you," Delphick pointed out. "And strings of glass beads to placate the natives." Bob choked.

Kebby looked aggrieved. "I'm not a smocks-and-gumboots chap any more than the rest of my team. We'd stand out like snowflakes in a coal mine. You want someone undercover, they've got to look the part."

Delphick sobered. "Of course. I apologise. By all means telephone Evesham—but I remain intrigued by the puzzle of those strait-jacketed sheep. If, in the course of further investigation, word should reach the Yard of unorthodox behaviour on the part of any sheep, no matter the size of the flock, in any western part of the country, perhaps you could let me know." He coughed. "It might just help to narrow the area of search."

"Or," said Jasper Kebby glumly, "it might not."

Chapter Five

In the directors' office of a factory on the outskirts of Glastonbury, at the end of the working day, four people met in formal conference. The surviving shareholders of Callender's Coats still had a problem, and very different opinions as to how it should be resolved.

Crispin, the more organised of the two brothers, glanced at the pencilled notes for which he had no real need. It had all been discussed before, more than once, on the telephone and face to face: but this was the first time there had been a serious meeting of Guy Callender's children in which decisions had to be made.

"With luck," he began, "it shouldn't take much longer for the grant of probate to go through. Everything was left in equal shares between us. Rather than owning ten per cent each as we do now, it will soon be twenty-five per cent. This means the four of us will be outright owners of the company, the factory—and the field. We can't keep dithering. We have to make up our minds about Janner and his sheep."

"We want to expand," growled Bill. "We want him gone. We need that field."

"It's good grazing land," objected Valentine, as she had repeatedly told her siblings over the past few days. "It's not right to cover good grazing land with concrete."

"We can't find anywhere else," said Bill, "if we want to expand the way Dad wanted."

Everyone looked towards Octavia. "You said," said Crispin, "you'd looked further into this Act of Parliament about farm tenancies." She nodded. "Let's have it, then."

Octavia Callender prided herself on the image she had built up. Today her flowing locks were capped by a pull-on knitted cloche in shades of gold, green, and brown, to match her caftan. In the same free spirit that saw her wear no wristwatch, she took pains to carry no handbag. Lengths of psychedelic cloth had been torn by Valentine into narrow strips and woven into fabric that, cut to size and brightly stitched, made a remarkable, unique and bulky tote bag, into which the owner now delved to retrieve her notebook and pencil.

She looked at Crispin, whose own pencil was poised to make additional notes. This was no time for doodling: he was all businessman now. Octavia hid a smile, winked at the other two, and solemnly cleared her throat before declaiming from the open page: "The Agriculture (Miscellaneous Provisions) Act, 1976. Of course," she went on in her normal voice, "until it's passed it's a Bill, rather than an Act, but all the discussions I've been able to find in newspapers and so forth show pretty clearly what will happen once it becomes law, some time next year. What it boils down to is that if someone who's been renting a piece of land dies, then any close relative who's worked on that piece of land for the previous five years, and regards it as his—or her—main source of income, will be able to take over tenancy of the land under the same terms and conditions as before."

"Then the sooner we get Janner out, the better," said Bill.

"The sooner," insisted Valentine, "we sort out a new rental agreement, the better. With the extra money—any tribunal would have to agree the rent's been set far too low for far too long—anyway, if Janner pays us more we might then be able to afford somewhere for the new factory that *isn't* top-grade farming land."

"We certainly could do with some cash," conceded Bill. "The insurance people are dragging their feet and everything else will be tied up in the business." It was the first hint he had given that he might be prepared to negotiate.

"Coming to a new agreement would take time." Octavia consulted her notes. "If there's an argument, and it goes to arbitration—which you can bet it will—it might take two, three years. Or longer. Could we afford to delay expansion by another couple of years?"

"No," chorused Bill and Crispin. Bill was forceful, Crispin a little hesitant in his reply, but both were agreed that waiting was out of the question.

Valentine looked unhappy, Octavia resigned. Once more she consulted her notes. "In *Farmers Weekly* a while back, in discussions about a ploughing tenancy, they mentioned that under the Agricultural Holdings Act of 1948, if you let land for grazing only, for a period of 364 days at a time, because it isn't a full year it doesn't seem to count as a permanent agreement. Boiled down again, of course, and we'd have to take legal advice—"

"Lawyers cost money," interposed Crispin.

"Money we haven't got," Bill reminded everyone. "Until the insurance pays out—"

"Perhaps," broke in Octavia, "without increasing the rent, we might try to renegotiate Janner's tenancy on a

364-day period so that Young Jan couldn't end up with squatter's rights, or whatever you want to call it—"

"And they won't agree to that," snapped Bill. "Why should they?"

Val continued to look unhappy. "What about Susan?" she asked her sister. "You said *his or her main source of income* and that's what it must be for Susan, I mean Brenda, as well as for Jan. Does that mean she'd have as good a—a squatter's claim as his?"

"Her main source of income—oh, yes. Does she work on the land? No, she doesn't." Octavia was brisk. "All the poor girl does, now she's gone off her head, is wander about the place looking for Arthurian symbols and ley lines, and dance about in long white robes claiming direct descent from the Lady of the Lake."

"Takes one to know one," said Valentine, with her first smile of the meeting. "You're not exactly in plain clothes yourself, Tavy."

"Sell the books, look the part," returned her sister, with a hint of irritation. "If it comes to that, you aren't exactly subfusc yourself."

"Oooh, the benefits of a college education." Val chuckled richly. "If you mean I'm every bit as colourful as you, there's no need to bamboozle me with posh words. The boys can wear collar and tie if they want, it's their working uniform—but I'm a walking advertisement for my work just as you are for your shop."

"Pipe down, you two," snapped Bill.

"Girls, girls," said Crispin. "And what's all this about Brenda?"

"Susan," began Valentine, as the other two stared. "Jan told me the other day," she went on, with a faint pinkening of her plump cheeks. "She's apparently talked about swearing a deed, or something, to make it official."

Octavia, the best-educated and best-read of the siblings, frowned. "Deed poll, I think you mean, but there's no need for all that fuss if she's not planning to commit any crime or defraud anybody—unless anyone who buys her book accuses her of selling them a lot of nonsense. Which in Glastonbury seems unlikely."

"As you know, to your considerable profit," pointed out Crispin, with a chuckle in which the other three joined.

"Modest profit," she corrected him, "but every little helps." She shrugged. "I still have a few of her pamphlets left, poor thing. Of course I'll peddle any amount of nonsense if it sells, but I do prefer it to be well-written nonsense and Susan—beg her pardon, Brenda—Brenda!—isn't what you could call either literate or fluent, when it comes to putting words down on paper." She drew a deep breath. "Just because people read books and write letters, they think it's an easy matter to *write* books. It isn't. The ability to string words together in a coherent argument—"

"Pipe down, Tavy," commanded her elder brother. "We're talking about Janner's rent of the family field, not the literary ambitions of his offspring." Bill's mouth twisted in a reluctant grimace. "But I've got to ask—why Brenda?"

"It means *sword*," Valentine told him. "According to Jan she hunted through a book of names and their meanings, and—well, with all this research she's been doing on the Three Swords of Arthur, she thought it would be more appropriate."

"According to Jan," said Crispin with a grin, in which even Bill shared. Octavia hurried to the relief of her sister.

"She's been researching King Arthur's three swords for what seems like years. She buys books from me occasionally—I let her know if anything likely comes along—and she borrows heaps from the library. If that book of hers is ever finished—and published—I'll stock it—I did promise—but she keeps finding more things to include, and her notes are a real mess. She showed me once, and dropped a few hints about helping her to sort them, but I told her I'd had quite enough of that sort of thing in my college days, besides having no free time with the bookshop." Her eyes glittered. "I dug out an entire quarter's invoices and general paperwork from the files and told her it was a week's worth. She got the message, though she's been a bit standoffish since then."

"Clever," said Crispin with reluctant admiration.

"You should have refused straight out. I'd have said No and left it," said Bill.

Val shook her head. "It was kind as well as clever of Tavy to let her down gently, even if it meant telling a few white lies. It's so much better not to stir up any more trouble than—well, than we've already got."

"And plenty more where that came from," said Bill. "From what you say, Young Jan seems happy enough to think about an independent rent tribunal, but Janner's not happy at all and the agreement's in his name. He says the terms were good enough for him and his brother, and we shouldn't be taking advantage of Dad's death until a decent interval's gone by. Not respectful to his memory, Janner says—or to the squire and old Ebenezer."

"Never mind the past," interposed Crispin. "Does he know about this Act of Parliament next year, d'you reckon?"

"We didn't talk long enough. You know he hates the phone at the best of times—which talking with me wasn't."

"You lost your temper," deduced his brother. Bill glared, then grinned.

"Well, maybe I did, the stubborn old idiot. Kept on about family feeling—when he and Dad hadn't spoken for almost twenty years, on account of Granddad's tombstone! I told him he was a ..." He recalled the presence of his sisters. "A something something hypocrite," he temporised. Octavia chuckled, Valentine sighed. Both they and Crispin knew the volatile nature of their older brother's moods.

"It was the final straw when he talked about poor Dad being barely cold in his grave," continued Bill after a pause. "I told him there was no need to remind me what had happened and, brother or not, it wasn't for him to make jokes about it, and as for showing respect ..." Again he glanced at his sisters. "And that was when he hung up on me."

"And bang went our chances of a rent tribunal, or a 364-day tenancy," said Octavia. "Oh, Bill, couldn't you have tried—just once—to play things cool? Or couldn't you have asked Cris to talk to him instead?"

"Bill's the head of the family," said Crispin. "Janner wouldn't dream of negotiating any sort of terms with me, partner in the business or not. Bill's the eldest, and Janner has a—a patriarchal streak in him a mile wide."

"And a stubborn streak even wider," muttered Bill.

"Takes one to know one," said Valentine, trying to make peace before a minor disagreement should turn into a full-blown row. Octavia, whose face had begun to assume an exasperated expression, suddenly laughed.

"At least he's not wearing a caftan," she said. The other three smiled at this neat echo of their sister's earlier remark. "But it does look as if we may have to propose any further negotiations through the legal types, after all. No matter how willing Jan might be to talk about the field, he's our cousin, not our uncle. His father's the one whose signature is on the paperwork—at least, I assume there's something signed? It wasn't all done on a handshake, and trusting to goodwill?"

Crispin shook his head. "You forget that at first, before Dad and Janner were of age, it was the trustees of old Ebenezer's will who saw to the business side of things." He sounded regretful. "It was all properly signed, sealed and delivered the same week Janner left school at fifteen in 1927 to start keeping geese. The lease doesn't specify anything beyond grazing rights and restriction to agricultural use, so when he expanded into sheep and took on the County Council farm tenancy next door, all it took was a few legal twiddles and the field was as much his as ever."

"Except that it was really Dad's," said Bill.

"If only he hadn't died," said Val, with a quivering sigh. "So young ..."

"And in such a ghastly way," said Crispin, whose imagination was a lively one.

"Perhaps Janner will have an accident, too," suggested Bill. "He can be as stubborn as he wants for as long as he likes, but if ... anything ... happens to him before the end of this year, it would solve our difficulties nicely—and," with a quick look at Valentine, "no need to upset Young Jan, either."

Val looked reproachful, Octavia startled; Crispin, thoughtful. "Three score and ten," he murmured as he roughed out a family tree on his notepad. "Old Ebenezer was seventy when he died, Granddad Peter seventy-four, Dad a mere sixty-five because of the accident. And Janner is ... no more than sixty-three."

"And could live another ten years," said Octavia.

"A decade after the new legislation comes in," said Bill.

"Unless," said Crispin, contemplating the family tree, "he meets with an accident, too."

On a desk in an office on the umpteenth floor of New Scotland Yard, the telephone rang. Delphick sighed, and kept his head resolutely bent over his paperwork. "Bob."

Detective Sergeant Ranger abandoned his own studies—since the recent arrival of a new broom in a newly created department these had involved, with the Oracle's reluctant permission, the summarising of summaries of reports they'd both believed long since dealt with, stamped as unsolvable, and archived—and reached for the shrilling handset. "Chief Superintendent Delphick's office," he told the handset. It quacked at him. "Yes, sir, but a bit tied up at the moment. Could I get him to call you back?"

The handset squawked electronically, forcefully, and at some length. Bob sighed. "Just one moment, sir." He put his hand over the mouthpiece and spoke quietly. "Narcotics, sir, Superintendent Snowe. He says Superintendent Kebby put him on to you."

"Kebby?" The Oracle abandoned all pretence at paperwork, and sat up. "News of the kidnap—Garth's been found? Is that how Snowe became involved—the drugs connection?"

"You'd better speak to him yourself, sir. Mr. Kebby was most insistent, Mr. Snowe says."

Delphick, about to reach for his telephone, hesitated. "I wonder why Kebby hasn't called me himself. We really must indent for another telephone, Bob. You could be stalling persistent callers on one line while I tried to find out on the other what was going on—"

There was a brisk bang outside. The office door crashed open, propelled by the small tornado that was Superintendent Kebby. "Has he told you yet?" he demanded as he strode into the room. "What do you think? Is it worth—? Oh." He had just noticed the telephone in Bob's hand. "Sorry." He dropped, moustache a-quiver, on a visitor's chair and waved to the others to carry on.

"Er—yes, sir," Bob informed the handset, which had resumed its electronic squawking. "Yes, he has. Just this minute. And here's Mr. Delphick for you now, sir."

"Snowe?" The Oracle smiled into the mouthpiece. "Yes, it was. How did you guess?" He looked at the moustache sitting opposite. "Your intuition is not at fault. The superintendent is with me as we speak." Kebby met his eye, and with a rueful grin mouthed a silent apology as Delphick began listening to the torrent of squawks and electronic chirrups the telephone insisted he should hear. At one point in the outpouring the chief superintendent sat bolt upright, but the telephone rushed on with its story before he had time to express verbally the emotion it was plain he felt.

"I see," he said at last, his voice controlled. "Your concern, I would say, is entirely understandable." He glanced at his visitor, who was once more quivering with suppressed excitement. "Kebby and I will consult together, after which consultation he will doubtless be in touch with you again."

After brief valedictions he dropped the receiver back on its cradle, and allowed himself the faintest of grins. Bob, who in the presence of Superintendent Kebby had refrained from listening on the extension, looked a query. Kebby shook his head.

"I know what he's told you, and I've heard it myself, but I still don't believe it—and I can't believe your lady-friend could possibly have known before it happened—but she did, didn't she? If I ever wore a hat I'd have to take it off to her, because she was spot on about the craziness even if we're no farther forrard over the kidnapping. No doubt it's our fault for not—not translating her crazy doodles into the right crazy language."

Bob stifled a guffaw. So Miss Seeton had come up with the goods, or at least some of them, yet again. He looked at Delphick. He'd like to know what had set the Oracle all of a fizz like that mid-conversation, if conversation it could be called when he'd hardly had the chance to squeeze in a word until the end. He looked again at Delphick, who recognised the look, and nodded.

"Your inference, Sergeant Ranger, is correct. Miss Seeton has again shown herself to be on top form. Superintendent Snowe would be one of her most fervent admirers if only what she's drawn didn't seem guaranteed to involve his department in a great deal of unexpected work—and worry," he added in a more serious tone.

"If he's right and there's worse to come," said Kebby, "then *worry* is an understatement—but that's for Narcotics. I'm here on my own behalf as well as Nick Snowe's. I need another dekko at those sketches you brought back from Kent. Snowe may be looking at a drugs breakthrough, but the kidnap's no closer to being solved, and it's a priority case. We need further inspiration. A second look."

Bob was almost bursting to ask what had happened. Delphick took pity on him.

"You may be interested to know, Sergeant, that the strait-jacketed sheep recently drawn by Miss Seeton manifested themselves in person—that is, in reality—down in

Somerset a day or so ago. Incidentally, Kebby, why was I not told of this before?"

"Only heard about it myself when Narcotics called to put me—huh!—in the picture. Crossed wires, messages not getting through—you know the sort of thing." Delphick knew only too well that policemen of every rank were always overworked and couldn't be expected to think of everything, and murmured a soothing reply to that effect.

"These blasted sheep," Kebby snatched up the narrative thread, "went on some kind of psychotic rampage out in the middle of nowhere—ran riot through a cluster of half-a-dozen cottages playing merry hell with the place—barged through hedges, broke down gates, even jumped walls when they weren't too high—huh!" He turned to Bob, who had emitted another guffaw and been unable to suppress it.

"It's no laughing matter, young man. *High* is the operative word. Those sheep were stuffed to the gizzard with cannabis, if sheep have gizzards—I don't need a natural history lesson, thanks—and one of them nearly caused an accident by finishing its garden snack and leaping back out into the road to work off the calories by prancing about right in front of a car. Fortunately it was a local driver, not a tourist. He'd already slowed down for some bend or other, and was able to stop in time rather than end up overturned in the ditch or skidding into a wall. Or even," he added, "hitting the sheep, which apparently just trumpeted a bit at him and carried on with the dance."

A resolute silence filled the office as even Kebby struggled not to laugh at the picture conjured up by his words.

"It—it sounds a bit way out, sir," said Bob at last, the first to sober though his shoulders still shook.

"Quite so," said Delphick after a moment or two for deep breathing. "A masterly précis, Sergeant Ranger."

Kebby allowed himself a grin. "*Far out* I think you mean, Ranger, though check the proper lingo with Superintendent Snowe. The point is that your Miss Seeton apparently predicted, several days ago, that somebody, somewhere in the West Country, was about to dump a sizeable accumulation of cannabis plants for a flock of sheep to gobble up, with predictable results—and they did. The locals caught 'em, penned 'em and got 'em sober, but word reached the cops in Glastonbury—" Delphick and Bob exchanged looks— "and they thought they'd better nose around. Tracked the most likely route from damage done on the way, found what was left of the plants half-hidden a short distance from an unused barn. Which turned out, when they got inside, to have been in use not long before. Seems someone'd been growing cannabis there in considerable quantity, and scarpered with most of it but couldn't take it all. It's rained a lot in that part of the world these past few days, and half of Somerset's no more than an inch above sea level anyway. Area they call The Levels, three guesses why. Too damp to burn the stuff they didn't take with 'em, evidently no time to dig a hole and bury it and wait for it to rot."

He paused for breath. "The imagination boggles," said Delphick, "at what could result should the plants eventually become usable compost. We may yet see triffids stalk the countryside. And cannabis, we should remember, derives from hemp, which was of course once used to make hangmen's and other ropes. One would therefore expect some degree of, forgive me, stringiness to the product—irrelevant no doubt if one smokes it, or stews it in soup or makes a tisane, but, given that it probably takes longer than most plants to compost, does on this particular occasion seem to hint at a degree of haste in the dumping of it. This would further suggest something in the nature of panic—prompted, may I venture to guess, by the search, clearly less discreet than you would have liked, of the area for a place where Christy Garth may or may not be being held prisoner?"

"Spot on," agreed Kebby. "You should hear Nick Snowe—and I'm none too pleased myself, having drawn a total blank in the kidnap, which was the whole object of the exercise—but he's seriously worried that if the chummies can afford to dump stuff as potent as this, the stuff they took with 'em is likely to be far stronger and'll cause far more trouble, once it's out there among the users." He rushed on before Delphick could respond. "Yes, I know he should be grateful for having the alarm raised so early, but it's alarmed the chummies, too. They'll hide their new factory even better than they hid this one, and the minute the Somerset cops decide on another search they'll move again. The lads did their best to keep it all under wraps, but it's just not the same way of life, out in the sticks. Sneeze by yourself in your bedroom at midnight, first thing next morning you're offered friar's balsam and aspirin. You can't keep anything quiet."

"Or secret," said Delphick. "Yes, I see how it happened—and incidentally, moving on from cannabis and hemp, did you know that Somerset is famous for its willows, from which aspirin is derived? An idle thought, merely," he added as Kebby began to bristle. "Somerset was, I take it, the only western sheep-farming area searched where any—" he dared not meet Kebby's eye—"any untoward event occurred?"

"Far as I know, yes, but my team are busy double-checking in case any other bits of paper with notes on 'em have been accidentally swept under the blotter or shoved straight in the files before reading." There was a note in Kebby's voice that combined impatience with apology. The superintendent preferred action to inaction, and all he could do at the moment was look at drawings he'd already seen once, and ask the Oracle to make a second guess at what Miss Seeton had really meant.

Delphick was willing to assist, but gave due warning that his colleague would this time be looking at photocopies, rather than Miss Seeton's originals. "You can't keep anything quiet," he said with a wry smile, "in Scotland Yard any more than you can in the depths of the countryside. The ACC found out about my trip to Kent, and was after me within five minutes of my return." Sir Hubert Everleigh, Assistant Commissioner (Crime), was a connoisseur who had very early seen the investment potential of Miss Seeton's lightning sketches, and also admired them for their own sake. No amount of insistence on the part of Chief Superintendent Delphick that, paid for by the Yard, the sketches were the property of the Metropolitan Police and might at any time be required as evidence, could deter Sir Heavily from dropping broad hints, and asking what had been done with the little woman's latest creation. He had met Miss Seeton—liked her—wouldn't wish to disappoint her by letting her think her work was not appreciated. Retainer fees and cheques were, after all, only money. A creative person wanted rather more acknowledgement of her talent than that.

Delphick knew that to the determined collector no holds are permanently barred. Every time the matter came under discussion, he insisted that the sketches were in a safe place, and that Sir Hubert had no cause to be concerned. Miss Seeton, and her work, were fully appreciated by all those who had occasion to thank her; after so many years their number was large—and increasing.

Superintendent Kebby, however, had as yet no particular incentive to join that number. As he'd pointed out, the westerly searches inspired by the Traffic Jam and the Crazy Sheep had drawn a total blank in his own case, even if it had prompted Narcotics in the person of Superintendent Snowe to pay particular interest to activities in the Glastonbury area.

"He plans to send one of his men down there undercover," said Kebby, "rather than rely on the Somerset lot to find someone suitable. Far more likely a local'd be spotted as a cop than one of ours, especially as some of the London druggies have started disappearing for a while and then popping up again flashing the cash. Nick Snowe thinks they head off to the sticks to set up new distribution routes and outlets, then come back to the Smoke once things are running well enough for them to just sit back and rake in the money. His undercover lad can keep his eyes open for anything of that sort at the same time he's dropping hints about top-quality cannabis and flashing some cash of his own."

"Or Scotland Yard's," amended Delphick, taking the copies of Miss Seeton's sketches from his desk drawer and setting them before Superintendent Kebby. "Tell him to grow his hair, hang a bell round his neck, sew flares in his trousers and wear sandals." He looked towards his enormous sidekick, six foot seven and seventeen stone, neat in collar and tie and dark grey jacket. "Tell him he'll get nowhere if he stands out from the crowd."

Bob grinned, and the three detectives settled to a further study of Miss Seeton's drawings, hoping the possible whereabouts of Christy Garth might somehow be revealed.

"And your guess, Jasper," concluded Delphick, "would really be little better than either of ours, at this stage. We might even wonder if she wasn't thinking of the kidnap at all, but somehow picked up on the drugs business before it happened—while as for the other ..."

He glanced at Bob, who was slowly shaking his head. Miss Seeton's adopted nephew had never really been able to make sense of her doodles the way the Oracle could. Once they were explained to him—oh, yes, he could see what was going on, but left to his own imagination they were mostly ... well, the scribbles she often called them, though he could chuckle with her over the Traffic Jam play on words just as he'd once seen the funny side of her lascivious nude with suitcases that she'd called Abandoned Baggage. Bob smiled at the memory. Superintendent Kebby shot him a look. He explained.

"Likes a good laugh, does she? You starting to think that might be all that's behind this row of jam-jars?"

"No," Delphick replied, as Bob subsided beneath the tornado's blast. "I don't believe we are. No fresh interpretation, however, comes to mind as yet. On balance, knowing Miss Seeton, I'm willing to hazard a guess that Evesham may come into your case, but it's all somewhat vague and we need more to go on—always assuming the false teeth aren't, as we first wondered, hinting that the kidnap story is likewise false. I think we—you—need further information upon which to rely."

Superintendent Kebby shot another look at Bob Ranger, then began to twirl his moustache. "See here, Oracle, I've already trespassed on your good nature by taking up your time with these sketches, but I'd like to trespass further and borrow your young giant here for a while. I want him to take notes when I have a chat with the sister—brother too, if we can catch him, though I know he's tied up at work. It will save time, and for all we know time's fast running out for Christy Garth. Trying to explain your lady-friend's doodles and why they make me have doubts about the whole kidnap story would take too long even for my sidekick, and he's been around almost as long as young Ranger here. But Ranger already has an inkling of why I'd want to know what I'm going to ask 'em. He'll be able to keep an eye open for anything odd in the responses."

"And can then report to me," Delphick finished, "should anything, odd or otherwise, make sense in the context of Miss Seeton's drawings. Be off with you, Sergeant Ranger. Consider yourself temporarily sub-contracted to Mr. Kebby. Produce your own doodles in the form of short-hand pothooks as he applies the third degree to the Garth sister, and possibly brother, and leave me to resume my work in peace. Who knows? By the time you come back, I might even have an in-tray that is merely full, as opposed to overflowing."

The superintendent, pausing with his hand on the door-knob, looked over his shoulder. Unable to see around, through, and especially not over his huge escort, he uttered a quick "Huh!" before whisking himself, and Bob, out of Delphick's office, leaving as he went a faint echo of thanks in the turbulent air behind him.

Letty Garth was slim and pale, her blue eyes darkly shadowed, her face puffy from lack of sleep. On hearing that Mr. Kebby brought no definite news of the missing Christy, even more colour had drained from her cheeks and her hands fluttered up to tug at her long, blonde hair, twiddling it round her fingers. Bob felt that if she'd been a few years younger she would have chewed the ends.

"Isn't there anything we can do?" she begged the two policemen as they settled themselves on not-too-comfortable chairs; Bob discreetly out of sight in a corner with his notebook and pencil, Kebby with a small table between himself and Miss Garth. "There must be something! All this waiting—it's been so long, and we've heard nothing. We did our best to pay the ransom—it wasn't our fault it went wrong! They surely wouldn't ... they wouldn't harm Christy when it wasn't his fault any more than it was ours—would they?" Her knuckles whitening under the pressure, she knotted her fingers together. Kebby saw how the nails that on his previous visit had been smooth, expensively manicured ovals were now ragged-edged, nibbled close to the quick. The graceful butterfly who flitted with her social conscience from homeless shelter to charity auction was almost unrecognisable in this taut, unhappy figure. "He'll—be all right, won't he?"

"I hope so, Miss Garth." Kebby was grave. "I hope so, but you must understand I can't promise. We've heard nothing new, and I take it you've heard nothing either." Letty shook her head, and once more twisted her fingers. "You'd tell us, wouldn't you?" urged the superintendent. "You'd not go behind our backs and try to make private arrangements?"

Letty sat up. "With a tap on our phone and our letters being opened, that wouldn't be easy," she reminded him, with the most fleeting of smiles. He smiled back. Bob could hardly believe the whirlwind force of the superintendent's personality could be so quickly muted. Letty's cheeks even held a little colour as she relaxed, and unlocked her fingers to spread wide her hands. "Honestly, Mr. Kebby, if we knew anything more we would tell you at once. Honestly."

"Your brother, too?"

"Ben can't be here—he's at head office—but he'd say the same, I promise you. If you'd arranged to come later in the evening you could have asked him yourself. We can't tell you anything you don't already know, either of us."

He nodded. "Then it's time for a different approach, Miss Garth—Letty?" She returned his smile with one of her own, and inclined her head. "I'm sorry, Letty. There *is* something you can do, though it won't be pleasant. Of course, we know of Christy's problems. His drug habit's no secret any more than your father's threats to cut him off without a penny if he doesn't pull himself together— and you said last time that he'd actually gone and done it. Please don't think I'm trying to insult your older brother, but is it possible that Christy might have—well, faked his own kidnap as a means of getting easy money from the rest of the family, with your parents both away?"

Letty did not tug her hair, knot her fingers, or express outrage. She sat very still, silent for several moments. "We did wonder," she said at last. Sadly. "Dad wanted him to have treatment—thought about hiring people to—to scoop him up somehow and force him into a clinic, but the doctors he consulted said that unless a ..." Her voice shook. She blinked rapidly, and took a deep breath. "Unless an addict really wanted to cure his addiction, there'd be no point in—well, in kidnapping him, no matter how well-intentioned it was. He would just ... go back to his old habits once he was out again. Christy isn't under age.

He's legally free to live his own life—to go to the devil in his own way ..."

"He's certainly raised a fair bit of hell in his time," agreed Kebby.

Letty sighed. Her shoulders, her whole body, drooped as she sat. "I can't really think of a time when my parents weren't worried about him," she said. "He's so much older than me, and he was never particularly close to Ben, though of course there's an age difference there, too. They even went to different schools. Dad could afford so much more for us younger ones by the time ..." She swallowed further tears as once more her voice began to shake. "It's awful to say such things of your brother, but Christy did seem to—to resent us both for having the opportunities he hadn't been given himself. You could never persuade him it wasn't—wasn't favouritism so much as the fact there was more money around later on than there'd been earlier. He said if that was true, his share ought to be larger to—to make up for what he hadn't had in the past ..."

"And your parents listened to him," said Kebby, trying not to frown.

She drooped still more. "Yes, for a while—for too long, they agreed afterwards, but by then it—it was too late. He'd got in with a fast-living crowd and they introduced him to drugs. He—he's perhaps not as strong as he likes to think he is. I don't know how long it takes to—to hook someone into dependence, but I believe Christy was hooked pretty quickly." She sat up, and took another deep breath. "Superintendent, I've never said this to anyone before, but I sometimes think—wonder—if he might not have done it deliberately, out of spite. It must sound silly to you ..."

"Why should it? It's the way a child would think." Kebby thought back to what Delphick had told him of Miss Seeton's impression of Christy Garth. "A child has little self-discipline, Letty. *It's not fair. I'll show the grown-ups!* I wouldn't say your brother has ever shown much common sense or self-discipline, would you? Hardly adult behaviour to sulk or throw tantrums when the family fortunes change. Better late than never, you'd hope he'd think. Well done to the old folks for having made it big, hard work paying off at last and so on. You'd hope that even if he'd started going to the bad, he'd try to pull himself together when the chance was offered—as you say it was." His tone mingled regret and sternness. "But he's not a child, he's an adult. He made his choice."

"Some of his friends did come to their senses as they grew older. Not many, but I remember Christy complaining some of them had been—been got at, and moved on, and even if he did ever see them, they weren't fun any more." Her eyes flashed. "Fun! What a—a stupid thing to say!"

"Drugs and drug addiction aren't fun," agreed the superintendent. "You said yourself, people go to the devil in their own way—but far too often other people are involved. Innocent people like your family—and there's crime, too. Not just the dealers and suppliers, but the addicts, having to steal or burgle, or worse, to get stuff to sell to pay for their next fix. Which is why I had to wonder, Letty, if this whole kidnap business might have been faked by your brother for the money. And now you tell me you've been wondering, too."

Chapter Six

"Here we are! Farside Hotel." The taxi pulled up outside the pleasant guest-house chosen by Miss Seeton from the directories and gazetteers in Crabbe's Garage—a public service instigated by Jack Crabbe for the benefit of any Plummergenite wishing to travel beyond the limits imposed by a day trip. And it had taken almost a day, even with a taxi at both ends of two main line trains connected by a cross-London cab, for Miss Seeton to travel from Kent to Somerset; but on the whole she had enjoyed the experience. So much easier to have the sandwiches Martha insisted she took, rather than make her way to the dining car and find somewhere to sit when she was so comfortable where she was, in her Reserved seat (again at Martha's insistence) in a second class carriage. And the hotel, now that she saw it in reality rather than a photograph, looked every bit as comfortable as she had expected.

"Good gracious." Miss Seeton, as the driver prepared to open the door for her and take her case from the boot, blinked. "Surely not." She blinked again. On the top step of the Farside Hotel sat a large—it rose, yawned, and stretched—no, a very large pale tabby cat that looked familiar. Surely Tibs, the cherished pet of young Amelia Potter at the police house, had not—could not have—followed her here?

"Hi there, moggy," said the cab driver, escorting Miss Seeton to the foot of the steps and waiting for her to ring the bell. The cat returned this impertinent salute with a long, green-eyed stare of disdain and sat down again, curling its tail away from careless feet.

The door was opened by a tall, grey-haired woman wearing large spectacles above a friendly smile. "Miss McConchie?" Miss Seeton smiled up at the spectacles.

"Miss Seeton? Yes, I'm Lyn McConchie. Hello, Ted. Here." Miss McConchie took Miss Seeton's case before its owner, burrowing in her capacious handbag for her purse, had time to protest. "Now, you settle up with Ted while I put the kettle on. You've been travelling for hours—you must be parched. I'll take you up to your room, and by the time tea's ready you can sit down quietly with me in the kitchen, if you've no objection."

"None at all," Miss Seeton assured her. "That would be most kind." Once more she smiled. "Thank you." One might almost be at home. Such a warm welcome. She hoped Miss McConchie's tea would not be too strong, but it was clear she was the sort of person one could happily ask to add more hot water to the pot, or at least to one's cup; and sugar was always left to personal choice, so that would be all right, too.

Her taxi driver duly thanked with a tip and another smile, Miss Seeton trotted into the lobby of the Farside Hotel. Sounds of movement and the hiss of steam drew her to the small kitchen at the back of what had once been a private house. Edwardian, she rather thought, or late Victorian: a family home where the family would by now have fallen on hard times, or died out. Miss Seeton had read as much about Somerset as the limitations of a Kent library system would, in the time available, permit. This house perhaps had been requisitioned during the war, maybe for evacuees, more likely for workers in various sheepskin and other key local factories: the Royal Air Force in the Second World War had used a great number of sheepskins, for airmen's boots and bomber jackets and probably, she thought, for the ear-flapped flying helmets one saw in old films, as well ...

Miss Seeton found the kitchen door half open, tapped, and pushed it wide to see Lyn McConchie busy with boiling water and a brown earthenware teapot. Miss Seeton said nothing to distract her hostess, and Miss McConchie called over her shoulder, "Hang on a jiffy and I'll show you your room."

Miss Seeton hung on. Miss McConchie finished swilling water round to warm the pot, emptied it away, set down the pot and opened a battered tin tea caddy decorated with bright female figures that were vaguely Chinese, swaying gracefully with long tunics and parasols. She dropped a generous two spoons of loose leaves into the pot, poured in more boiling water, clattered the lid into place and slipped a cosy made from vivid crochet squares over the brown earthenware globe; and at last turned back to her guest.

"We'll have cake as well," she promised, "once you're settled."

Once settled, Miss Seeton enjoyed a slightly strong but definitely unsugared cup of tea in the kitchen, listening as Miss McConchie chattered her happy explanations of anything Miss Seeton might wish to know. The tabby cat was called Hodge "because his mother lives with the Johnson family". Miss Seeton nodded her appreciation of this pleasing whimsy. "He can be a little standoffish, but he's friendly enough—he doesn't scratch my guests, or fight other cats, which sounds very different from your Tibs."

Miss Seeton smiled. "Indeed, yes. Tibs seems fond of Amelia, but of few others, though of course cats by their very nature are said to be rather more distant creatures than dogs." She returned Miss McConchie's literary allusion with one of her own. "The cat that walked by himself, for instance, waving his wild tail."

"Through the wild, wet woods on his wild lone." Miss McConchie likewise knew and loved her Kipling. "It's certainly been wild and wet over the past week or so. Lots of heavy rain, and rain on grass makes it slippery at best, a quagmire at worst. If you plan to climb the Tor, I hope you've brought a pair of good stout shoes with you." Miss Seeton frowned. "Don't worry if you haven't, there are a couple of outdoor clothing shops in the High Street. There's sometimes talk of concrete steps, but it's more than five hundred feet to the top, and whether the idea will ever come to anything is anyone's guess."

"I had thought," said Miss Seeton, "of visiting the Abbey first, as it is closer, and also to see the tomb, or rather the site of the tomb, of King Arthur and Guinevere." She explained the reasons for her interest, and Miss McConchie's eyes gleamed.

"Friends of the Abbey Ruins!" She jumped to her feet and hurried to the large pine dresser that stood against one wall. From the left-hand drawer she retrieved a bundle of raffle ticket booklets. "Everyone who stays here has to buy at least one," she said, "or their breakfast toast is charcoal, I promise you." Miss Seeton returned the landlady's mischievous threat with a smile. "It's for a good cause, preserving and maintaining the Abbey ruins—and a book of ten tickets costs the price of nine singles, so you get one free. There are some splendid prizes, too. Just look."

Miss Seeton accepted one of the raffle-ticket books and studied the list. "Certainly," she agreed, feeling even more at home than ever. Plummergen, just like Glastonbury, would in a good cause cheerfully tempt the charitable with a pair of tickets for a Mystery Coach Tour, or a bottle of whisky; a hamper of groceries, or a rich Dundee cake; a meal for two at a well-known hostelry (she was pleased to see that Glastonbury also had its George) or a feather cushion in a crazy patchwork slipcover. But ...

"A ride in a hot air balloon," she breathed. "Good gracious. How very unusual—and how interesting it would be to view the earth from so different an aspect. Some time ago a small aeroplane flew over my village and took photographs, which we were given the chance to buy, but an aeroplane flies so much higher and faster than one supposes a balloon would do, and some of the houses were hardly ... distinct." She paused. Her own dear cottage had seemed so insignificant, from the air. "One could, of course, charter—if that is the word—a helicopter, as they can hover, but as far as I know the chance to ride in a balloon is rare, unless one happens to know somebody who owns one."

"Vincent Weaver," said Miss McConchie at once. "His father is Weaver's Consolidated Northern Industrials. Our Vince will tell you he used to be quite a tearaway until he grew up, and came to his senses, and came here. He hang-glides as well, but he prefers the balloon. Like your

97

aeroplane, he takes photos—he can afford the best equipment, and he knows how to use it. You may have noticed his work when I showed you your room." Miss Seeton had indeed wondered about the creator of such splendid images. Miss McConchie continued to enthuse. "Elongated shadows at sunrise and sunset, flocks of birds in the nature reserve, huge murmurations of starlings in the autumn, reflections of light from ditches and rhynes." She pronounced this last as *reens* and explained, in answer to Miss Seeton's query, that rhynes are the major drainage channels for the peat moors and levels of Somerset, the first phase having been begun by thirteenth-century monks, to be followed by further work in the 1700s, and again after the Second World War.

"It looks like a huge patchwork quilt, from the air," went on Miss McConchie. "Squares and oblongs in different shades of green, all joined together by strips of silver."

"Sashing," murmured Miss Seeton, but Miss McConchie did not hear.

"There's one of his prints in each bedroom as well as up the stairs. A local craft shop sells them on his behalf and donates ten per cent to charity—which reminds me," she added, brandishing the rest of the raffle tickets in the direction of the one book held by Miss Seeton. "Are you tempted?"

Miss Seeton recalled the landlady's earlier threat, and smiled. "Dear me, as I don't care at all for burned toast, and you have made me so welcome that I really shouldn't wish to move to a different hotel, I will certainly buy, now let me see ..." She opened her handbag to find her purse.

Lyn McConchie smiled back, deliberately misunderstanding. "A different hotel? You mean bigger? I'd love to expand, but the house next door, which would have been perfect, was rented out right under my nose before I even knew it was on the market. So I still have no more than five rooms, which means ten people at most, and there are plenty of singles, like you—not that I mind," as Miss Seeton began to frame an apology. "Not at all. I enjoy meeting my guests and making new friends, but ..." She sighed. "I could have taken down part of the fence at the back and built a little walkway with a roof for when it rained, which would save having to knock holes in the dividing wall—but there it is, I missed my chance." She fixed Miss Seeton with a stern eye. "But you mustn't miss yours, Miss Seeton. How many raffle tickets would you like?"

After this pleasant transaction had been concluded the teacups were refilled, more cake was cut, and Miss McConchie proceeded to advise her guest of what else she must be sure to see after her visit to the Abbey ruins. She explained that her stock of tourist leaflets was not extensive, space being limited, and suggested a visit to one of the local bookshops. "Bedivere Books is the closest, halfway up the High Street near the church, on the same side. You can't miss it."

She saw Miss Seeton's twinkle of amusement. "You really can't," she insisted. "It has a sort of balustrade thingy—a decorated line of hollow stone triangles, right across the top. She stocks a fair selection of guide books, as well as the more ..." She hesitated. "The more unorthodox sort, for hippies and suchlike—people on the fringes of logic, with quaint ideas." She laughed. "I once walked up the High Street and overheard a tourist say to her companion, 'Isn't there anybody normal in this place?' and I could have told her, all right! Don't be surprised to see people wandering about in long robes and beads, or if you catch a whiff of incense from shop doorways. The Flower Power generation never lost a single one of its petals in Glastonbury, believe me!"

A tall, rangy, fair young man sporting a wispy beard, with a braided headband holding back tangled hair that brushed slim shoulders, drifted from the bench where he had been sitting to enjoy the sunshine, threw away the half-smoked aromatic cigarette on which he had been puffing, and climbed gracefully into the bus that wheezed to a halt at the nearby stop. He bought his ticket, commented unfavourably on the capitalist system, and dropped heavily on a seat as the driver told him he could always walk there and back if he wanted, couldn't he? The young man leaned against the seat, closing his eyes as if still dreaming of summer. The bus rattled on its way. The young man waited thirty seconds and then opened his eyes.

"Sheep," he muttered to himself, closing them again with a shudder. "Cows. Fields, hedges, wide blasted open spaces ..."

His eloquence was even greater once he had left the bus in the neighbouring town of Street, and ambled down a side road to a public telephone box standing out of the general sight. Here, he could let his sentiments rip—and did. "Talk about the ruddy sticks, sir," he summed up his miserable situation to the voice of authority at the other end of the line. "Huge great cows with shaggy red coats and enormous horns—"

"Highland cattle," interposed Authority, as eloquence failed and the young man drew breath. "On Wearyall Hill—they're famous, remember?"

"And sheep," moaned the young man, who, announcing himself as Detective Sergeant Brumby, had been put straight through to Authority by the switchboard. "If it isn't cows—beg pardon, cattle—it's sheep. They both eat grass, so it's all the same to me. And birds—you can't believe the racket birds make in the country!"

"No worse than the racket your generation makes with its pop concerts," countered Detective Superintendent Snowe of the Drugs Squad. "When you're safely back I'll see about fixing you a transfer to Mr. Kebby's lot. He's not too keen on nature, either."

Dick Brumby spluttered, but was ignored by Superintendent Snowe, whose fuse could be short. "Right, you've had your moan, now let's have your news. Anything doing?"

"I'm not sure, sir." Sergeant Brumby knew how far his superior could be pushed.

"Why not? Have you been spotted?"

"I don't think so. I've hung around a few likely places and met a few likely types, though it doesn't go beyond sharing the odd joint when they're in what you could call party mood. I've dropped one or two hints, but nobody's offered to supply me or introduce me to anyone—but they're not giving me the cold shoulder or trying to chase me out of town, either."

"They do say incomers are suspect for a lifetime, in the country," Snowe informed him brightly. "You can call me back in twenty or thirty years' time—say, around the turn of the new millennium."

"Ha bloody ha, sir," retorted Brumby. "With respect," he added, just in case, though he had heard Snowe's wicked chuckle at the other end of the line. "But what I have noticed is a house that seems rather too busy for its boots. Visitors of all shapes and sizes, but more or less the same sort, if you get me."

"Our sort," said the Drug Squad chief quickly.

"I think so, sir. From what I can gather, the house belonged to an old lady—last of her family, lived there for generations, died a few months back. The place never got on the open market, but someone bought it and rented it out ..."

"Curtains closed at the windows? Lights on day and night?"

"No, sir. I don't think it's a cannabis factory. I'd say it was the end of a supply chain, where you'd go to get your own fix and collect enough stuff to sell on to other idiots willing to pay the price, so that you yourself could pay for your next fix."

"A very vicious circle," growled Snowe. "Stupidity, dependence, greed." He snorted. "That the only lead you have? Nothing about what got dumped the other day and sent those sheep off their heads?"

"Only people saying it was a bit of a laugh and a waste of good weed. And hoping the better stuff shows up before long, but not an idea when it will, or where it'll come from."

"Just your over-busy house, then. I wonder the neighbours haven't reported it to the local cop shop. Neighbours generally spot unusual behaviour."

"And like to mind their own business, sir—or are far too busy themselves to notice."

"Or too scared," added Snowe. "What sort of area is it? Narrow streets, concrete gardens, broken windows?"

"Corner shop and des.res. mostly, sir. The neighbouring house to one side has been converted to bedsits, mostly students from the local college. Extra people wandering about would really have to stand out to be noticed. The other side's a small guest-house, landlady and a couple of part-timers, rushed off their feet half the time and putting their feet up the other half, at a guess."

"Too busy to notice," Snowe agreed. "Whoever chose the place, if you're right about what's going on, chose it well. I'd wonder about some of our own lads, the ones who keep doing the vanish-and-reappear act, but of course they'd have to be tipped off by someone with local knowledge. I wonder how the word got about the place was empty? A crooked solicitor? A dodgy estate agent? Or might it be squatters?"

"It might. I haven't looked too closely at the locks, but if they're new—or if there's any sign of broken windows—"

"Don't get too close," warned the superintendent. "Discretion, Brumby. Find out what you can without risking being seen. If anyone from the Smoke's involved, at least we'd stand a chance of bagging them even if the super-powered stuff you were meant to be after proves too elusive. Keep a watchful eye on things—and keep the other eye open for familiar faces, while you're watching."

Miss Seeton, with her bag and umbrella over one arm, with her sensible shoes and respectable tweeds marking her out as a tourist—only her hat struck that note of creative individuality for which Glastonbury is famed—walked with great interest up the High Street hill. So much to see, though less about King Arthur than she had expected. She now understood what Miss McConchie meant about unorthodox. Shops on both sides of the road displayed in their windows jewellery and gemstones, amulets, star charts and packs of Tarot cards. There were crystal balls for scrying; there were cauldrons, there were mysterious glass bottles with elaborate stoppers, there were books about witchcraft. There were candles in every size, shape—some very strange shapes indeed—and colour. There were shops selling statuettes of wizards and elves, of The Goddess, The Mother, The Green Man; there were shops selling costumes, robes, pointed hats and glittering crowns. It was all somewhat overwhelming, like the occasional whiff of incense on the gentle breeze. And—dear me—Miss Seeton's nose twitched—perhaps some other substances, as well. But not exactly unpleasant, in the way oil paints and cleaner fluids could be. Miss Seeton sneezed just once, and blinked.

It was a relief to reach Bedivere Books at last.

"Good gracious." There on the threshold, eyes glowing, tail curled, sat Hodge—no, now she looked more closely, not Hodge, but a very close resemblance. Plummergen's Tibs had notoriously loose morals, and after two illicit and productive unions had been denied the opportunity for a third. Could her progeny have travelled from Kent to Somerset? It seemed unlikely. "Excuse me," said Miss Seeton, and stepped carefully around the large, disdainful feline figure into the bookshop.

"Don't mind Graymalkin," called a woman's voice from above. Miss Seeton looked up to see a tall, willowy woman in sandals, a long caftan, several strings of beads and a necklace of tiny bells standing on a step-stool, busy shelving an assortment of volumes with bright covers. "He's friendly enough—he doesn't bite, or scratch—but he can be a bit standoffish sometimes, and this is one of them."

Miss Seeton recalled the comments of Miss McConchie. "Just like Hodge," she said. The willowy woman pushed the last book into place and jumped down, her hair drifting out from her headband in an explosion of gossamer blonde.

"You're staying at the Farside Hotel," she deduced. "Hodge is some sort of cousin to Graymalkin. They're often mistaken for each other. Did Lyn send you here? She's a star. Octavia Callender, by the way, in case she mentioned my name, and this is my shop. Do you want anything in particular, or shall I leave you to browse?"

She contemplated Miss Seeton, who was gazing about her with interest at some of the more blatant titles ranged around the various display units and shelves. "At a guess, you're after a guidebook. Over here." She placed a gentle arm on Miss Seeton's shoulder and steered her to a set of shelves beside the till. "Anything else you want, just ask."

Miss Seeton smiled her thanks, and began to browse. A book with photographs, she had decided, and certainly with a reliable index, though nothing too bulky ... Octavia settled herself behind the counter, repositioned a green glass vase of tissue-paper flowers, and set about unpacking the next layer from a large, half-empty box of books on the floor. She began cross-checking one title after another against a list on flimsy paper, marking them in pencil, a slight frown between her brows as she concentrated.

"Move, you." The voice from outside the shop was male, and peevish. A thick-set man in late middle age trod stiffly into Bedivere Books to confront the owner as she rose from her chair to face him, with a smile, across the counter.

"I've read those books you sold me the other day," he informed Octavia in a voice Miss Seeton, disturbed from her browsing, felt held a challenge, if not a direct accusation, though of what and for what reason she had no idea. Was it not, after all, the job of a bookshop owner to sell books?

"The whole thing is nonsense," said the middle-aged man. "I thought it would be!"

Miss Seeton's quick ears thought she heard a sigh from Miss Callender, quickly stifled.

"Not so much nonsense, perhaps, as something seen from a different point of view," said Octavia. "A very different point of view, I agree," at which the middle-aged man snorted, "but many people believe in the Zodiac, and say they can see it—only, in the same way some people are tone deaf, not everyone is in tune with the necessary vibes. With the natural sympathies of the landscape."

"Natural poppycock!" snapped the middle-aged man. "This Maltwood female said she had a vision of a supremely important mystic secret that had been kept hidden for hundreds if not thousands of years. Well," and he leaned forward, wincing, to fix Octavia with a stern glare, "if these secrets were so important, why write books telling everyone about them?"

"The Age of Aquarius was about to dawn. The time was at last right for their revelation to the world," said Octavia.

"Time? The very word, young woman! I've been to your Museum. I've read all about the archaeological digs, I've seen the Lake Village finds. They date from the Iron Age, not more than a couple of hundred years BC at the very earliest. Until then, the Lake Village swamp was never anything but sea! At the very time Katherine Maltwood said the ancients were mapping out the constellations of a giant Zodiac on the ground, more than half that ground was under water!"

His face was turning red. Octavia reached to pull a tissue flower from the green glass vase, and held it out. "Peace, my friend," she said kindly as he automatically took the delicate stem from her hand. "Just cool it. Open your mind and let the flowers bring you peace, as the negative vibrations fade away."

"Mrs. Maltwood," he persisted in a marginally less aggrieved tone, "couldn't even make up her mind about when these ancients were supposed to have laid the figures out. In one book she says it was two thousand seven hundred years BC, but in the next book she takes off a full seven hundred years!"

"Her calculations were refined as her researches progressed," countered Octavia.

"If it's genuine, an inspired vision ought to be accurate the first time, young woman." He tossed the flower down on the counter and dusted his hands, drawing a deep breath. "Then along comes some other woman and starts to refine, as you call it, the Maltwood figures to her own design—and even draws one of them completely the other way round!"

"Scorpio," murmured Octavia, but he rushed on.

"Scorpio? According to these Zodiac people the original Scorpio was twice the size, and made smaller later to accommodate Libra—and what kind of astronomer, astrologer, whatever you want to call the Chaldeans—what kind of person works with a system that has to divide by eleven?"

"I think you may have misunder—"

"And if that isn't bad enough, Libra isn't seen—if it's seen at all, which I take leave to doubt—as a pair of scales the way everyone knows it. Oh, no. Not a balance, but a bird—a dove, for pity's sake! And Cancer, the crab, is a boat—a boat! Why?"

"The tradition of the hobby-horse—"

"It's all nonsense, I tell you!"

Octavia managed another smile. "But intriguing nonsense, wouldn't you say? You've clearly read everything most thoroughly and found it all of interest, whether or not you agree with the ideas expressed. I hope you're not going to ask for your money back. My second-hand section—"

"It's not the money." He waved a hand, winced again, and scowled. "It's the—the barefaced lunacy of the whole ridiculous concept that you peddle to unwary fools more easily gulled than I am! How you can sell this rubbish with a clear conscience, I don't know."

"I do sell other books." Octavia likewise waved a hand. "For instance, there's Richard Muir, *Riddles In The British Landscape*—it has a wonderful teddy-bear produced by using an Ordnance Survey map in just the same way as the Zodiac figures were found."

"Supposedly found," sniffed the middle-aged man, yet found himself following her across to the appropriate shelves. Miss Seeton, who could hardly regard it as eavesdropping when the conversation had been so very public, hid a smile. Miss Callender seemed to know exactly what she was doing. It was a pleasure to watch an expert at work.

"Or Lesley Vibert's *Tangled Tales: Fact Or Fiction?* which has chapters both for and against the idea of Glastonbury Tor as an entrance to Annwn, the original Celtic underworld, and the Maltwood proposal that her Zodiac could have been the Cauldron of Wisdom before it became King Arthur's Holy Grail." Octavia pulled a third book from the stand. "And here's *The Secret Strength of Seven* in which Septimus Hepton examines the relevance of the number of stars in the Plough, the days of the week, the five main planets with the sun and moon, and the supposedly druidic labyrinth that girdles the Tor with seven earthwork semi-circles—my goodness, only wait a couple of years for the seventh of July 1977 ..."

As she spoke she was piling books, one at a time, into the man's fascinated hands, and he was not refusing them. Miss Seeton, similarly fascinated, continued to observe.

"This Tor," the near-hypnotised customer managed to bring out, even as he accepted yet another title from Octavia and did no more than glance at the cover. "I've climbed it. If it's so sacred and special in all this mythology of yours, why isn't it right at the centre of the Zodiac Circle rather than out on the edge? Why's the centre some place called Butleigh nobody's ever heard of?"

"To keep it safe," said Octavia, "until the time was right for the secret to be revealed. Which is where we—you— came in." She retreated behind the counter and reached for the eight or ten books he carried, having refused not a single one. She nodded and smiled. "There are some well-reasoned arguments and counter-theories in all of those books, and if you want to make a detailed study of the subject I have plenty more, but they should be enough to be going on with. Shall I ring them up for you?"

Miss Seeton, an admiring observer, was not in the least surprised to see the hitherto testy customer leave Bedivere Books clutching a brown paper carrier containing a dozen expensive volumes, with another tissue flower in his hand.

Chapter Seven

Miss Seeton regarded Miss Callender with approval, even as the younger woman sank back on her chair to brush a hand across her forehead. The beads of her many long strings clattered together; the little bells of her necklace tinkled. Miss Seeton smiled.

"My dear, you are not exactly as you seem to be, are you?"

Octavia sat up, regarding her with a wary eye. "The flowers," enlarged Miss Seeton. "The—forgive me—the language, or perhaps one should say jargon; the fancy dress. You have a part to play, and you play it very well."

Octavia let out a long breath, glanced towards the door, saw no-one there, and laughed. "Don't you dare let on to a soul, but you're right. I'm a Callender, remember—Callender's Coats, you may have seen the family shop in the High Street—but I didn't want to go into the family business even though I seem to have inherited the family business brain. Tourists do expect the weird in Glastonbury, that's why they come. As a born-and-bred local I'd hate to disappoint them, so you see it's no more than good business sense to act the part. Which I try to do, and thank you for the compliment."

Miss Seeton expressed genteel dismay at any hint of family discord, but Octavia was quick to reassure her.

"Oh, we all rub along pretty well together, but my brothers and sister are a lot older than me, and after college—I'm the only one who went—I thought I should try striking out on my own. My sister Val has, too. She works with wool—spinning, weaving." She laughed again. "Valentine. She was born on the fourteenth of February." She contemplated Miss Seeton with a twinkle, inviting her to share the little joke.

"Callender," said Miss Seeton, after a pause. "Dear me, yes. And your brothers?"

"Crispin, whose birthday is the twenty-fifth of October. Cry God for Harry, England and Saint George! And Bill—definitely not William. He came at the end of the month, as they always do. New Year's Eve, in fact. And I," she prompted, "am Octavia ..."

Miss Seeton envisaged the year-at-a-glance page of her pocket diary. "The eighth of August?"

Octavia laughed again. "You can guess how the purists worry about me, the same way they do about poor Bill. They ask what the other seven are called, and get upset when I say I'm the youngest of four—but then, our whole family is used to explaining names. My cousin Susan, now. She's asking to be called Brenda in future. Brenda means 'sword', and she's trying to write a book on the Three Swords of King Arthur. She sees herself as a reincarnation of the Lady of the Lake, the one who presented him with Excalibur—only she calls it Caliburn."

Miss Seeton's interest had quickened at the mention of King Arthur—after all, was he not the reason for her visit to Glastonbury?—but she was puzzled. "My reading around the subject has not as yet been extensive," she admitted, "but I never realised that Arthur had any sword other than Excalibur."

"Oh, Susan—I mean, Brenda—has read all the texts and done a Katherine Maltwood, looking at maps and aerial photos and following roads and features in the landscape. She swears she's found a giant sword nobody else knows about." She smiled. "If you like I'll show you, but cousin or not there's no obligation to buy."

Octavia moved to a shadowed corner, rummaged on the bottom shelf, and pulled out a handful of papers stapled together. "She's going to work up this little pamphlet into a full-sized book one day, she says." She sighed. "How many times have I heard that! If I had a pound ... Still, I agreed to keep this in stock and tell people about it, and now I've told you." She riffled through the dozen or so photocopied pages until she found a map. "Look at this. Near Taunton, that's our county town, is a place called Thornfalcon. A falchion is a type of sword—and everyone knows about the Holy Thorn planted by Joseph of Arimathea when he came here after the Crucifixion. Our Susan looked for other places named Thorn and they lined up, as you see, pointing to the prehistoric Sweet Track the history people discovered just a few years ago. It's the oldest wooden walkway in the world."

Miss Seeton, accepting the photocopied pages, followed the line joining Thornfalcon with Thorngrove, and on towards the black-and-white line that was the disused railway. Doubtfully, she looked at Octavia.

"The Sweet Track has been covered up again to preserve it, but its position forms the hilt of the landscape sword," said Miss Callender, keeping a straight face. "The blade, you see, is a dead straight line pointing to Pomparles Bridge."

Miss Seeton continued to look puzzled. Octavia shook her head. "For a friend of Lyn's you don't know much about the place you're visiting. Didn't she tell you how Pomparles is a corruption of *Pons Perilous*, the bridge where Sir Bedivere stood to throw Excalibur—sorry, Caliburn—into the lake? Didn't you know—" her finger stabbed at the blurred photocopy map in Miss Seeton's hands—"there's a village called Meare which, before the rhynes and drainage channels were dug, was the original Lake?"

Miss Seeton caught the twinkle behind the sorrowful tone, and smiled. "No, I didn't, but it sounds … interesting. Your cousin is clearly an enthusiast, and of course I should be happy to buy the booklet even though," honesty made her add, "I cannot promise to be converted to her ideas." She glanced down. "I notice a Thorney Moor on the map, and a place called Thorne Coffin, but neither of these is anywhere near the others."

Octavia winked. "It's a secret, but that's what they do—pick and choose to suit their argument, and to hell with logic and common sense." She shrugged. "But it's a harmless enough hobby, I guess, and helps keep me in business. If Susan ever does finish her book, I dare say it will sell—but really, you don't have to buy the pamphlet. You seem an unlikely candidate, to me."

"I must buy a guidebook too." Miss Seeton, holding firmly to Susan/Brenda's stapled pages, moved back to the shelves she had been studying when the middle-aged Zodiac scoffer had entered the shop. "I am unable to make up my mind between these two. Which would you recommend?"

"A trip to the local library and save your money," Octavia told her frankly. "There's an excellent reference section, and the museum people down at the Tribunal—one of the oldest buildings in town—are very helpful, too. Borrow a couple of books for a few days and take notes, and with some tourist leaflets you'll be fine."

Miss Seeton, who could see very well how cleverly Miss Callender was teasing her into further purchases, nevertheless remained impressed by the bookshop owner's commercial expertise. "A library card from Kent will be of little help in Somerset, I fear. And you have been so helpful that I have no wish to take advantage of your kindness by buying nothing beyond your cousin's ... unusual publication."

"You've talked yourself into it," said Octavia, "but don't say I forced you! There's little to choose between these two, I'd say. This one would fit better in your handbag, but the index to this one is rather more comprehensive."

As Miss Seeton made her purchases she noticed a pile of raffle tickets beside the till. Octavia followed her glance. "I'll bet Lyn's already sold you some." Miss Seeton nodded. "Then I wouldn't dream—" began Octavia, but broke off as a shadow darkened the open doorway. A stout young man with a heavy beard, wearing jeans and a tie-dyed teeshirt, came in with a brass bell on a ribbon round his neck, a plaited cord encircling his throat, and his face, arms and bare feet as brown as the leather of his sandals.

"Peace and pleasant reading, friend," said Octavia, slipping Miss Seeton's choice in a paper bag and handing it over. "May you find enlightenment here." As the man with the beard studied the contents of the shop she found time to favour Miss Seeton with a quick wink, then sobered. "A flower for you. Your spirit will blossom as your heart will sing."

Miss Seeton left Bedivere Books with a high opinion for the professional skills of Miss Octavia Callender.

As she adjusted her handbag and umbrella she considered the sky, heavy with clouds. There had been, Miss McConchie had explained, a lot of rain over the past few days. This was England; it was more than likely to rain again. Miss Seeton's shoes, stout enough for walking round the town, or for exploring the Abbey ruins on their level site, might not be sufficiently stout for climbing the Tor as she planned to do the following day, once she had found her bearings. How strange that, though she could see it clearly as her taxi approached the town, she had as yet been unable to see the Tor from Glastonbury itself. The buildings and trees blocked the view, she supposed.

Over five hundred feet high, steep and grass-covered, with wandering sheep to nibble the turf where a machine could not safely mow, Glastonbury Tor, with its ruined church tower at the very summit, dominated the countryside for miles around. It was a popular climb, Miss McConchie had said. One day there might be concrete steps or an asphalt path, but for the moment there was nothing but grass. In wet weather this could soon turn to mud, and of course would be slippery even before it became muddy. Miss Seeton sighed with regret for the heavier shoes in which she had tramped the Scottish moors and Lakeland fells during her recent northern holiday—and had left behind in Plummergen. It would be wise, before climbing the Tor, to find a local shop that specialised in outdoor equipment. Extravagant, of course, and she would not tell Martha, who was likely to scold her not just for extravagance and forgetfulness, but even more for climbing steep hills by herself. According to Miss McConchie, it was a popular climb and there were sure to be other climbers to assist her should she encounter any difficulties.

Miss Seeton went on her way up the High Street, continuing to marvel at the varied contents of shop windows—one could not, of course, properly call those dragons lifelike, as dragons were mythical creatures, but they certainly looked most realistic—and the colourful costumes worn by so many of the passers-by. The young—so carefree and uninhibited, so quick to smile and so very much ... themselves, approved Miss Seeton, who never thought of herself as anything other than conventional but had in her art college days learned that genius would flourish among spirits that were truly free. Mere talent—she sighed for her own limitations—remained within conventional boundaries, restricted in a way genius, which knew no bounds, never was. Her nose twitched. One could not, of course, condone the taking of drugs to enlarge one's creative scope—what was the modern phrase? to blow one's mind—but the general atmosphere of relaxed creativity she could sense all about her was surely to be encouraged. In moderation.

She reached the top of the High Street, and stopped. A signpost, indicating Wells to the left, Shepton Mallett to the right. No mention of the way to the Tor, which she still could not see. An optical illusion, some might say; Miss Seeton, artist, thought at once of perspective, and lines of sight. She smiled. Miss Callender would doubtless inform her customers that the magical hill was visible only at certain times of day, certain phases of the moon—even, perhaps, only to the initiated. And then she would recommend some books ...

Still smiling, Miss Seeton turned, crossed the High Street, and began her slow descent in search of an appropriate shop. Callender's Coats, perhaps? A coat, after all, was worn out of doors and the shoes she required were surely outdoor wear—

"Ugh!"

"Oh, dear, I am so sorry." Miss Seeton in her abstraction had drifted across the path of a thick-set man of late middle age, burdened with a carrier bag that, caught by the careless lurch of her umbrella, ripped across one side and spilled its contents on the pavement. "Oh, dear—your books ..."

She had bumped into the very man who, scoffing at the landscape Zodiac, had been sold a further selection of reading by Octavia Callender. Blushing, Miss Seeton bent to pick up a solid volume with a cover depicting a brown horse in the green-field foreground, a white chalk horse carved into the hill behind, under a sky of flawless blue. With horrified fingers she smoothed the paper jacket back in place. "I am so sorry—this book, at least, appears to have suffered no injury, but—oh, dear ..."

"No thanks to you," said the man, who with an effort had stooped to pick up and was now dusting down the rest of his property. He glared, then seemed to recognise her. "Well," he temporised, "I suppose my mind was wandering, too. That Zodiac nonsense. I've bought some large-scale Ordnance Survey maps and a pocket compass from the outdoor shop down the road. Now I need a stationer's, for pencils and a ruler." He contemplated the tattered state of his brown paper carrier. "And some sticky tape as well, I think. I've got to carry all this lot back to my hotel." He crammed the slim card-covered maps into the pocket of his jacket—Miss Seeton winced for the strain on the fabric—and shoved the compass after them. The books he piled together. He no longer, she was even at this moment faintly amused to see, had the paper flower in his possession.

"No need to laugh," he grumbled, rubbing his lumbar region. She blushed again.

"I fear there is no suitable shop further up the hill," she said contritely. "Please allow me to accompany you on your search, and of course I will pay for the sticky tape, but perhaps at the same time you could show me where you made your purchases?"

"Peace, love, and a replacement bag? If I go back to that young woman she'll only sell me more books. She's tougher than she looks, for all her bells and beads. There's a glint in her eye ... She'll go a long way, that one."

Miss Seeton, who could not disagree, nodded even as she explained that, more than willing as she was to pay for the sticky tape—indeed, she insisted—or even a new carrier bag, if one could be bought, she was in fact looking for a shop that might sell shoes appropriate for climbing the Tor, which she intended to do tomorrow once she had explored the ruined Abbey and seen King Arthur's grave.

The thick-set man stared. "And she's not the only one who's tougher than she looks," he observed. "If you don't mind me saying so." This little hen talked about climbing the Tor as if it was a stroll in the park. He'd already done that climb, and knew it wasn't. His legs were tender after yesterday's effort, his back ached. Did she understand what she'd be letting herself in for? She didn't look or sound at all dotty or doolally, though she was no spring chicken, but still ... He looked again at Miss Seeton, and decided that she understood very well. "Hope it stays fine for you," was all he said aloud.

"I will have my umbrella—" she began, then remembered how the umbrella had been the cause of the original collision, and blushed for a third time. "Sticky tape," she hurried on. "We really must find a stationer, or a newsagent."

"Oh, well, I can borrow a pencil, and it's not far to where I'm staying. I'll wrap what's left of the bag round the books and put 'em under my arm. After yesterday I've had enough walking on hills, thanks. You'll find the shop half-a-dozen doors along." He pointed down the High Street. "Good luck—and enjoy yourself tomorrow!"

He walked stiffly on his way before Miss Seeton had time to thank him.

The evening, decided two Callenders as one, had grown too late to spend longer at the factory, poring over balance sheets and market forecasts. The directors had pushed papers and studied charts far beyond the usual clock-off hour observed by their workers. Their eyes were tired, their brains weary. Their local pub began to call to Bill and Crispin. Bachelors both, these dedicated businessmen held the view that fish-and-chip meals, scampi in a basket, or a pie and a pint at the end of a working day were more than adequate supplements to the wholesome food served in their small factory canteen. Northload Street and The Lamb & Butcher beckoned as stomachs that had survived since the middle of the day on no more than biscuits and cups of strong, sweet tea began to grumble.

"Enough's enough," said Bill, stretching. "The Lamb?"

"See you there," agreed Crispin. He owned a car, Bill a motorbike, and both lived far enough from the factory to justify the expense, especially in bad weather. Valentine could not agree, and nagged them sometimes for not using bicycles, as so many people with far greater consideration for the environment did. Petrol (insisted Val) wasn't eco-friendly.

Her elder brothers naturally scoffed at their sister, but found a compromise by agreeing not to pollute the Somerset air by driving to the Lamb even if it rained. The daily exercise, they said, did them good. Changed from semi-formal to casual attire, in his leather biking jacket (a Callender line that sold very well) and denim jeans, Bill Callender pushed open the pub door and glanced about him.

Crispin, who was a little more careful of his appearance and rated it almost above his comfort, rarely arrived first and had not now. Bill nodded to several acquaintances, grinned at a few friends, and waved to the landlord with a call for *The usual, please* while he found himself an empty table.

With a glass of cider conveniently placed, he was skimming the tabloid newspaper for which he never found time during the day when the door opened again. A tanned, sturdy man of about Bill's age trod in heavy boots into the public bar. He glanced about him. He nodded to several acquaintances, grinned at a few friends, and then froze as his glance fell upon Bill at his table, the newspaper half concealing his face.

"Bill Callender, I bin wanting a word," said the newcomer. He trod purposefully across the bare wooden planks of the floor. Glasses rattled on nearby tables. "And you'll not hide from me behind that bloody paper!"

"I'm not hiding, Jan." Bill put down his newspaper. "I'm having a quiet drink and waiting for Crispin."

"Nothing to do with Crispin," said the younger John Callender, son of that John known as Janner who was half-uncle to Bill and his siblings. "It's you who's the eldest, so it's you who's got the bloody authority to set letters from bloody solicitors on to my father. Don't you go blaming it on the rest of your bloody family!"

Bill's eyes narrowed as he looked at his cousin. He spoke with slow emphasis. "No need to be so—bloody—rude, Jan. Our solicitor wrote to your father. Janner's the one who signed that lease. It has nothing to do with you."

"Nothing to do with me if you turn us off the land we've farmed since Dad left school and set up on his own account? It's got all to do with me—and Susan, too, when you go sending letters to rob an old man and his children of their inheritance!"

"Your father's not yet sixty-five—and he's not being robbed." Bill crunched his newspaper into a ball and tossed it in the fireless grate beside him. He pushed back his chair, and stood up. "If anyone's been robbed it's our family, with your father paying the same rent since 1927 and never an increase. That's almost fifty years, Jan Callender, all from a handshake between brothers and the trustees agreeing and nothing even properly signed until he came of age!"

"A handshake was good enough then, and if you'd not tried to threaten us wi' solicitors we might've come to some agreement now and shook hands again—but letters is another matter entirely and distressful to family feeling, your father not even cold in his grave—"

"Which has nothing to do with the case! Your father runs sheep on land he said backalong would be for keeping geese, and my father from the goodness of his heart let him be when he made the change—and ever since—but there should have been an increase in the rent when that change was made, only Dad was too soft-hearted and it went on too long. But better late than never is what we say, the four of us," which he knew was stretching a point, "and we're only asking for what's our due," which he knew even Val would accept. "If your father's not agreeable to a tribunal, as would be the fairest way, then we'll have him and his sheep off the land as is our right, and make better use of it ourselves—"

"If you'd not sent that bloody letter—"

"If your father hadn't refused to talk to me—"

"Building on good grazing land—"

"Taking advantage—"

The argument had steamed to boiling point. Jan Callender snatched up Bill's glass of cider, hurled the contents in his face and the container past his head into the fireplace. It smashed and splintered there while he seized the table and tossed it aside. He and his equally angry cousin stood face to face. Jan was a working farmer, but the office-bound Bill raced his motorbike most weekends and did the repairs himself, single handed. If it came to trading blows, the fight would be closer than an outsider might expect.

"That's enough of that! I thought you two was s'posed to be grown up now." William Hoare, landlord of The Lamb & Butcher, had known the cousins since their childhood. "If you'm lookin' for a place to break up you'd best go home. Or get out thik door and play yer damfool games in the car park."

"Games?" interposed another voice, as Crispin appeared behind him, the spectators to this family squabble parting to let him by. "Bill—Jan—what the hell are you playing at?"

Bill, Jan, and several spectators all began to tell him at once. Deafened, he looked towards William Hoare. The landlord, moving to right the overturned table, rolled his eyes as he picked it up in one large hand. Crispin took his brother by the arm and firmly shook him.

"Stop it. Stop! If it's about the field, this is no place for business talk, and if it's not then you still shouldn't make such a display of yourselves. I'll knock your stupid heads together if you don't shut up this minute."

William Hoare grinned. "They'd make mincemeat of 'ee, lad, but should you ask it I'd be happy enough to knock 'em together on thy behalf—before I chuck 'em out." William, despite his years, remained a fine figure of a man. "And chuck them out I will, you may be sure, if they go on upsettin' folk with their bloody nonsense."

Bill and Jan stood and glared at each other. Neither spoke. Both breathed heavily.

William Hoare knew human nature, as a successful landlord must. "Then—outside," he commanded. "Car park—and the winner to come back and pay for that broken glass or I'll ban the bloody lot of you for life!"

"Sit down and shut up," Crispin advised his brother and his cousin. They continued to glare. Reluctantly, he accepted the landlord's better judgement of the situation. "Then—outside," he echoed, with a sigh.

"Nobody else, mind," said William, glaring in his turn as the spectators began to shuffle. "'Tis nothing to the rest of you if a pair o' fools chooses to make even bigger fools of theirselves." He folded his arms and looked sternly around, so that as the three Callenders headed for the door they went alone.

For relaxation, Crispin preferred books to newspapers and enjoyed, among others, the works of P.G. Wodehouse. With vague memories of the fight between Mike and Adair, as overseen by Psmith, he wondered about finding a stop-watch but guessed that such refinement would be thought unnecessary by his simmering relatives. They simply wanted to thump each other until one of them backed down. The Callenders, he reflected, stayed true to their heritage even unto the third and fourth quarrelsome generation.

And this time around it was all because Guy Callender had left it too late to make his brother sign a new tenancy agreement when he decided to farm sheep instead of geese.

The next morning dawned clear, sunny and bright. The rain-washed air almost sparkled. Dark shadows were cast by trees, houses, and garden walls across paths and roads. Miss Seeton was amused to watch, on the ground, ravens dancing along the roof and perching on the chimneys of the Farside Hotel.

Hodge, on the window sill, lashed his tail and emitted little creaks of irritation, knowing from experience that the ravens, no matter how close to his hopeful claws they might appear to be, were in truth far out of reach. Lyn McConchie smiled as she loaded a faintly protesting Miss Seeton's plate with scrambled egg into which more than a taste of smoked haddock had been stirred, because she had decided to climb the Tor that morning.

"Then you'll need something to keep you going," said Miss McConchie, "and what's left I've put in Hodge's bowl, so there's nothing wasted if that's what you're worried about."

"Oh, no, thank you. You are very kind, but ..." It would be ungrateful and, indeed, rude to refuse such kindness, but when one was accustomed to no more than a single boiled egg, a little toast with jam, or a small bowl of porridge for breakfast, this breakfast seemed more like luncheon. Miss McConchie produced a generous rack of toast. Oh, dear. Like lunch and afternoon tea together.

"It's a fair old haul to the top," said the landlady, seeing her guest about to protest again. "We can't have you fainting from hunger halfway there—nor halfway back, either. Protein's what you want, so you eat it all up now. And you're doing the right thing giving the Abbey a miss for later. There's no arguing with the weather, and it's the best day for viewing we've had for some time. When conditions are this good you can see forty miles all round, across the Bristol Channel into Wales and right down into Devon." She chuckled. "Pity not to give those smart new boots of yours an airing!"

Miss Seeton, struggling to clear her plate, smiled for Miss McConchie's encouragement. They were an extravagant purchase, but the shop assistant had been most persuasive and, indeed, these unusual alpine boots were so very comfortable, soft yet supportive, that although one would probably have little need for them at home, for more energetic excursions they might even outdo the walking boots she had taken north with her for tramping the Scottish Highlands.

She sipped tea and realised, from the landlady's expression, that she must eat at least one slice of buttered toast to reassure her that she would not faint from hunger halfway up or down Glastonbury Tor.

"There was much of great interest," she began, as she reached for the smallest slice, "in the books I purchased from your friend Miss Callender, although there was so much that in the end, I fear, I could only dip into them rather than read every word." Sternly, Miss McConchie pushed the butter closer. Oh, dear. A few moments for the scrambled eggs to settle would have been welcome. "But all most interesting," persisted Miss Seeton. "And she was so entertaining about her family names."

"She tells a good tale, does Octavia." A silver dish with a blue glass lining, filled with strawberry jam, was set firmly beside the butter. Miss Seeton drew a deep breath, rallied, and sipped more tea.

"Her cousin, she tells me," she went on, "is writing a book on King Arthur. When she showed me the pamphlet I bought it, as well as the guide books and, of course, a map from the outdoor shop where I found my new boots.

They will be most useful, I feel sure." Miss McConchie, who already knew of her guest's particular interest in King Arthur, suspected her of diversionary tactics and fixed Miss Seeton with a warning eye. Miss Seeton drained her cup and meekly buttered her toast. Miss McConchie smiled ...

Miss McConchie laughed out loud. "You're never taking that umbrella with you on a lovely day like this! There's not a cloud for miles, Miss Seeton!"

Miss Seeton smiled back, but said nothing. She patted the crook-handled brolly over her arm and slipped her capacious handbag to rest beside it. "I have here my sketchbook and pencils," she told the landlady, "though not my binoculars, which I did not bring. One does tend to think of them for watching birds rather than scenery. My eyesight is excellent, and I shall of course make copious notes. One of the books mentions King Arthur as having some connection with Wales, and Miss Callender spoke of the Tor as a gateway to the Celtic underworld, although forty miles does seem rather a long way to tunnel ..."

As she left the hotel she looked up and blinked at the bright clarity of the sun-filled blue, smiled once more at the row of dancing shadow-ravens on the road. Black birds, black shadows. Darkness as dark as the underworld tunnel—or was it, she wondered, red with fire, grey with smoke? Her dipping into various books had not made this entirely clear.

In the deepest of the dark shadows the still, silent watcher emitted a gasp that he tried to stifle with a swift hand. The sudden careless movement cracked his elbow on the lamp-post beside which he had concealed himself. He cursed out loud and fell back against the wall, falling from shadow to sunshine.

In the house he had been watching, curtains twitched.

Chapter Eight

In her neatly-laced new boots Miss Seeton, having consulted the map in the middle of her town guide, arrived safely at the foot of Dod Lane. Here she paused to reflect on the fate of Richard Whiting, last abbot of Glastonbury. Having displeased Henry VIII (something all too easy to do) the elderly abbot had been arrested on a trumped-up charge and, found guilty after a show trial, strapped spread-eagled to a rough hurdle that was dragged by horses through the town to the very summit of the Tor, where he was hanged in the unpleasant manner of the time, with two other monks beside him.

They might, mused Miss Seeton as she set off again, have come this way, though it seemed from the map more likely they had not. It was possible to climb one side of the Tor and descend the other; she had chosen to make the shorter, steeper ascent first while her knees, as one might say, were still fresh. Coming back down past Chalice Well would lead her towards the Abbey, so it was probable the unhappy abbot and his followers would have made their final journey along that more straightforward route. But longer, according to the map, and therefore slower. Miss Seeton shook her head for the misfortunes of history, and trod onward as the steepness of the path steadily increased.

As she climbed she would pause, not to catch her breath—how thankful she was for the *Yoga and Younger Every Day* regime she had followed for so many years—but to sketch the swift likeness of a windswept tree, a gleam of water on the moors below, a bird lazily riding the currents of air rising with the warmth of the sun. This was where King Arthur had come to be healed of his wounds. She breathed deeply, savouring the glorious freshness. The Isle of Avalon. Yes, in King Arthur's time the Tor would indeed have been an island retreat. As for his castle—would she be able to see Camelot once she reached the top, or would the distant hills beyond blur the castle into their own misty blue?

She thought again of Abbot Whiting. Small consolation to a condemned man that the last he would see of the world would be a view of the countryside for forty miles around. But it was a splendid view. Miss Seeton arrived at the ruined tower of St Michael's Church, and saw that she was not alone. Ignored by grazing sheep, people were taking photographs, looking through binoculars, even sketching or making notes as they studied maps. A group of enthusiasts in long robes walked barefoot around, then through, then around the tower again, flowers in their hands and a muted chant on their lips.

"Take no notice," said a scornful voice behind her. "The sunshine brings them out—these last few days must have driven them crazy! They'd never have got themselves properly clean of the mud and the grass-stains, living in caravans as they do."

Miss Seeton turned towards the voice. It belonged to a small, thin, bespectacled girl wearing denim jeans and a shirt of some flimsy cream fabric, patterned with flowers. Miss Seeton smiled politely and said good morning.

"Oh, isn't it?" The girl flung out her arms to embrace the sunshine. "*Such* a morning—you can see for miles!" She beamed at Miss Seeton. "Did you climb all this way by yourself? My goodness," as Miss Seeton nodded. The girl, intent on friendliness, rushed on. "Have you been up here before?" Miss Seeton shook her head. "Do you want to know what you can see?" Her voice throbbed suddenly, and deepened. The rush of words slowed, and her spectacles shone. "Are you looking for ... the Zodiac?"

"I have heard of the Zodiac," admitted Miss Seeton, who from the corner of her eye had observed the barefoot chanters cease their procession and begin to seat themselves in a circle at the base of the ruined tower. Miss Seeton approved the elegance of some of the lotus positions, but hoped nobody would sit for too long on such damp ground. So unwise, even if the sun was shining.

The old lady had heard of the Zodiac. It was enough. "Let me show you! My name's Grace, by the way. Grace Howe." She gave Miss Seeton no time to reciprocate. "I come up here most days when it's fine, just to—to feel, and to be here." She took Miss Seeton's arm. "Come away from those unbelievers!"

She led her startled captive a few yards down the slope. With an eager pounce she unhooked Miss Seeton's brolly from her arm and, holding it as a pointer, began her lecture. "We're right in the centre of the Phoenix of Aquarius here." The ferrule of the umbrella described a series of vital movements. "Chalice Hill down there is part of the body—the Abbey ruins are on the tail—the Pilgrims' Path is the edge of the beak—just look towards Wells, and see how the two ancient tracks make one wing ..."

Dutifully Miss Seeton looked, but could see nothing beyond the expected hills, hedges, roads and a distant gleam of water. Water! "I had always thought," she ventured as Grace drew breath, "that the sign for Aquarius was a man pouring water from an urn or a jar. But you said a phoenix. I'm sorry, but I fear I don't—"

"Or an eagle," broke in the lecturer quickly. "The symbolism is what's important."

Miss Seeton knew nothing of the symbolism, and murmured to that effect.

"The moon goblet of Chalice Well—the Holy Grail in one of its earliest incarnations—was illuminated at the summer solstice five thousand years ago. Five thousand years!" Grace appeared to think this was explanation enough. Miss Seeton felt it was not, but knew the fault must lie with herself for having hitherto believed there to be only one Holy Grail (if, indeed, any at all) and for her ignorance as to what the moon goblet had to do with it. In whatever incarnation. Really, Glastonbury was quite as confusing as she'd been warned by Miss McConchie. Three swords for King Arthur—more than one Holy Grail ...

"... the castle of the Fisher King." Grace Howe's bemused audience forced herself to pay attention. "They say Wearyall Hill is named for Joseph of Arimathea, that it's where he fell asleep for his staff to take root and grow into the Holy Thorn, but not everyone understands that, as one of the Fish in Pisces, it has a far deeper symbolism ..." Miss Seeton couldn't help it. Her mind wandered again as she struggled with the Phoenician fish-god, with

Poseidon, with Babylonian seals and the Celtic salmon of knowledge ...

One really did not wish to break into such enthusiasm, but there were eleven further signs of the Zodiac—even a normal Zodiac—and Miss Howe had just spoken of a whale and a dove as well, not to mention—

"Arthur?" Eagerly Miss Seeton broke in as Grace paused to jab the umbrella in another direction. "I have a particular interest in King Arthur," she was thankful to be able to say, without appearing too rude.

The glasses in their gold wire frames flashed. "Hercules!" cried Miss Howe, with Miss Seeton's umbrella continuing to outline on the landscape below figures that Miss Seeton simply could not see. "Hercules the star-god on his charger—the constellation Sagittarius depicting the High King Arthur on his horse, with the rest of the constellations his knights, the Zodiac his Round Table—"

"And Camelot?" gasped the desperate Miss Seeton. "Can you show me Camelot?"

Grace turned to point the umbrella. "Cadbury Castle—over there, with all those trees round the base." Miss Seeton peered in that direction. Doubtfully, she nodded. Miss Howe laughed in sympathy. "I know, a bit of a disappointment, isn't it? They're ten miles apart, and they say you can see Avalon easily enough from Camelot, but you can't really see Camelot from Avalon because of the higher ground behind."

"Everything," agreed Miss Seeton thankfully, "is blue and blurred." She gazed about her, hoping to deflect this young enthusiast from yet further bewildering assaults on her unprepared mind. One tried, naturally, to keep one's mind open to new ideas, but one did prefer to have sufficient time in which to absorb and contemplate them.

Miss Howe, bursting with information about the earthly Temple of the Stars, had not yet learned how to present that information in manageable mental paragraphs.

"Is it possible to go to Cadbury Castle?" Miss Seeton wanted to know. "A day trip by coach, perhaps?"

Grace, about to unleash a further explanatory torrent, stayed the umbrella and shook her head. "It's just an Iron Age hill-fort. There's nothing much to see, and it isn't part of the Zodiac, which lies in the other direction—a circle ten miles in diameter—we're on the edge of the circle here …"

Miss Seeton blinked as her umbrella darted through the air, still sketching shapes she could not see, though it was clear that Miss Howe could. Or (Miss Seeton privately amended) believed she could. She had now moved on from Camelot to Scorpio, the Water Gate of Death, and Virgo, the Earth Gate of Life. It seemed they lay between Avalon and Camelot … for reasons Miss Seeton realised she would never understand.

Her bewilderment must have shown, for Grace suddenly laughed, lowered the umbrella, and hung it over her own arm. "You don't know what I'm talking about and you can't see any of it, can you?"

"Well, no," confessed Miss Seeton. "Though you make it all sound most interesting. One does, of course, try to keep an open mind, even when the concept is unfamiliar. There are books, I know, and perhaps if I could read one at my leisure I might better understand the principle, but as I am here for only a few days I rather fear there will be insufficient time, when it is King Arthur who is of especial interest to me."

"Have you been to Bedivere Books?" Miss Seeton said she had. "She knows her stuff, does Octavia, but she never gives discounts, not even for regular customers, and it's almost impossible to go in there and come out again without having spent a lot more money than you meant to."

Miss Seeton, with a smile, admitted that she, too, had thought much the same, although when Miss Callender learned she had already bought raffle tickets to help the Abbey she had not pressed her to buy more.

"Vincent Weaver's balloon." Grace sighed. "I've bought as many as I can afford, for the chance to win that flight—I'd love to see the Zodiac properly, from above, the way it was meant to be seen. Maps and photographs just aren't the same."

Miss Seeton braced herself, as Miss Howe unhooked the umbrella, for more information about the Zodiac, but there was no need. The brolly was handed back to her with a smile.

"If it's fated—if it's in the stars—then one of my tickets will win," said Grace bravely. "If it isn't meant to be, then I'll have to wait. My time will come, even if the circle must turn more than once." She contemplated Miss Seeton, nodded, and then spoke in a throbbing voice. "You have listened, and not laughed. You have kept—unlike some—an open mind. Such courtesy merits good fortune. You may well be the lucky winner and then, from high above, you will be able to see the truth I have been trying to share with you."

Before Miss Seeton could answer, the umbrella was snatched back as Miss Howe's mood suddenly lightened. She began once more to point into the distance.

"See those ugly square buildings beside the Bristol Channel over there? The concrete bunkers?" Miss Seeton could not deny that the Brutalist architecture was all too visible from the top of Tor Hill. "That's Hinkley Point nuclear power station. Entirely the wrong sort of power, of course. You would hope, with the dawning of the Age of Aquarius, the promise of enlightenment, that it shouldn't take too long to initiate those who have set themselves in control of the world's destiny, but they just don't seem to listen ..."

Again Miss Seeton braced herself for another burst of bewildering enthusiasm as the umbrella stabbed further down the coast. "That hill is Dunkery Beacon—on Exmoor, almost forty miles away beyond the Quantocks—you know, Wordsworth and Coleridge and the person from Porlock?" Miss Seeton nodded with relief; this was something she did know.

Another stab. "Miles away over there, though you can't see it, is St Michael's Mount in Cornwall." Miss Seeton knew of the Mount, and of its even more spectacular counterpart in Mont Saint Michel, off the coast of France. "St Michael's Mount," said Grace, "is linked by the ley line of the Dragon directly to St Michael's ruined church on Burrow Mump over there—and to St Michael's tower here on Tor Hill—and then on through Creech St Michael and beyond, as far as the Norfolk coast!"

Miss Seeton smiled, and for good measure nodded. To her new acquaintance the information was clearly significant, and Miss Seeton still felt guilty at having allowed her attention to wander at the start of the discourse. She must acknowledge this significance in the only truthful way she could. But it was really very puzzling. The coast of Norfolk was several hundred miles from Somerset. Young Miss Howe, undeniably an enthusiast, nevertheless seemed to dart from fact to—well, fiction, supposed Miss Seeton, and back again in a—well, one had to say, an almost incoherent fashion. She was, however, young. With some young people it took longer than with others to learn the wisdom of ordering one's thoughts. Had her ideas been better organised, better presented, a newcomer might more readily grasp—"Burrow Mump," announced Miss Howe with another stab of the umbrella. "It is the hill that forms the muzzle of the Great Dog of Langport." Miss Seeton blinked. Once more Miss Howe's voice throbbed and deepened.

"The Great Dog guards the entrance to the Zodiac, between Cancer and Gemini, just as Cerberus guarded the entrance to the underworld. King Alfred burning the cakes is based on an ancient truth, you know. Oh, the legend has become distorted over time, but Alfred, for all his Christian piety, knew enough of the old ways to make sacrifice and offerings to the holy hound when asking for help in his coming battle with the Saxon invaders ..."

At long last the umbrella, having stabbed and pointed and described the holder's somewhat overwhelming knowledge in a breathless, all-enveloping circle, was handed back to its owner with an apologetic twinkle. "I do hope I haven't bored you," said Miss Howe, a little wistfully. Miss Seeton shook a truthful head. She had been overwhelmed, bemused, and puzzled, but she had not been bored.

Grace beamed. "I tend to get carried away if there's a sympathetic listener, and while I think you do not know it, you have just such sympathy—and something more. You have a true insight into the greater truth—into the reality that is hidden from less enlightened eyes." Upon Miss Seeton's startled brow a quick pucker flashed, and was gone. She had suddenly been reminded of Chief Superintendent Delphick, and the strange things he sometimes said. A coincidence, no more, but one had to wonder if—

"Promise me," urged Miss Howe, "that if you are fortunate enough to win the balloon flight you will scan the ground beneath for signs of the Zodiac figures I've tried to show you. There are so many books—promise me you'll go on trying to keep an open mind, and not dismiss the Zodiac as no more than—than barefaced lunacy!"

Again Miss Seeton's memory fleetingly stirred. Miss Howe's mention of books—there had been something— some *one* ...

"Bedivere Books," she murmured.

Grace was quick to catch the reference. She beamed more brightly than ever. "Go and see Octavia Callender again," she urged. "If you told her before that you were looking for Arthurian background I expect you didn't buy anything beyond Susan's little effort on the Three Swords and a history book or two—or three, knowing Octavia." Miss Seeton had to twinkle back for the accuracy of the mischievous guess.

"But all most interesting," she hastened to add. "As listening to you has also been, my dear." This, at least, was true. But perhaps one ought to drop a gentle hint, for the benefit of future chance-met strangers? "Rather a lot to take in at once, of course," kindly, "yet I feel sure that, should I find time to read more on the subject, I will regard the landscape with—with even greater ... interest." Honesty could not let her say that she *would* read more, only to suggest that she *might*.

And yet, remembering Octavia Callender, Miss Seeton felt sure that a second visit to Bedivere Books would result in plenty of reading matter on the subject of the Glastonbury Zodiac.

Superintendent Kebby was a worried man. Even his moustache seemed to droop.

"The sister sneaked us the latest missive disguised as a note put out for the milkman. He's been one of ours since we started keeping watch on the family home—and whoever missed that package being chucked over the garden wall is due the biggest rollocking of his career. When I find out who it was, I'll make mincemeat of him."

"I may well join you in the good work." Delphick had smoothed the bottle-curved print on his desk and held it flat under a rotary pencil sharpener, a box of paperclips, a stapler and a china mug filled with pencils. "This does, unfortunately, look genuine."

In stark black and white, Christy Garth sat with his elbows resting on a bare wooden table holding, its date and headlines clear, a recent edition of a national newspaper in both hands. One was heavily bandaged, the other as bruised as Christy's face. His eyes were dark-rimmed and sunken, his expression hollow.

"It could be faked," said Kebby, "but he does look thinner than he did. Those wrist bones seem genuine, and you'd need to be pretty smart at fakery for that. They won't be starving him into submission, exactly, but keeping him short of grub and knocking him about does put a lot more pressure on the family to pay up."

"You wouldn't entrust a photograph of this type to an ordinary chemist for developing and printing," said the Oracle slowly. "Whoever took this knew what he or she was doing. Of course, any professional can be blackmailed or otherwise coerced, but ... This is a wild guess, Jasper, for a possible starting point. Do we know of any criminals inclined towards kidnap, whether for fund raising or for revenge, who boast amateur photography as an apparently harmless pastime? Family members or other close connections who could make similar boasts?"

Kebby made a note. "We'll ask that mechanical monster in the basement to churn through its punch-cards, and I'll try a few human elephants as well for likely memories, but somehow I think it's a dead end. You said it yourself. Anyone can be coerced into almost anything, if sufficient pressure's applied. We need another lead—and soon. I don't like the look of this photo, and the message they didn't send with it makes me worry all the more."

"Yes." Delphick removed the office impedimenta and picked up the photograph. "One would have expected an anonymous typed note, perhaps on the back, with demands for further payment and instructions on how it should be made, together with threats as to what will happen if the demands are not met. But apart from this disturbing portrait the rest, I fear, is a most uncomfortable silence."

"They must have worked out by now that the family's come to us for help," said Kebby. "They could have taken that photo and killed young Garth the same day. They could be turning the screw just for the fun of it, now."

"Fun? Another question for the computer, perhaps—always assuming that psychological analysis and interpretation are included among the facts that have been fed into the wretched thing."

"Trick cyclists," muttered Kebby. "Long words, educated guesswork and some common sense, that's how they work it."

"Copper's instinct," countered Delphick. "Different terminology and no string of letters after our names, but we ourselves have worked that trick for years."

Kebby brightened. "Yes, with enough experience you can usually spot a wrong 'un. Instinct. The very word." He looked towards the Oracle, then reached for the photograph. "Yes, there's always that ... special feeling," he prompted. "Instinctive."

"She's on holiday, Jasper." Delphick glanced for the first time across the office to the corner graced by the enormous but tactfully silent form of Detective Sergeant Ranger. "Any idea when Miss Seeton's due back, Bob?"

"End of the week, I think, sir. It all depends on the weather, but I know she didn't plan to be away too long because she wants to make a proper start on her sketches in good time for them to be scaled up for the scenery painters."

Delphick nodded. "There are a great many West Country connections to King Arthur. If she's on a sightseeing spree we could waste more time chasing around Somerset to find her than if we leave it to the end of the week. The local bobby can let me know when she's due back, and I'll go straight down to Kent. That's the best we can offer at present, I fear."

"And so do I fear," returned Kebby. "Rather a lot. For Christy Garth, I mean."

"You're not alone in that," he was assured.

It all depended on the weather. Miss Seeton had revelled in her sunshine climb of Glastonbury Tor, her meeting with Grace Howe and the subsequent, half-smiling, return to Bedivere Books to enquire after a book—or at least no more than two—about the Zodiac for leisure reading, once she was home again. Octavia had looked surprised, then returned the smile on hearing of Grace's lecture, and sold just one small paperback and a hand-drawn map to this remarkable customer before warning that it looked like rain tomorrow, and Miss Seeton might find herself reading about the Zodiac rather sooner than expected.

The rain began as drizzle later that evening. Miss McConchie's Hodge, in the cautious manner of cats, put a tentative nose out of doors, flicked his ears, retreated, and sneezed. He shook one forepaw after another, and lashed his tail.

"What a shame." Miss McConchie favoured her guest with a regretful look. "You just wait, there'll be a proper downpour by tomorrow morning. Hodge is better than any amount of Met Office forecasts. Weren't you lucky to climb the Tor when you did?"

"Indeed I was." Miss Seeton twinkled at the dignified tabby sitting beside his mistress. "If Hodge is correct—I trust he will forgive me for doubting him—but if he is correct in his suspicions about tomorrow's weather I think I might undertake a short journey by bus to Wells. In the guidebooks it appears most interesting, and looks delightful."

She set off next day with every intention of enjoying herself. Why should she not? She had stout shoes, her umbrella, and (as reassured by her landlady) plenty of shops into which to pop should the downpour pour down even harder.

The guidebooks had already prepared Miss Seeton for the sight of water pouring down the wide stone gutters of the main shopping street in the small cathedral city. A mediaeval bishop of Wells had ordered the great springs that gave the place its name to be diverted into channels as a clean and permanent water supply for the general populace; further diversions had created the moat around the Bishop's Palace. Miss Seeton wondered if the celebrated swans, whose predecessors were trained by the daughters of a Victorian bishop to ask for food by ringing a bell, would be swimming or taking shelter. Then she smiled at her folly in supposing that swans or, indeed, any water birds would mind a few drops of rain.

"Lover-ly weather for ducks," carolled Miss Seeton as she trotted blithely up the gentle hill, ignoring the smiles of passers-by. "Lover-ly weather for ducks!"

Others out and about that day found the weather less pleasing. A thick-set man in late middle age was trudging across green, waterlogged ground miles from, but within sight of, Glastonbury Tor. On his aching back the bulky rucksack was stained dark where it had leaked. His tweed cap was sodden; his trousers clung wetly to his legs and were splashed with mud to his knees. The maps and notebooks he had intended to consult were useless in such conditions. He could rely only upon his pocket compass, and his memory.

Hawley Bowyer's landlady had urged him to wait for tomorrow's promised improvement in the weather before making this expedition, but Mr. Bowyer's trust in the official forecast was no greater than his belief in the landscape Zodiac. He liked to check his facts and make up his own mind. He judged it would be even wetter next day, and the ground thus even more difficult underfoot. His legs were still weary from that climb to the Tor summit. Keep moving, circulate the blood, and the ache would all the sooner be gone. Stagnate indoors, and the middle-aged body would become cramped, stiff, and unable to explore.

Yet just at present he might have welcomed a brief spell indoors. Shelter would mean he could consult his map

141

and refresh his memory from his notes. For some time he hadn't been as sure of where he was as he ought to be. Horizon-stretching pastures, wide straight ditches, and hedges interspersed with gates and willow trees were very difficult to distinguish from any other pastures, ditches, hedges. Ah. Hawley brightened. Beyond the next hedge, in the near distance he could just make out through the sight-blurring monsoon a cluster of low, tumbled walls and sagging ridge-tiles. Farm buildings, abandoned by a farmer who had fallen on hard times. No, not entirely abandoned, he realised as he drew closer. One tiled roof had been patched with so many sheets of corrugated iron that it was more galvanised grey now than ruddy tile. Good. He slipped the compass into his pocket and trod on across the fields, his rucksack bumping with every labouring step.

He reached the door, and opened it. He stepped inside. He stopped. "Oh ..."

Hawley Bowyer was entirely unprepared for what happened next.

A tall, rangy, fair young man with a wispy beard, a braided headband holding back shining hair that brushed slim shoulders, was reporting in person to his Scotland Yard superior.

"It does all seem to fit the usual pattern, sir. A short-term let while they make the connections and set up the network, selling the stuff nice and cheap at first to hook local mugs so deep in debt they'll have to become the next generation of dealers or risk something nasty happening to them. They've not yet moved on to Stage Two, when the deepest-hooked locals get their homes taken over a few weeks at a time so the distribution centre never stays anywhere long enough to be traced."

Superintendent Snowe looked glum. "They'll move now, and fast. They'll be out of there even shorter term, which will surprise the letting agents—though not so much as spotting you on the prowl must have surprised the druggies. Careless, Brumby. I told you not to take any chances."

"Yes, sir, and I'm sorry to have blown my cover, but I was surprised too. You said to keep an eye open for familiar faces, and I thought I'd spotted one of our friends from the Smoke going into the place and was hoping to make sure when he came back, but I didn't expect Miss Seeton to come popping out of the house next door the way she did, and—"

"What?" cried Superintendent Snowe. "Who did you say?"

"Miss Seeton, sir." Dick Brumby was puzzled. "The Oracle's—I mean Chief Superintendent Delphick's—Miss-Ess. A grand undercover agent, looking like everyone's favourite auntie the way she does. The Battling Brolly, sir," he persisted. "That's how I spotted her, because that time she came up to the Yard I only saw her down a corridor, not face to face. But it was a bright sunny day—lots of nice deep shadows for me to hide in—and she was carrying an umbrella, so of course it caught my attention when there wasn't a cloud in the sky. I was so startled, I let out a yelp. That's how they saw me from the house, I'm sure. Well, I'd have liked to be told she'd be on the case with me, but I'm not so conceited I can't take a little help when it's offered—not that the Brolly offered, not even to let me know she'd seen me. She's really good, sir. So, knowing she had things under control, I legged it in the opposite direction so as not to interfere, and before I'd gone a hundred yards a couple of bods were on my trail." He spread his hands in apologetic resignation. "There seemed no point in hanging around to get thumped, or worse, once they'd seen me, so I kept going until I found a convenient shop, ducked in with my ID and asked them to phone for a taxi."

Snowe permitted himself a wry grin. "From what you tell me about Glastonbury they'd have taken it in their stride with no ID and you asking for a helicopter," he said. "Or a witch's broom with a tank full of magic."

Dick grinned back, relieved that the rollocking—understandable, but a tad unfair—was past the worst. "I thought I'd seen it all here in Town, sir, but now I just don't know. There's some strange people in those parts—not to mention the wide open spaces and the sheep and the cows and the birds. If I want a wildlife fix, I'll take our home-grown maniacs over life with the country bumpkins any day."

But Superintendent Snowe was no longer listening, his fingers busy with the dial of the telephone on his desk. "Ranger? Snowe, Narcotics. The Oracle there? I'd like a word ... See here, Oracle, why didn't you warn me you meant to go poaching on my preserves? You could've let me know. One of my men's just had a narrow escape from being done over by a pair of drugged-up thugs down in Somerset, all because he tripped over your Battling Brolly going solo, and was so surprised he blew his cover ..."

The chief superintendent was as surprised as Dick Brumby had been. "Miss Seeton's there on holiday, Nick, not working for me or, as far as I know, for anyone else."

"Holiday? Right next door to a drugs den?"

"Holiday," insisted Delphick. "People do take them, from time to time. Not work. For some reason the professionally perplexed would rather approach her through me, or my sergeant, than make any direct official request. I'm sure I would have heard about it, had anything changed." He cleared his throat, and frowned at Bob Ranger, who in his corner was turning pink about the ears.

"Moreover," Delphick went on, "I am confident that the Yard's efficient grapevine must have informed me had Miss Seeton's professional services been requested by any, shall we say, outside authority. As for the inside variety, Superintendent Kebby has asked if I will visit Miss Seeton for further consultation the moment her short holiday is over and she is back at home—but that's as far as it goes."

Superintendent Snowe counted silently to ten. "My lad got out by the skin of his teeth, but from what I hear that woman of yours is a born survivor. So if—when—she makes it safely home, you might just ask her if while she was down in the west she happened to spot anything that could have to do with drugs. Or even those dancing sheep of hers. As you'll be seeing her anyway. Once she's back," he ended bitterly, "from her holiday."

Chapter Nine

Miss Seeton poured the first round of tea and topped up the pot as she pressed sponge cake upon a thoughtful Delphick, gingerbread upon an eager Bob. The Oracle, ill at ease over the course he had been asked to pursue, had arranged an early start from London. Over the stressful motorway miles, and along the wandering roads of Kent, the memory of breakfast soon faded; even so, he had less appetite than usual.

"We have time for just one slice," he warned, "before we settle to our professional consultation, Miss Seeton." A consultation he was reluctant to begin; he forced a smile. "With your permission we'll send Bob out to the kitchen to make a fresh pot while I ..." Miss Seeton regarded him with curiosity. Such uncertainty was unlike dear Mr. Delphick.

"While I discuss the kidnap with you," he finished. "I regret to say that matters seem to have taken a turn for the worse." Miss Seeton was shocked. "But I regret also that on this occasion, there is more. While the kidnapping has to be our main concern my colleague, Superintendent Snowe, would very much like your opinion of another case."

He had protested; Snowe had insisted. *That woman with her dancing sheep knew all about the drugs before we had any idea. Why should it confuse her to ask if she knows any more? You afraid it will tangle her vibrations? At least give it a whirl. It's an offbeat case, and your MissEss with her psychic scribbles is as offbeat as they come ...*

Unable to refuse a colleague's plea for help, Delphick finally agreed. Miss Seeton might, for all he knew, be capable of sketching the solutions to a dozen cases at once without tangling her vibrations. On the other hand, she might not. There was only one way to find out. He must ask her, and hope that disentangling the various solutions would not prove impossible when the time came.

"Superintendent Snowe?" Miss Seeton looked doubtful.

Was she worried about her ability to deal with two cases at the same time? Had his anxieties been justified? Then the more obvious answer came to him. "The powers that be haven't demoted me," he reassured her, "or told me to take early retirement." He sensed, rather than saw, her relief. He smiled. "We aren't all as lucky as you, inheriting a cottage in the country and having Premium Bond wins."

She smiled back. "A modest win, but after so many years with nothing, most gratifying. It was a pleasure to visit another delightful part of the country even if, it now appears, most of my little artistic efforts were in vain."

Both men were detectives. "You mean the Padders aren't doing King Arthur after all?" burst from Bob, while Delphick echoed the question.

Miss Seeton hesitated. "Not exactly. Mr. Jessyp tells me the new story is part of the Arthurian canon and takes place at Christmas, and is therefore perhaps more suitable than Malory for turning into a pantomime. The first scene of *Sir Gawain and the Green Knight* is set in the great hall of Camelot, at the height of the twelve days of festivities.

The Green Knight enters and challenges someone to behead him with his own axe, which Mr. Jessyp insists must be of cardboard, though Mr. Eggleden has offered to make a blunt one. A blacksmith is naturally able to wield a metal implement with great skill, and indeed he is to play the Knight, a man of gigantic stature, if he can only be persuaded to allow himself to be painted green. Cardboard is far safer. People when acting do sometimes tend to become carried away by the part."

"It may be as well they decided against Malory," said Delphick. "Eggleden might have forged Excalibur for Arthur to pull out of the stone, and even a blunt metal sword can do a lot of damage."

"Forgive me, Mr. Delphick, but I think you mean Caliburn." Miss Seeton spoke with a hint of deferential amusement. "In Glastonbury I bought a most interesting little publication about swords, and it seems that King Arthur had three. Excalibur is merely the later, more poetical name for one of these"

Bob wasn't bothered about the number or names of the swords. It was the green paint. As a child he had seen "The Wizard of Oz" and been scared by the witch; as an adult he had read of how the first Tin Man was poisoned, though not fatally, by his aluminium makeup. He could understand the blacksmith's reluctance. "Just the few bits that show, I hope," he muttered, his imagination boggling. Had he known his Longfellow he would have agreed that *a mighty man* described Dan Eggleden perfectly and that *iron bands* was an understatement when applied to the strength of his muscles. But painted bright green—Christmas or no Christmas, it didn't bear thinking about.

Miss Seeton, deep in explanation, had missed her adopted nephew's muffled hope as she ended with the news that Jack Crabbe, famed in Plummergen for the witty and cryptic crosswords he composed, was to supply some of the jokes while Mr. Jessyp wrote the main script. Delphick, his doubts receding, laughed.

"And splendidly terrible jokes they will be, as I recall from a previous production. Are you able to share any of them, to forewarn us?"

Miss Seeton hesitated. "What is the centre of gravity?" she said at last. "The question is asked when the Green Knight's head falls to the ground—to give him time to pick it up, as it will be of papier mâché and might bounce, or roll too far."

"I'll buy it," said Delphick. "Nothing too scientific, I trust."

"The letter V," came the answer.

Bob, who had surfaced from his green paint nightmare, joined his superior in groaning. Miss Seeton was encouraged by her success. "Which two letters of the alphabet indicate the most pleasant people in the world? The riddle is asked in the scene when the Green Knight's wife has to flirt with Sir Gawain, while her husband is out hunting—and," a slight twinkle, "could be likewise applied to your visit here."

There were no takers. "U and I," she announced, to further appreciative groans. "And what," she concluded with a definite twinkle, "have X, Y and D in common?"

Silence. Shaken heads. "It is when Sir Gawain is riding west the following Christmas," prompted Miss Seeton. Further silence.

"They are all rivers! The Exe, down in Devon; the Wye in Herefordshire; and the Dee in Scotland, which of course is to the north, but they are all rivers. He might well have crossed the Wye through a ford, or on a bridge, when heading for his encounter with the Green Knight at the mysterious chapel in the Wirral."

"So he might," agreed Delphick. "After which, with your permission, Miss Seeton, I feel a second pot of tea is in order. To the kitchen, Sergeant Ranger!"

While crockery clattered and water splashed, Delphick grew serious. So too did his hostess. He took the familiar stiff brown envelope from his pocket, and she sighed.

"During my little holiday, Chief Superintendent, while I did not entirely forget him I fear that the young man who was kidnapped did slip to the back of my mind. I must regret that my sketch was of less help than you had hoped. You said there was further news ..."

"There is. Another message, visual and potent." He laid before her the photograph of Christy with the newspaper.

Miss Seeton caught her breath. "His bandaged hand and bruised face would appear to suggest some degree of violence, would they not? Poor young man, although it seems from the newspaper he holds that he was alive and well on that particular date, which must be some encouragement to his family." Delphick noted her use of the conditional. Even now she seemed to have doubts as to the genuineness of Christy Garth's abduction.

"Further encouragement might be given by another of your sketches," he suggested gently. "Your holiday will have refreshed your imagination. Perhaps you could study this new picture in company with these others you saw before." He shook out the contents of the envelope. "I'll go and make sure Bob isn't putting salt in the sugar bowl or miscounting the number of spoons for the pot—or dropping the tea caddy on the floor."

When the two policemen returned, Bob carrying the tray, Miss Seeton was putting the final touches to her drawing. She heard the steady footsteps, angled the point of her pencil for a last swirl of movement, and then sat back, shaking her head.

"Tea," said Delphick, "and sympathy, Miss Seeton. I can tell you're dissatisfied with your efforts and I do understand, but, I assure you on behalf of my colleague, we are unlikely to share your dissatisfaction. May I see?"

The picture she had just completed showed a small and lively flock of sheep dancing in a meadow dotted not with flowers, but with letters of the alphabet. "I am so sorry to have allowed the pantomime jokes to distract me." The artist's cheeks were pink. Delphick said nothing. The sketch resembled her earlier effort, but ... "I fear that I misled you, when the matter is so important." She was determined to explain, even if she could not justify, such misleading. "Jack Crabbe will indeed supply most of the jokes, but those foolish riddles are—are mine, or rather my Cousin Flora's. That is, they originally belonged to her mother, who left her the riddle book I later inherited. In Victorian times it was common for young ladies to assemble them. She stitched and bound it herself, pasting in cartoons from *Punch* and similar journals. I chanced upon it while helping Martha the other day, and when I opened it at random the first riddle I saw concerned an umbrella, which naturally caught my attention. When Mr. Jessyp said that Jack was compiling jokes for King Arthur I wondered if there might be anything he could use, and lent it to him—to Jack, I mean—the book, not my umbrella—and there was. And he said he would."

Delphick looked up from the dancing sheep. He had realised the great difference between this and the previous sketch: they were no longer wearing strait jackets, or those manic, toothy grins. Perhaps a false kidnap had after all become real; but the riddle-letters puzzled him. "What particular joke originally caught your attention?" he enquired.

Miss Seeton again turned pink. "At which season of the year is one most likely to lose an umbrella?"

"Winter," said Bob, "because of carrying it in the snow and leaving it on the bus."

"Summer," said Delphick, "because it's a trick question. There's nothing to say it cannot be used as a sunshade before you leave it on the bus."

They both looked at their hostess. "When it is Lent," she said.

"Polonius," said Delphick at last. "A warning to us all." Bob stared. Delphick took pity on him. "A prosy old gentleman in *Hamlet*, full of good advice but more than tedious in its delivery. He considered it unwise either to borrow ... or *to lend*."

He and Miss Seeton waited for light to dawn. It did. Bob forced a chuckle. The other two exchanged smiles. Bob drank tea; Delphick leafed backwards through the sketchbook, curious as to what aspects of her Somerset holiday had made the greatest impression on Miss Seeton.

"What prompted this?" he enquired of a stately cleric in mitre, cape, and gumboots. Around his head shone a nimbus of multiple figure sevens; in one hand he held an umbrella in place of a crozier, in the other a bottle. "Did you meet a bishop boozing in the rain?"

"Good gracious, no. I went to Wells and visited the cathedral, and the Bishop's Palace with the swans on the moat, but I returned to my hotel in a very damp condition because it was so wet—the weather, that is, for of course a moat is already full of water—and Miss McConchie was most kind." The landlady had brewed a stiff concoction of hot chocolate, rum, and Worcester sauce and stood over Miss Seeton while she drank it. Miss Seeton's very toes had tingled, and she slept unusually well that night.

"And the sevens?"

Miss Seeton told him of Octavia Callender's remarks concerning the approach of the seventh of July, 1977 "to which some significance is attached, I believe, by many persons in the town" and the sevenfold earthwork maze around Glastonbury Tor. Delphick kept his thoughts to himself.

"A handsome specimen," he observed, having flipped past several worthy sketches of Arthurian scenery to the next inspiration, a likeness of a sturdy bull that filled almost the whole page, majestic in frame, its head huge on strong shoulders, its body supported by powerful legs. "It looks very like a Hereford, with its white face and chest, but surely their horns are somewhat less prominent?"

"Just outside Glastonbury," said Miss Seeton, "a herd of Highland cattle grazes on Wearyall Hill, where Joseph of Arimathea is said to have planted the holy thorn. A most distinctive sight—such enormous horns, and their coats so shaggy one has to wonder how they manage in prolonged spells of hot weather when they do not, as far as I know, moult in the summer. The stomach, I believe, is larger than that of any other breed."

Delphick tried to ignore Bob, who was discreetly reaching for his third, or was it his fourth, slice of gingerbread.

"A bishop and a Hereford bull," said the chief superintendent to himself. "Hereford ..."

The next swift holiday sketch had Miss Seeton exclaiming at the coincidence. "Our talk of swords, and dear Daniel Eggleden—it was in her bookshop—a most unusual mix of the normal with what one might call the esoteric—that I learned of Caliburn and the rest, and was persuaded to buy her cousin's little pamphlet. She is a clever actress and a remarkable businesswoman, with considerable understanding of human nature." She smiled. "It was hard to resist her ... sales pitch, I believe is the term. While King Arthur may no longer be the main focus of our theatrical endeavours they are still of interest—the books, that is—and once I have read them I will give them to Mr. Jessyp. He has more space, and a growing library on a variety of fascinating historical subjects."

A tall woman in flowing robes, her long hair bound back from a face covered by a mask, stood rubbing her hands together while an indistinct feline shape watched from the shadows cast by a guttering candle.

"Lady Macbeth," said Delphick.

Miss Seeton nodded. "Although Miss Callender named her cat Graymalkin, somehow I could not envisage her as one of the witches."

"You mean that she acts the part of a hippy shopkeeper but in reality is something more?" Miss Seeton nodded again. Delphick thought of Superintendent Snowe, and his drugs enquiry. Strange costumes and esoteric books could make excellent stage props for attracting the right—or rather, the wrong—people.

"I would imagine," he said slowly, "Miss Callender is far from the only person in town to adopt an unorthodox fashion in dress. I take it hers is not the only ... unusual shop?"

"There are a great many. With some remarkable window decorations," she added. "Candles in the form of skulls, the Dead Man's Hand in wax, and similar black magic foolishness, as well as crystal balls and witches' hats, or possibly wizards', for there were carved staffs and other such—such pantomime trickery, although if one does not take it seriously I suppose it may do less harm than, let us say, the taking of drugs." Delphick looked at her. "There were, you see, such very peculiar smells coming from some of the shops, and from the windows above them."

Superintendent Snowe had been forceful on the matter of his undercover agent's cover having been blown by the unexpected presence of Miss Seeton. "From any of the houses?" Delphick enquired. "Did you notice anything ... peculiar where you were staying?"

"Oh, no. Miss McConchie is most charming. Her little bed-and-breakfast, while small, is a model of efficiency and a delightful place to stay. She wishes to expand, she tells me, and I am sure she deserves to succeed. It was a sad disappointment for her when the house next door was sold, or possibly rented, before she knew about it because she could have knocked it through, or at least built a walkway between the gardens."

Yes, thought Delphick, it fits. She's noticed what's important without really noticing. Nick Snowe's chap was on the right track. I'll ask her what she thinks, and the Glastonbury cops can investigate—though by now the birds, at a guess, will have flown ...

But in Glastonbury the police had important matters of their own to concern them.

The body had been moved. "Marked post mortem discolouration." The police doctor knelt on damp ground beside the thick-set man of late middle age who lay crumpled beneath a hedge. "Indicating to the meanest intelligence that the man must be dead, or it couldn't be *post* mortem." He creaked from his knees to a standing position, and sighed as he dusted his trousers down. "Killed yesterday. I'll have a better idea of time once he's on the slab. Brought here in a vehicle of some sort—not a car, the boot would be too cramped for the way he's been lying. A small van or a farm trailer, at an educated guess."

"You can't beat the benefits of a good education," agreed the chief inspector, who with his small team of professionals had worked all this out within minutes of their arrival at the scene. Since childhood Tom Faggus had heard jokes about highwaymen and *Lorna Doone*, and accepted that all he could do was laugh with his tormentors. He was now able to find the humour in almost any situation. "Thanks, doc, we can take it from here now you've done your bit. Shame about your trousers, though. But they'll wash."

"Dry cleaning," emphasised the doctor, "costs money. I'll bring my own tarpaulin next time, and to hell with protecting the scene of the crime." He squelched back to his car. The official photographer took several shots of what, should they come out as he hoped, he would submit to the Art Society's annual exhibition as a study in dejection.

Chief Inspector Faggus addressed the newest member of his team. "You said you thought you knew who he was, Hannaford, and then the doc arrived to confirm the death officially. Now he's pushed off you can tell us what you know."

Detective Constable Hannaford hesitated. "I can't be *sure* I know who he is, sir, but I've seen him around and I think I know where he's been staying. Our Mum was chattin' with Mrs. Beck the other day and she said about some new boarder who'd come here just to see the landscape Zodiac, and how she had to chivvy him out of the kitchen when he wanted the table for his maps and charts, then he tried the dining room and it upset the other guests when the meals started being late because he wouldn't pack up."

"If he was looking for the Zodiac, he's way off target here." Faggus glance at his two companions in detection; the photographer had packed his equipment and was making for his car. "Why he was moved, d'you reckon? To put us off the scent?"

"It's thirty miles round," said Sergeant Bloxham. "I'm told," he added quickly. "Could've bin brought from almost anywhere, if such was indeed his purpose for wanderin' the moors in all that rain."

"If I had a corpse in the back of my car I'd not want to drive too far with it," said the chief inspector. "Especially in the rain. Mud and field run-off on the roads, gurt big puddles all over—I might skid into a ditch, and then where'd I be?"

"Discovered," supplied his sergeant promptly. "Caught red-handed by whoever come along to pull you out."

DC Hannaford ventured that a corpse covered by, say, old sacks, or the doctor's tarp, might go unnoticed when all that was supposed to happen would be a tow on the chief inspector's vehicle and then being waved on his way by his unsuspecting rescuer.

"Suppose I knocked meself out on the dashboard and they found me slumped over the wheel with concussion?" objected Faggus.

Hannaford, pondering, said that the chief inspector had been coerced into transporting the corpse. When the ditch entered into the equation, the murderer had coshed him to make good his escape, thus leaving him with the blame.

Tom Faggus had thought from the start the lad showed promise: Jem Hannaford was a welcome addition to the team. Bloxham was getting no younger, while he himself was too close to fifty for comfort. "Buying time," he nodded with approval. "They'd see in the end I didn't do it, but by then our guilty party could be miles away."

"Acting on impulse," said Sergeant Bloxham. "And that's what I reckon he really did. The weather we've had of late, you'd not choose to be left with a corpse on account of the difficulty in getting rid of it. Like that cannabis, right? Too damp to burn, too long a time to bury. This poor chap, he'll have stumbled across summat way out on the moors, and was silenced in a panic and then brought here when, you'd be right in your thinking, sir, our lad'll not want to carry him far, just far enough to be away from where he was killed because of what he must have seen."

All three considered this. The chief inspector nodded slowly. "Reckon you could be right. It's a lot o' trouble to go to, else. But what he could have seen, and where ..."

"His maps," said Hannaford. "They'd show us. Dozens of 'em he had, so Mrs. Beck told Mum—notebooks, too. Into his knapsack each morning with a flask and some sandwiches, then off researching and ... Oh."

The three detectives stared together at the body under the hedge. Fully clothed, it wore a weatherproof jacket and trousers, and sturdy boots. Of notebooks, maps, or a knapsack to hold them they saw no sign.

"Check his pockets, young Jem." Theatrically, Tom Faggus rubbed the base of his spine. "The sergeant and I are getting too old for this caper."

DC Hannaford diligently rummaged. "A pocket compass and that's about it, sir, apart from a wodge of paper hankies where the waterproofing must've leaked." He straightened, soggy tissues in one hand, compass in the other. Idly, he glanced down. He stared. "Well now." Without thinking he let the tissues fall, to tap gently on the glass of the compass as he looked towards the unmistakeable landmark of St Michael's tower on the summit of the Tor. "A shame, the glass cracked that way. And fancy puttin' it on a metal key-ring!"

"Let's see." Chief Inspector Faggus in his turn made the alignment, and tapped. "Ah. The needle's readin' wrong. That crack looks as if he dropped it—could be the reason for the key-ring. Daft, though, to go looking for Zodiacs and suchlike with a compass fitted to a hunk of metal. You'd think he'd of noticed when he checked against his maps."

"Pouring with rain it was, all yesterday," Sergeant Bloxham reminded him. "Unfold a map in such weather and you'll end up with as much of a mess as young Hannaford's made wi' them paper hanks now contaminating the scene of the crime."

Blushing furiously, Hannaford scooped up the soggy tissues and, after hesitating, tidied them into his own jacket pocket. Chief Inspector Faggus saw no need for further rebuke, and with an approving nod passed the faulty compass to his sergeant.

"Looks as if we guessed right, between us," he said as Bloxham began the tapping routine. "Couldn't check his map, so he'll have done what most folk would do and trusted to his memory for where he was heading, but he didn't realise his compass was on the blink and ended up miles from where he meant to be. And then …"

"And then, wallop," supplied Bloxham.

"Wallop," Faggus agreed. "And *then*—well, it's up to us to find out why. And who."

Mrs. Beck had been loud in her sorrow for the death of her boarder, though sorrow was tinged with relief that she would no longer need to keep nagging him to take his paperwork from the table and be herself nagged by full-board guests who wanted their meals on time.

"And it weren't just us here the poor man upset," said Mrs. Beck, shaking her head.

Unable to name names, because she hoped she had more sense than to credit such twaddle, the landlady could only suggest that Faggus and his men should talk to those who really believed in the Glastonbury Zodiac, or who might know the likely believers.

"There's some chap who takes folk on guided walks, sir," volunteered DC Hannaford. "But I dunno who he is, nor how to find him."

"There'll be a poster or two about," said Sergeant Bloxham, "if they've not been washed away by the rain."

"Or you could ask in the most likely shops," suggested the chief inspector, preparing to head back to the police station to set the investigation on a proper footing.

Bedivere Books, an obvious port of call, was closed until half-past three.

"Funny time to have dinner," said Hannaford. "Not like Tavy, to be shut when there's a chance to do a spot of business." He remembered Octavia from school.

"Three o'clock, end of hospital visiting," said Bloxham. "That's when she'll be back."

Hannaford looked surprised. "She ill? That's not like her, either."

The sergeant shook his head. "You got to keep your ears open as well as your eyes in this job, my son. You not heard about Janner Callender's accident? Octavia's visitin' her uncle, no doubt, blood being thicker'n water when all's said and done, even if the families don't get on so well day to day. But the ambulance was up to the farm a bit back, when his tractor overturned. Could've been very nasty, they say."

"Tavy Callender won't have shed a tear in sympathy," said Jem. "She'd rather he'd been killed outright, wouldn't she?" Among locals born and bred, the rental dispute was widely known; there was sympathy for both sides.

"That family's just started a run of bad luck," prophesied Sergeant Bloxham. "First her father dead, then her uncle hurt. Dangerous place, a farm can be for accidents. Let's hope the third, when it comes, ain't so serious."

"Hawley Bowyer's dead," soothed DC Hannaford, less superstitious than the older man. "If we count him, doesn't that break the run and bring better luck?"

"You aren't hit on the head and dumped under a hedge by accident, my son."

In thoughtful silence they reached a shop with window-hangings spangled with stars and a luminous crescent moon. They looked at each other, nodded, and went in.

"Yes, I act as a guide for those who are inspired to seek out the Zodiac sites." Torry Salt, when they tracked him down, was a thin, well-spoken young man in the process

161

of growing his hair. He wore a faded paisley shirt, a hand-knitted coat that reached to his knees, and jeans. Earnest spectacles perched on his aristocratic nose. Giving his full name he admitted to Torquil, but said it was his intention, having now found his true path in life, to put his old life behind him. "Only, so many of my belongings are initialled. Property, we know, is theft, but I have to accept that my spiritual journey will be slow as I struggle to lose my sad bourgeois habits." Sergeant Bloxham privately gave him a year at most before he went home; six months, if winter turned out as wet as the autumn had been. "The rest of my time is spent in furthering my researches." With a sweep of his hand Torry indicated a shelf of books and a large box crammed with maps and leaflets. Bloxham wondered how many, if any, of these had been acquired at second hand. Not many, was his guess.

"Plenty of people inspired, are they?" The sergeant was genuinely curious, even as he kept a sideways eye on DC Hannaford, taking discreet shorthand notes.

Torry smiled. "Enough. The Zodiac signs and their original purpose are deep mysteries for which not all are prepared, and which not all can see or understand ... but enough people have sufficient curiosity and openness of mind to make the tours I have planned—on which I have spent much time and effort—worth running."

"You mean they pay you to take them round and about." Bloxham stated this, rather than putting it as a question.

"One must live." Torry smiled. "Katherine Maltwood herself was an artist and sculptor, as well as a visionary writer—and, to quote Dr. Johnson, no man but a blockhead ever wrote, except for money. There's the upkeep of the van, for instance."

Two pairs of constabulary ears pricked up. "A van?" Sergeant Bloxham was casual. "I'd have thought you'd be protecting the environment and walking everywhere."

"The Temple of the Stars is set in a circle ten miles across and thirty miles in circumference. Few people have the time, or the physical stamina, to walk the entire Zodiac. We drive to the nearest convenient point, park, and then travel the lanes and pathways of our chosen sign on foot. We walk in single file, both to reduce the impact of our steps on the sacred ground, and to reinforce our one-ness with the whole. When we arrive at the very heart of the Zodiac figure we light candles and undertake a ceremony of silent communing with the spirits of the star-gods—silent, because the Zodiac means many different things to different people, and in essence all are equally true. The clamour of voices would distort the serenity of the shared experience."

The clamour of Sergeant Bloxham broke into Torry's intended rapturising on the tying of ribbons, the scattering of seeds, the communing of spirits. "And you walk back to your van."

Torry emerged from his rhapsody, and blinked. "Well ... eventually, yes, although there will be detours from the main delineations should anyone be inspired to take them."

"Inspired. Suppose some of these walkers of yours aren't so much inspired to believe in the Zodiac as to make fun of it? What d'you do then? Give 'em a refund?"

Torry Salt favoured him with a look that was close to pity. "If anyone has made such an effort in the first place, it must surely show that interest has already been kindled, and they are but taking the very first steps along the path.

With further knowledge, understanding and acceptance will come."

"By paying for another of your tours."

"Possibly." Torry spoke carelessly. "Or buying books, maps, magazines. Those who doubt and debunk, just as those who believe, read and research many sources. The Zodiac has a far wider influence than is generally realised. In time, the truth becomes known." He favoured Sergeant Bloxham with another pitying look. "We have heard of the death of the man who scorned the Zodiac. Any man's death diminishes me, because I am involved in mankind—but it would the more greatly diminish me or, indeed, any of us who believe, to deprive a man of his life simply because he made fun of our beliefs. He had not, as yet, been welcomed on one of my tours, but he would have been welcome indeed had he chosen to attend. From what I have heard he showed a true spirit of enquiry and thoroughness in his researches. I feel sure that with time he would have come to, if not a full, but certainly a far deeper, understanding."

"Then, sir," said Sergeant Bloxham happily, "you won't mind us takin' a look at your van, will you?"

Chapter Ten

"Farside Hotel," said the taxi driver. Miss Seeton felt a thrill of excitement as she took out her purse to add a larger tip than usual. When the Hon. Secretary, Friends of the Abbey Ruins had telephoned to say her raffle ticket had won first prize, Miss Seeton could hardly believe her recent good fortune. First her Premium Bond, now this! The weather outlook (said the Hon. Sec.) was fine; the Friends on Miss Seeton's behalf had booked a room with Miss McConchie, who had sold her the winning ticket and, sadly, won nothing for herself.

"Don't be silly, Miss Seeton." Lyn McConchie brushed aside her guest's tentative offer to retire. "You won it, fair and square. If I wanted, I'm sure I could ask Vince Weaver to take me up with him one day. He's not allowed to ask people for money, but he often obliges his friends." She chuckled. "If anyone wants to swap a few well-cooked meals or a week of free housework for a ride in the balloon, he says why should the authorities need to know about it, though of course he could pay for the licence easily enough, if he wanted."

Miss Seeton hesitated, but said nothing. Some form of tax evasion? But that would be wrong. Yet it was hardly her place to criticise the morals of complete strangers. No doubt she had misunderstood.

The landlady failed to realise that it was the legal aspect of the flight that bothered her guest. "Remember, he's the son of Weaver's Consolidated Northern Industrials. Pots of money, as you can imagine." Miss Seeton had no need to use imagination. The financial pages of her newspaper always referred to Weaver's Consolidated as one of the century's success stories. "A bit of a drop-out a few years ago," Miss McConchie went on. "You know how they can be, at that age." Miss Seeton, retired teacher, nodded. "Took off to California surfing and so on—learned to hang-glide—but he's his father's son and the hippy phase didn't last long. When he came to his senses, his father told him to find a job and he turned up here. He says it's excellent for photography—remember his photos?—and it was when he changed to a balloon that he could take really good wildlife pictures, because of the noise."

Miss Seeton's hesitation this time resulted from her failure to follow the logic.

"Hang-gliders make a noise all the time," said Miss McConchie. "Hot air balloons don't."

After the Hon. Sec. of the Friends rang Miss Seeton had telephoned Martin Jessyp to ask what, if anything, he knew of hot air balloons. "There is a burner, I understand," she now said. "Does the gas not make a noise as it burns?"

"Roars like a lion, they say, only not all the time. When the wind's right he drifts along so quietly you can hear the birds singing below you, dogs barking, even people talking if you aren't too high." Miss McConchie sighed. "It might

166

be fun to see the world from above—except," she added quickly, watching the guilt rise again in Miss Seeton's eyes, "I don't like heights. A friend of mine looked through the wicker floor of the basket and said it gave her quite a turn, watching the ground go backwards as the balloon took off. Don't you do that, Miss Seeton!"

The artist in Miss Seeton protested that the experience must give one a very interesting and different perspective on the world; but something still bothered her. "About the licence," she ventured. Lyn McConchie laughed.

"Oh, if they insist he'll pay for one, but he's still a bit of a free spirit at heart. He says if and when they catch up with him he'll make it legal, but he does like to poke a bit of fun at the authorities even now, when really he's old enough to know better. Nobody round here pays any attention, especially after the local paper ran a piece on him a couple of years ago and nothing happened when he said he sometimes took his friends up with him—and the Friends of the Abbey Ruins are certainly friends! But," as Miss Seeton continued doubtful, "he can explain it all to you better than I can. If," she added with a chuckle, "you're up to it so early in the morning." Miss Seeton looked a question.

"I'll have to call you at half-past four," said Miss McConchie.

Miss Seeton was so startled that the matter of the licence was driven from her mind.

Concern for the legality of her prize-winning flight returned as the kindly taxi driver, refusing an even larger tip despite the hour, delivered Miss Seeton to the edge of a large field where a stout wicker basket squatted beside a steadily inflating heap of bright fabric. People moved about, being very busy and calling to each other. The taxi driver tootled a cheerful farewell, waved, and drove off. Miss Seeton hesitated, took firm hold of her bag and umbrella, and made her way over the dew-damp grass towards the bustle of activity.

A sturdy young man with curly black hair, a flowered shirt, and a leather thong about his neck had stopped supervising the busy-ness at the sound of the car horn, and detached himself from the group, hurrying across to this final passenger. "Miss Seeton?" His smile held just a hint of doubt. "The one as won the raffle? Vincent Weaver, that's me, and yon's my balloon—and I'm right pleased to see your shoes. I forgot to tell them to warn you we might have to set down in a field of stubble." His Lancashire—or was it Yorkshire?—accent seemed to come and go. "The ladies tell me that can come scratchy on the ankles."

Miss Seeton, shaking his hand, said that she had bought the soft alpine boots on her previous visit to Glastonbury, as recommended by the outdoor shop for climbing the Tor.

Vincent blinked. "You climbed the Tor?"

Miss Seeton could guess what he was thinking. "Yes, indeed. It is not something I would have dared to attempt, a few years ago," honesty made her add. "But since I undertook a modest programme of yoga exercises my knees are so much more supple that I felt confident I could do it and—well, I did."

Vincent smiled with genuine pleasure and admiration. Like many in Glastonbury he knew the power of yoga, but had no intention of prying into a matter so individual to each practitioner. And this little duck was certainly an individual—that hat! He tried for a lighter touch. "Your brolly might come in handy if the wind should drop," he told her. "We could always try it for a rudder, to steer us out of trouble—nay, only joking. Sorry, Miss Seeton. Not that funny—downright daft, in fact, if this is your first time aloft."

She continued to regard him gravely, doubting in her turn. One could hardly ask him if he were planning to break the law, but ... "Would it be legal?" she enquired, as they trod together through the dew.

"A gamp used for a rudder? Never been tried before, so far as I know." He saw that she was still doubtful, and addressed her seriously. "Are you worrying about this flight, Miss Seeton? You've no cause, believe me. Though I says it as shouldn't, I'm pretty much an expert, after a lifetime. My Dad brought me up to it, see, being keen on aeronautics himself and teaching me in his own balloon when I was nobbut a nipper. Even called me Vincent, after the great Lunardi himself." He grinned at her. "Mind you, me mam took on so about him forgetting her father, he agreed to pay extra to have granddad's name added later." He saw Miss Seeton's doubt turn to bewilderment, and laughed.

"Now, I know you'll think the fifteenth of September's Battle of Britain Day, and so it is, but to the likes of me and my Dad it's also the anniversary of the day in 1784 when Vincenzo Lunardi took off in a hydrogen balloon from the Royal Artillery Ground in London, and flew twenty-six miles to Colliers End in two and a quarter hours, and made history!"

Miss Seeton looked suitably impressed, though still doubtful.

They had halted their walk across the grass as he tried to reassure her, and as there was nobody within earshot she felt she must try again.

"Forgive me," she began, "but—though I may have misunderstood, of course, but—that is, I have been told of the—the need for a—for a licence, and I cannot help wondering—"

Vincenzo Lunardi's namesake burst out laughing, then thumped rather than patted her on the shoulder. "Been tattling about me in town, have they?" Miss Seeton, pink-cheeked, had indeed been so discourteous as to discuss him behind his back. Vincent gave her no time to explain or excuse, but thumped her cheerfully once more. "Can you keep a secret, Miss Seeton?" She nodded again. He looked towards his friends. They were all too occupied about the balloon to pay any attention.

"I've had my Commercial Pilot's licence ever since they told me I should get one," he confided. "Everything fully paid up, properly insured, the lot. But it doesn't fit the image, sticking to the letter of the law when Glastonbury's that full of free spirits every other person you meet is floating higher than the clouds." He winked. Miss Seeton relaxed. The young. So mischievous; taking such delight in their teasing. A little naughty, at Mr. Weaver's age—he must be nearly thirty—but how he reminded her of Nigel Colveden, whose own sense of humour still held more than a hint of mischief. She wondered, briefly, if Mr. Weaver, like Nigel, was married.

Vincent's smile was so infectious that she found herself smiling happily back, and they resumed their walk to the centre of activity, the balloon's owner continuing his exposition on the unspoken benefits of being seen as a free spirit. "That was grand publicity they gave me in the local paper a year or so since. Everyone wanted to know about my photos, and folk started buying them. My dad, see,

170

told me to get a paying job and earn for myself, and so I have. Now I even get commissions for people's homes and farms at the right time of day, when the shadows, and the shine of the water in the rhynes—" like Lyn McConchie, he said *reens*—"and drainage ditches criss-crossing the moors look like a great net laid over the landscape, made from black lace and silver cobwebs."

Miss Seeton caught her breath at this picturesque imagery. Somehow, she knew just what he meant. "I have brought my sketching block with me," she said as they drew near the slowly burgeoning balloon. "What a splendid experience it will be!"

They reached the giant basket, where several people, by means of ropes, now stood guiding the rising canopy into position. "Now, listen up," said Vincent. "Some of you've flown with me before, but Miss Seeton, here, hasn't—Alison Midney," he waved a further quick introduction, "Susan—sorry, Brenda, Callender—" Miss Seeton recognised the name, and knew why Susan wore a long white robe—"but you'll have the safety talk same as if none of you'd been near a balloon in your lives. It might just save your lives if owt should go wrong. Not that it will, of course, but you can never be too careful. Right?"

He was especially proud of the basket, which he had himself designed and woven from scratch and Somerset willow. "Some folk use steps to climb inside. See how I've made me own steps, by them foot-holes?"

Miss Seeton, recalling some of the Art and Handiwork classes she had attended, was impressed. Susan Callender remarked that her cousin Valentine was likewise a self-taught weaver, although wool wasn't so hard on the hands.

Alison Midney added that wool was also easier to dye, and in rather more colours than the three basic willow shades of stripped bark, boiled, or with the bark left on.

"... canvas pockets on the sides," concluded Vincent. "Alison's Dave's staying behind wi' Tracy and Trevor to finish up today, while Ned and Dylan follow us with the champagne. I'll not travel with owt made of glass in case we tip too far on landing and things get broken. But I'll remind you all of what's to happen at the appropriate time. Any questions?" There were none. "Then, as we're almost ready ..."

Vincent went first and, knowing of her yoga, was unsurprised to watch Miss Seeton step nimbly from one foothole to another and, balancing herself with her umbrella, jump down to join him in the basket. The other watchers, who had been waiting for this little old lady to request at least a little help, were open-mouthed with admiration.

Susan struggled with folds of white fabric; Alison was an elegant last. At some point in the proceedings the balloon guiders had set their free hands firmly on the leather-bound rim of the basket, released their guide ropes, and gripped the basket with both hands, holding it fast.

Vincent gazed up at the balloon's wide mouth as it gulped the hot air roaring from the burner. He waited; then he ordered, "Hands off!" and those who had been holding down the basket raised their arms. The balloon immediately rose to bump against their palms. "Stand back!" cried Vincent, and the balloon was free.

Cheers came from Dave, Tracy and Trevor, while the other two basket holders turned as one and ran to an estate car parked, with a large trailer attached, about a hundred yards away. "The retrievers wi' the champagne," said Vincent, once he had checked his watch and made some quick calculations in a pocket-book. "You need one to read the map and one to drive the car, when you follow a balloon. They'll help us pack everything up once we've landed, and squash in the back when we drive home again."

Already the three cheering and waving on the ground were far below the quartet in the balloon. Miss Seeton had been so interested to watch all that happened that looking down through the wicker floor had quite slipped her mind. She felt soft air brush her cheek as the basket continued to rise, then with the sudden silence as Vincent turned down the burner she felt, surprisingly, a gentle warmth, and absolute stillness—apart from Vincent's unexpected action in tossing over the side two stout canvas bags that joined the array of cloth and leather pockets already slung against the wickerwork.

"There's clutter enough in here that has to stay in here," he told Miss Seeton, observing her interest. "Four gas cylinders and the four of us, for starters! So once we're airborne, I clear the decks." He pointed over the side. "Yon's the trail rope, in the largest bag. Useful to slow us down and hold us steady, if needful. T'other bag's the handling line. If the wind should drop and there's a dead calm holding us over a place it's not safe to come down—high voltage cables, a river, a busy main road—then I give a blast on my bugle, there, to attract attention. There's always someone as comes out to gawp as we go by. I shout down to ask if they'll take the end of the rope and pull us clear—and once we're safely down they get a share in the champagne."

Miss Seeton dug in her capacious handbag for sketchbook and pencils. Every moment of this unique experience must be captured. Her friends would hardly credit her adventures, and she, herself, would fear to miss or risk forgetting a single moment. In the drifting hush, the whole world was somehow ... intensified—smells and scents rising from the earth, the rich colours of sky, clouds, trees, fields; the brightness of the light, the clear song of birds, the barking of dogs, even the hum of a distant tractor as the balloon traversed a stubble field of bronze-dark gold, where the harvest had been safely gathered in.

"Sorry to disturb you, but we're going up a bit more." Vincent broke apologetically into Miss Seeton's silent rapture as she dashed off lines, shapes, forms of vivid concentration. "Susan, sorry, Brenda wants to try flying over her Sword. Mind your ears!"

There came a thunderous roar from the burner; the balloon rose and, again to Miss Seeton's surprise, slightly changed direction. She had taken Mr. Weaver's earlier remark about using her umbrella as a rudder for a joke. Mr. Jessyp, discussing her raffle prize after he had checked his encyclopaedia, had explained that without a motor it was not possible to steer a balloon—ah. He had also explained that at different heights, the currents of air might flow in different directions ...

"Yes," breathed Susan in a rapture of her own. "Thank you, Vince—look, there it is!" Standing beside Miss Seeton, it was Miss Seeton's arm she grabbed to turn her to gaze down and follow the direction of her pointing finger. "See that long, straight road? Where the railway line used to run before Dr. Beeching wielded his axe. But the railway would have taken the most obvious route—an old, an ancient path—the path marked out by our Dark Age ancestors to celebrate one of the Three Swords of Arthur!"

She regarded her captive with an almost challenging look, then relaxed her hold as Miss Seeton did no more than nod, and smile, and say: "I have studied your little pamphlet with some interest, Miss Callender."

Susan blinked in surprise, then laughed. "You've been to Bedivere Books, of course. And our Tavy would never miss the chance of making money, even if the family's not exactly on speaking terms at the moment." Alison chuckled; Vincent uttered a meaningful snort. Susan ignored them both. "Did you understand what I was trying to tell you—to tell the world?" she asked, her eyes glowing with belief.

"Until reading your book I had certainly not known—understood—that King Arthur had more than one sword," temporised Miss Seeton.

Pointing again, Susan-now-Brenda continued to ignore her sceptical friends as she enlarged on her theories to this new acquaintance who already grasped the basics. "Sir Thomas Malory in the fifteenth-century *Le Morte D'Arthur* writes of Mirandoise, the sword young Arthur drew from the miraculous stone to prove himself the rightful king. Wace had already described in the twelfth century how Caliburn was given to King Arthur by the Lady of the Lake." Susan took a deep breath, struck a pose, and straightened her robes. "And in the Alliterative *Morte Arthure* of the fourteenth century the writer explains how—" she closed her eyes, reciting from memory—"Clarente was Arthur's 'daintiest darling sword and held full dear', and kept for ceremonial purposes only, until his treacherous wife Gaynor gave it to Modred, and Arthur laments that now Clarente and Caliburne will meet in the final battle."

She opened her eyes, which brimmed with tears. Alison and Vincent were tactfully silent. Miss Seeton murmured that it sounded interesting, and must have involved Miss Callender in much reading and research.

Susan sniffed, dabbed at her eyes, and beamed. "It was the discovery of the Sweet Track just a few years ago, in

1970, that first revealed the truth," she enthused. Miss Seeton approved of enthusiasm, and gave her an encouraging smile.

"Our ancestors," said Susan, "had deeper knowledge than we can ever possess. What little we now know can be only the faintest shadow of enlightenment concerning the ancient wisdom. The Sweet Track is thought to be the oldest wooden walkway in the world—and could those who built it have been unaware that in due course of time it would run directly across the railway road that followed a pathway only a little less ancient than their own creation? The road denotes the blade of the sword—the Sweet Track forms the hilt." Tears once again filled her glowing eyes. "And I am the one destined to rediscover its secret—just as Katherine Maltwood rediscovered the Temple of the Stars!"

Miss Seeton braced herself for further outpourings on the Glastonbury Zodiac, but the other two in the balloon evidently knew Susan of old, and hurried to the rescue. Vincent applied himself to the burner, and Alison, when he turned it off again, began to show Miss Seeton the old peat workings that were being turned into a nature reserve.

"People worry about my plant nursery, and despoiling the environment, but there's talk of an experimental enzyme to turn shredded tree-bark into compost," she said. "Susan's cousin Octavia tipped us the wink, so we're keeping our eyes open for when it becomes commercially available. There's no shortage of willow trees around here."

"Tavy worries about things like that," Susan said. "She took a First in Biology, after all, so she knows what she's talking about." She sighed. "I used to admire her so much, for not taking the easy route and going into the family firm—and now she hardly talks to me!"

Vincent patted her on the shoulder. "When Tavy makes up her mind, it stays made up. There was no changing her when she said we were finished, though truth to tell I wasn't heartbroken, liking the peaceful life but not liking having to give way all the time to get it. But I'm glad she set me on the right path with my photography and all. I've no mind to be a tycoon just because me dad's by way of being one. To each his own—or hers, of course. She'll make a go of that bookshop, or bust—and you should cut her a bit of slack, lass. You can't blame her for sticking by her immediate family, right or wrong as they may be about that field—not that I want to know," hastily, "for it's no business of mine, but give them a chance, can't you? They're all still in shock from losing their dad in such a way—"

"And this is hardly a cheerful topic of conversation," put in Alison, as Susan opened her mouth to interrupt. "Poor Miss Seeton has come to enjoy herself, not be forced to listen to local gossip. Tell her how you taught yourself to weave, Vince. Talk her into buying one of your baskets to take home."

Miss Seeton jumped. "A basket? I fear there would be no room in my cottage for one of this size, Mr. Weaver, splendid work though it undoubtedly is. Moreover, I doubt if it would be possible to take so large an item home with me on the train, even in the luggage van."

Even Susan laughed. The old dear was quicker than you'd think, for all she seemed so strait-laced and conventional. Apart from that hat, of course. Looked as if she took it all seriously, but able to crack a joke and keep a straight face at the same time.

Vincent grinned. "You're a card, Miss Seeton! Why, it'd be the balloon canopy taking up most of the luggage space, for the baskets I make to sell are no bigger'n two inches square. The whole outfit stands a foot high at most—or rather, hangs, for it's designed to be slung from a hook on the wall, even from the ceiling. But I'd guess it was a shopping basket Alison had in mind for you as a souvenir, being as I work only with genuine Somerset willow. If we were flying that way—" he pointed—"we'd pass over the withy beds, but we seem to be making for Cadbury Castle and with Susan, sorry, Brenda, so interested in King Arthur, if nobody has any objections that's where we'll probably go."

Nobody had any objections. Alison cheerfully discoursed upon other items that could be made of willow, such as garden features, pea-sticks, and eel traps. "And charcoal, of course. Somerset willow makes the very best charcoal for artists."

Miss Seeton slowed her sketching long enough to note the address of the shop.

The balloon drifted on, with only an occasional short burst from the burner to disturb the serenity of the flight. Far below, sheep and cattle scarcely raised their heads as the strange shadow traversed the grass on which they grazed. Dogs barked, horses whinnied and cantered; walkers paused to wave, and cyclists dismounted to do likewise, or rang their bells in greeting.

"Eh," sighed Vincent, "but this is the life for me! It's grand!" His three guests could not disagree. "Aye," he continued, "I'd be up every day, if I could, only there's always arrangements to be made, and finding people to help. That's the one thing I miss about California, the freedom. When I lived there, if I wasn't hang-gliding I was surfing— and we'll forget the rest," he added sternly. Both Alison and Susan had begun to giggle before recalling the presence of Miss Seeton, whose elderly ears would no doubt be shocked by even an oblique reference to the Flower Power counter-culture of free love, drugs, wild music and Doing Your Own Thing.

"But I had some rare good times, there's no denying," he went on dreamily. "Once, me and my pal Chris—but all that was years ago." Vincent shook himself. "You can't keep on like that for ever, not if you've any sense."

"If you mean Christy who's always in the news," put in Susan, "he doesn't seem to have come to his senses at all." Vincent, reddening, ignored her. "You should invite him here," she urged. "There's a healing spirit in the Vale of Avalon, otherwise why would Arthur have been taken there? The waters of the Chalice Well—"

"There's more than one Chris in the world," snapped Vincent. "And I'm not one to tell secrets. What's past is past. You'll oblige me by making no further comment, Susan, or over the side of the basket you go. Right now!"

This flash of unaccustomed temper startled his younger passengers, but Miss Seeton, still busy with her sketching, noted nothing beyond a brief disturbance of the general calm that embraced them all, and a jagged line or two in her depiction of the drifting clouds that cast fluffy shadows on the ground beneath. She wondered if it might signify a thunderstorm later.

Throughout the flight Vincent had checked his watch as he switched from one cylinder of gas to another. "Time to think about landing," he announced. "Camelot, here we come!"

The ancient hill-fort, with its bare grass summit and clustering fringe of trees, had been visible almost from the moment of take-off, once its darker shape had been pointed out against the merging blue haze of the hills behind.

Miss Seeton uttered a little murmur that combined pleasure with regret. For the rest of her life she would remember this experience. There would be her sketches, of course, but she somehow felt there would be no real need of any visual reminder ...

"Remember what I said about pulling down the seats." Vincent was busy scanning the ground for a likely-looking field. "I'll say when." He tugged thoughtfully on a rope, and the balloon began to sink. "Miss Seeton, you take the seat by the plate," he added.

She was surprised. Had he not explained that he carried nothing breakable with him, in case of accident? Then she recalled the mention of champagne. Maybe a picnic was to be enjoyed after landing? The plates must therefore be plastic.

As he tugged again to release more gas and send the balloon even lower, he saw her surprise, and chuckled. "A metal plate with my name and address," he explained. "That's the law." He winked, and put a finger to his lips. "Even for a free spirit like Vince Weaver."

The burner roared once more; the balloon rose to avoid a tall tree directly in its path. Then more air was released; the gentle drift to the ground resumed. "Take your seats, ladies," instructed Vincent, still busy with the rip cord. "Hold on to the top of the basket and don't let go." He switched off the burner. "When I tell you, start the countdown from ten." He leaned over the side to take a coil of stout rope from a canvas bag, and dropped it. "Trail rope, to keep us upright as possible," he told Miss Seeton, as the onward drift of the balloon slowed almost to a halt. "Right ... All together—ten, nine, eight ..."

When the countdown reached *one* he pulled hard on the rip cord, and as the deflating balloon continued on its way the basket bumped heavily to the ground, tilted, dragged a few yards and then rocked itself, upright, to a bumbling halt. The balloon, a shrunken wraith of its former glory, moved onward to slump at last in whispering wrinkles to the ground.

"And now count to twenty before you even think of moving!" Vincent's eyes were busy as he checked that all was well. At *nineteen* he nodded. At *twenty* he grinned. "Well done, all of you—and out you get. And especially well done you, Miss Seeton. I'd never have thought this was your first time, the way you took it all in your stride. Enjoy yourself?"

The two younger women scuffled slightly over who should leave the basket first, but Miss Seeton could only nod in answer to Vincent's remark. Her eyes sparkled. Her hands, released now from their clutch on the edge of the basket, moved quickly to open her bag for the sketchbook she had packed away before landing. She must capture before she forgot the sudden change from blissful calm to busy-ness and movement, from stillness in the air to the earthbound billowing of Susan's white robes, the disarray of her long hair by the wind, the rustle of breeze-rippled grass ...

" 'ere!"

Vincent, leaping from the basket without recourse to the footholds, left Miss Seeton to her happy sketching and joined his two lady-friends in preparing the now almost empty balloon for packing up. When the ground crew arrived they would manhandle the awkward bundle of fabric, rope and cable into the trailer towed behind the estate car, and everyone would enjoy a glass of champagne before the basket was added to the cargo and secured under a tarpaulin. Even Susan, a far less frequent flyer, knew (under instruction) what to do; Vincent had many, more than willing, helpers who took turns to stay on the ground as the others in their turn took to the skies.

" 'ere, young man!" The rapidly approaching voice was loud, male, and indignant. "What's all this then, you and that heathen contraption dropping on my land without so much as a by your leave?"

"Oh, heck," muttered Mr. Weaver. "I'd clean forgotten where we were. Wildfell Farm."

"Oh, dear," said Alison, who had been on the previous flight to arrive there.

"Oh?" said Susan, who hadn't.

Wasting no time in enlightening her, the balloonist advanced to greet the older man who, as Miss Seeton saw, carried a shotgun broken over one arm. She supposed he had been hunting rabbits or other pests, as Nigel and Sir George so often did; she was glad to see that, angry though he sounded, he had taken quite as much care of his weapon as ever the Colvedens would. In moments of confusion accidents could so easily occur, and she supposed that the unexpected landing of a hot air balloon would certainly confuse the one who farmed the land on which the balloon had, well, landed.

"Mr. Huntingdon," Vincent began, "I'm very sorry, but—"

"Never you mind wi' your but-butting, young Weaver. Din't I tell 'ee last time as I don't hold with it? Which I still don't, an' never shall." Arthur Huntingdon had now come up to the balloon, and was scowling at the aeronauts. "If the good Lord had intended us to fly He would have graced us with wings, as He did the angels—but He in His wisdom clearly did not so intend, for we were not so graced. Why, 'tis nothing less nor blasphemy for you and

182

your friends to go a-gallivanting through the air pretending to be birds, scorning the ways of creation and making mock of the Commandments." His gaze flashed towards the innocently bystanding form of Miss Seeton, her pencil and sketchbook for the moment stilled.

"An' you," snapped the farmer, "old enough to know better! Older," he amended, after a closer look at her demure grey locks and decorous tweeds. "Taking to the skies at your age! Mimicking the birds, wi' they feathers in your hat! A fine example to be setting these idolatrous rapscallions—and worse, if a weaker vessel such as you has allowed them to lead you into wicked temptation!"

Miss Seeton was indignant on behalf, not of herself—a gentlewoman must never make, and should always ignore, a personal remark—but of her new young friends. "Nobody," she protested, "has led anyone anywhere. All I did was purchase a raffle ticket, and—"

"Oops," said Vincent.

Arthur Huntingdon turned purple. "Gambling!" he cried. "*Let us cast lots, that we may know for whose cause this evil is upon us*—and evil it is to waste hard-earned money on idle pleasure—on gluttony, and wanton drunkenness, and all manner of selfish pursuits when there is only too much room in this sinful world for charitable causes ..."

As he drew breath and brandished his shotgun a small, dumpy, red-cheeked woman in a wrap-around apron and heavy black gumboots arrived, breathless, at his side and tugged his other sleeve with a pink, damp hand and an urgent "Arthur!" on her lips.

"Let your women keep silence," he began, trying to shake her off; but she stood her ground and tugged more firmly.

"Arthur, enough!" Nell Huntingdon could quote scripture as readily as her husband. "You know full well the Book tells us how the wind bloweth where it listeth and there's nothing to be done, as Mr. Weaver explained before. I'm sure he didn't mean to land at Wildfell again— did you, Mr. Weaver?"

"I did not," said Vincent. Nobody doubted his sincerity. "It was only that we wanted a closer look at Cadbury Camp—King Arthur and his knights, and Camelot—and when I saw we were running short of fuel we had to come down here, though I promise you we'd have gone further if—" he shot an apologetic glance at Susan—"we'd not made a bit of a detour beforehand, which used more gas than I'd bargained for wi' climbing to take advantage of the currents higher up. But surely there's no real harm done? And we'll be off your land just as soon as the retrievers arrive—"

"I'll have no dogs on my farm!"

"—to help us pack everything away, same as they did before. I know you've no telephone, or they'd be here even quicker, but they've been following us in the estate car and I reckon it won't be too long before we're safely off your land."

"And your sinful drink with you!" Arthur Huntingdon did not forget the previous incident, when Vincent had offered him, for the inconvenience caused, a half-bottle of champagne as well as a coloured print of the balloon signed and dated by passengers and landowner alike.

Nell Huntingdon smiled kindly. "But we'd be glad of the picture, wouldn't we, Arthur?" Arthur muttered something inaudible. Miss Seeton found her fingers gripping her pencil ...

"And I told you last time," said the exasperated Vincent, "if the worst comes to the worst and you've suffered real damage, I'll speak to me father and he'll buy the whole blamed field from you! How can a man say fairer than that?"

"Not one inch of their land do the Huntingdons part with!" thundered Arthur.

"There have always," murmured Alison, "been Starkadders at Cold Comfort Farm ..."

"Excuse me," ventured Miss Seeton, who as the argument ebbed and flowed around her had been busy and absorbed in her work. "There was, as I recall, some mention of a picture. Might this be the sort of thing you had in mind?"

She handed her finished sketch to Vincent, who accepted it with automatic thanks, glanced quickly at it, paused to look again, and then handed it to Arthur Huntingdon. As the farmer scowled and his wife, leaning close, began to smile, Mr. Weaver clapped his helpful passenger on the shoulder and favoured her with a broad grin of relief.

"You're a grand lass, Miss Seeton, and thanks. Any time you fancy another flight wi' me you've only to say the word!" For Mr. Huntingdon's scowl had faded, and he joined his wife in exclaiming with pleasure at Miss Seeton's swift depiction of their distant farmhouse with a balloon hovering above. Although Vincent's party had not approached so close the sketch showed the farmhouse with surprising accuracy, and there were two small figures in the foreground, one with a shotgun and another with a laundry basket at her feet. Miss Seeton, decided Vincent, must with her artist's eye have had a better view than he, busy with burners and rip cords and ropes, had realised.

"We'll set this in a frame to match the photograph from last year," announced Nell Huntingdon. "And will 'ee sign it for us like a real picture, midear?" Miss Seeton turned a modest pink. "An' all the rest, you can write your names together on the back."

Nell spoke with such assurance that even her husband was nodding and agreeing with her pronouncement. Vincent grinned once more at Miss Seeton, then suppressed a cheer as the approaching rattle of an engine announced the arrival of Ned and Dylan, who had followed the balloon in the estate car. Arthur Huntingdon, to his own surprise, found that it did his god-fearing soul no particular harm to lend a hand in rolling and folding the fabric canopy into a manageable bundle. Nell Huntingdon, holding the broken shotgun, smiled as she watched him while Miss Seeton, asked by Vincent to chronicle the end of the excursion in further drawings, stood by her side and drew.

Nobody grudged Miss Seeton, sketching saviour of the situation, her place in the front passenger seat as they drove back to Glastonbury. Besides, she was the only one of them who did not already know the legends with which Vincent now regaled her. He told of how, on Midsummer Eve and at Christmas, King Arthur and his knights leave the hollow hill of Camelot through a massive iron gate, riding out on horses shod with silver. Listening ears will hear the hoof-beats but, look hard as any listener might, nothing can ever be seen.

"We know the hill must be hollow," he explained, "because if you blow a golden trumpet down Queen Anne's Well on one side, the sound echoes back up through King Arthur's Well on the other."

Miss Seeton was duly impressed. "And have you ever tried?" she enquired, with just the hint of a twinkle. "Your bugle would surely be ideal for the purpose."

"Nay, it must be a trumpet made of gold. My bugle's nowt but brass, from when me Dad changed the main factory to a silver band and replaced all the instruments. Some were too worn out to be worth passing on, and when all I needed was to attract attention, he said it would serve well enough. We don't go splashing our money about, up north."

Miss Seeton privately reflected that Mr. Weaver, on his father's behalf, had offered to purchase an entire field merely to keep one farmer happy. Evidently the very, very rich and successful had very, very different ideas of economy from her own.

"Oh," she exclaimed, as they passed a signpost. "Cats-gore. What an un—unusual name." She had almost said *unpleasant*, but perhaps she had misread it.

"Same as Kensington Gore," said Vincent. "A gore's nobbut a triangular piece of land. Over Bristol way there's the Gordano—" he pronounced it Gor-day-no—"Valley: same word again. As for the Cat, well, nobody knows if it's someone's name, or commemorating where the wildcats used to roam in savage packs, terrorising the countryside, killing the cattle and sheep, carrying off small children ..."

Miss Seeton, deliciously shuddering, felt that Vincent Weaver, like his former girlfriend Octavia Callender, had rather more about him than he chose to let anyone know.

Chapter Eleven

Milicent Hattersley was busy in the police house kitchen, making six times the usual amount of her celebrated Black Treacle Bread for the Women's Institute Tea. Mrs. Hattersley's bread—thickly sliced, lavishly buttered—always went down well, even unto third and fourth helpings. There had never been a Tea when she wasn't asked for the recipe.

Milicent heard the roar of an approaching motorbike, a screech of brakes, a scurry of feet and a loud ring at the front door, accompanied by a quick tattoo on the knocker. Before she could dust her hands clean to greet this impatient visitor, the feet scurried away and the motorbike roared again, speeding from the house and faster still out of the village.

PC Ralph Hattersley clumped indoors from the garden, where he had been tending his vegetable patch. Harvest Festival was this weekend, and his prize marrow had been chosen for display beside the pulpit. The motorbike's roar had disturbed his peaceful pleasure in his work, but official work must come first.

"Mischief," he told his wife, who for once did not scold him for tracking mud into the house. "Not kids larking, from the sound of it. You stay by the phone, Millie, while I check outside. If there's any hint of trouble you call HQ at once, you hear me?"

"Yes, Ralph." Millie turned a little pale but said no more, watching her husband as he went cautiously to the door and opened it, standing well back.

Nothing happened.

PC Hattersley peered round the door. He saw something on the step. "A shoebox," he called down the hall to Millie, alert beside the telephone. "They've took off the lid and the top's all shiny—clear plastic, it looks like ... Oh."

He had peered a little closer. He retreated now to the umbrella stand and removed a stout walking stick. He reversed it, reached out, and hooked the box towards him. Now he could not only see what was inside on a nest of cotton wool—he could read the message that came with it.

"*Tell Scotland Yard,*" quoted Chief Inspector Kebby. "The blighters have guessed the family would be asking for our help by now. And *reference C.G.* just in case we're too thick to get the point."

Delphick took the photocopied note Kebby thrust across his desk. "The point being that Christy Garth has suffered a genuine physical attack, no matter what our earlier reservations may have been. I take it there's no doubt the severed finger is his?"

"They'd packed it in ice, and so did Hattersley when he found it. It's a bit the worse for wear and it's lucky the weather wasn't too hot—but of course his prints are on file, so unless he had an unknown identical twin drugging, causing affrays at nightclubs, drink-driving and being arrested in his place—yes, it's Garth's finger."

Delphick frowned. "His hand was bandaged in the photograph, which would appear to suggest that he lost the finger several days ago." His frown deepened. "The amputation could at that time have been faked, just as Miss Seeton hinted." Kebby stirred, but said nothing. The Oracle pondered.

"If," he said at last, "such is the case, I wonder what can have pushed them now to so drastic a measure? Did they simply tire of waiting, and hope by this action to apply further pressure? Or ..."

Kebby continued to fidget as Delphick continued to ponder. The Chief Inspector looked in the direction of Sergeant Ranger, who had not hitherto spoken or been approached. Bob, naturally curious but tactfully quiet, shook his head in response to Kebby's look.

"How long," said the Oracle, "will a severed finger ... as it were, survive?"

"I've checked with the medics," said Kebby, "and it's as you'd expect from any experts. They can't, or won't, give a straight answer."

"It all depends?" Delphick smiled, thinly, as Kebby nodded. "But it is entirely credible?"

"Oh, yes." Kebby sighed. "You know, for the first time in all this I'm starting to feel sorry for the chap, no matter what kind of life he's led and the amount of trouble he's caused."

"The loss of a thumb," said Delphick, "would have been far worse than that of a little finger. At least they spared him that."

"So far," groaned Kebby. "Heaven knows what they'll try next. This is getting urgent, Oracle—and the only lead we have is that the parcel was delivered to a bobby in a village near Leominster. They've got it in the fridge at Worcester now."

"Westward ho," murmured Delphick, even at so tense a moment amused that the city man knew enough of the wild open spaces to pronounce "Lemster" correctly.

Kebby nodded. "It does seem to bear out what his family told us of his original plans, as confirmed by your lady-friend with the sketchpad—but she didn't warn us it was going to turn nasty. Could even turn to murder if we can't get it sorted soon."

"We must hope that it does not, but I fear you may be right. Criminals who resort to kidnapping are seldom noted for patience or moderation. We should perhaps have guessed that when the Traffic Jam interfered with the ransom pick-up, they might well tighten the screw."

"And we haven't got even half a clue, beyond the West Country connection. There's a hell of a lot of the west, Oracle. I'd like you to talk to Miss Seeton again. You said we should have guessed. Well, inspired guesswork is her speciality. Is the old girl likely to boggle at the sight of Exhibit B? Tastefully photographed, of course."

Reaching for the telephone, Delphick paused to smile. "While at art college, Miss Seeton studied the human body in detail by frequent attendance at hospital dissection classes. She also survived the Blitz. A severed finger, even if delivered to her with garnish on a plate, is unlikely to bother her. A photograph, still less."

He heard the telephone ring in distant Plummergen, but from Sweetbriars there came no answer. "Martha's not there and MissEss is probably shopping," he decided. The police house was his next attempt.

A small, squeaky voice coughed as it tried to identify itself. "Wait," said Delphick, and identified himself before asking, "Amelia, is that you?"

Little Miss Potter wheezed that it was, off school with a cold. No, her father wasn't there. Nor her mother, out shopping for lemons and crystallised ginger to make a special drink. Could Amelia take a message? Delphick, rapidly reviewing possibilities, said he would try not to bother her again, and rang off.

It was third time lucky when he tried Rytham Hall. Martha Bloomer was working there that day, and explained that Miss Emily was down in Somerset again because her ticket had won first prize and she'd been flying somewhere in a balloon.

Delphick asked the Yard's switchboard to put him through to the Glastonbury police.

Chief Inspector Faggus and his small team were deeply involved with the murder of Hawley Bowyer. Torry Salt's van, a promising lead, had yielded no clues. The police were back almost where they had started, and as murder, in Glastonbury, was rare, their concentration was entirely directed upon the current investigation. That a Scotland Yard detective, no matter how high his rank or polite his request, wished him to find an unknown spinster visitor to the town as soon as possible did not register as perhaps it should have done. Sergeant Bloxham and Constable Hannaford could not be spared: the station sergeant was instructed to send a less vital officer to visit the Farside Hotel and if necessary to comb the streets and shops for Miss Emily Dorothea Seeton.

Young Constable Birch, the newest recruit, was keen. The desk sergeant issued quick instructions and sent him off on his quest with buttons shining and boots burnished, the badge on his proud helmet glittering in the autumn sun. Not five minutes on the job, and he was working with Scotland Yard!

At the Farside Hotel he learned that Miss Seeton was out shopping. Miss McConchie wasn't sure where, but she would back in time for a light lunch and the taxi she'd booked to catch the train.

The suspect was skipping town! "I'll wait," announced PC Birch.

"You're welcome," said Lyn McConchie. "How about a cup of tea while you're waiting?"

PC Birch hesitated.

"Would you prefer coffee? Herbal tea? Hot chocolate?"

Would he be caught at a disadvantage when Miss Seeton came back? Or would the sight of him with a drink and perhaps a biscuit or two lull her into thinking his visit was just for a casual chat? He might catch her off guard and trick a confession out of her. The sergeant had thought it must be on account of the murder he was being sent after her ...

When Miss Seeton trotted in with a wicker shopping basket for Martha over one arm, in which two packets of artist's charcoal and a model hot air balloon (to hang above Gideon Ranger's cot) were neatly packed, Police Constable Birch blinked. She looked like somebody's favourite aunt, not a suspect connected, however remotely, with a case of murder. And when he thought the matter over, how come they'd been able to work it all out in London before the folk down here, where the murder had been committed? There was obviously more to this little lady than he'd thought, being known to the Yard like that. Well, didn't they say appearances could be deceptive? And didn't this one just prove it!

He spoke in his best official tones. "I'd like you to come along of me, miss," he said after the preliminary courtesies had been observed. "To the station, toot sweet."

Miss Seeton glanced at the kitchen clock. "But my train doesn't—the taxi isn't—I still have my packing to finish," she protested, displaying her recent purchases to explain what, she feared, might have been misunderstood by this thoughtful young man as a rather abrupt dismissal of his kindly offer to assist her.

"The police station," said Constable Birch sternly. Trying to bluff it out, was she? "You can leave your luggage for the moment. We'll send someone to pick it up later." She might well be about to leave town as she'd planned, but perhaps not quite the way she'd planned—or where she'd planned to go.

Miss Seeton still seemed puzzled. She looked from her basket to Miss McConchie, and then at PC Birch. "I fear I don't quite understand," she began.

"I can put your last few bits away for you," offered the landlady. "You run along and see what they want. Probably," she added, as her guest remained confused, "they'll be asking about that balloon of Vince Weaver's. We always said the licensing people would catch up with him in the end."

Miss Seeton smiled. "Then it shouldn't take long, for I can assure them—" She recalled that she was sworn to secrecy about the balloonist's having obtained the necessary paperwork. "At least," she added, "I trust that I will be able to do so."

"It's Scotland Yard you'll have to satisfy," PC Birch warned, forgetting discretion.

Miss Seeton, to his surprise and the astonishment of Miss McConchie, smiled again, nodded, and set down Martha's basket on the kitchen table without a qualm. "No doubt," she said as she prepared to accompany PC Birch, "another IdentiKit picture is required. I do hope there will be time to catch my train, but of course it is my duty and perhaps, Miss McConchie, you would be kind enough to explain to the taxi driver, should I be delayed?"

Constable Birch kept a watchful eye on his captive as they made their way to the police station, but she showed no sign of making a break for freedom. From what this seeming innocent was telling him of how she'd climbed the Tor on a previous visit, she'd be fast enough on her feet if she wanted; he wasn't so sure he'd be able to stop her. Unless it was all a clever double-bluff, and she wanted him to think that, just to catch him off his guard, in the same way she'd given the impression that Scotland Yard didn't worry her at all. She'd murmured something he couldn't quite catch but that sounded a bit like "beatnik"—okay, out of date, but probably, in her terms, best suited to most of the long-haired people she would have seen wandering about the town with their bells and beads and flared trousers.

Entering the station, he nodded proudly to the desk sergeant and escorted Miss Seeton straight down the corridor to the Murder Incident Room. She'd talked of pictures—well, he'd show her some, and then she'd be the one to be caught off guard!

For once, the room was empty. PC Birch wandered casually across to the notice board with its maps, lists, and photographs. Politely, Miss Seeton wandered beside him.

"Oh, dear." She recognised the blank, soulless gaze of a dead face. "The poor man. How sad. I take it there has been an accident? I met him on the occasion of my previous visit." PC Birch stiffened. This was more like it! "A somewhat excitable temperament, I fear," she continued. "One can readily imagine how he might become distracted when traversing some of the steep hills in these parts, and tumble down. There has been so much rain of late that the grass can be most treacherous underfoot." She gave the staring countenance of Hawley Bowyer a second, sorrowful glance. "Is it a likeness of this poor man that the chief superintendent wishes me to draw?"

Chief superintendent? Who did she think was she kidding, trying to confuse him like this? "Chief inspector, miss. Mr. Faggus."

"Oh," said Miss Seeton, instinctively closing the handbag she'd automatically opened. She pondered. "But I suppose, if Mr. Delphick has made the arrangements ..."

They stared at each other, both equally perplexed. Behind them, the door opened.

"Ah, Birch, you found her. Good." Chief Inspector Faggus bustled into the room and held out his hand. "Miss Seeton? How d'you do, and it's good to meet you. The Oracle's told me all about you—put me in the picture, as you might say."

As he chuckled over his little joke Miss Seeton, shaking hands, blushed and murmured that dear Mr. Delphick was always so kind.

PC Birch stared as the chief inspector continued to put the suspect—no, a suspect she clearly wasn't—at her ease. What was that she must've said? Not *beatnik*, but *Delphick*—and from the way she and the old man were chatting together, she was either a friend or even a colleague of this man at the Yard, who wanted to talk to her about something important. And he'd gone and taken her for a wrong 'un!

As Faggus led the honoured guest to telephone from the privacy of his office, Police Constable Birch scratched his head, shook his head, and finally hung his head in bewildered shame. He'd got it all about as wrong as it could have been. He'd obviously misunderstood the original message—he wouldn't dream of blaming the sergeant—and badly misjudged Miss Seeton. He'd never make a copper. He wondered about resigning right now, before she had time to complain to old Faggus about how she'd been treated ...

As Birch trudged sadly towards it, the chief inspector opened his office door to usher Miss Seeton out. "Ah, Birch." As Miss Seeton smiled in renewed greeting, so his superior officer grinned. "Good man. Now, I don't know how long it will take, but when Miss Seeton's finished her business here she'd like to be driven across to catch the train, seeing as she's cancelled her taxi and she knows you." Again Miss Seeton smiled. "Nip along to her hotel for her luggage and then just hang around nearby until she gives the word, right?"

Birch blinked. "Er—right, sir. Miss Seeton. Is ... is everything okay?"

"Soon will be." Faggus winked at Miss Seeton as he escorted her back to the Incident Room. "Poaching on the Yard's preserves, I know, but it was Mr. Delphick's suggestion. He thinks a lot of you, Miss Seeton." Miss Seeton turned pink with pleasure. "And you can hurry up, my son!"

Smiling back at Miss Seeton, Birch hurried.

After making his request of the Glastonbury police, and apologising for his unwitting intrusion into a murder investigation, Delphick's professional conscience had troubled him. Glastonbury had said that they were busy and implied that they were baffled: they did not tell him outright that they needed help, but help might, he suspected, be welcome. Particularly if it came in a semi-official capacity rather than the official Calling In The Yard so wounding to local pride. Miss Seeton, surely, could wound nobody's pride ...

Miss Seeton considered. The chief inspector wanted her impressions of a man she had met just once—no, twice, on the same day. She thought him excitable, she said: a little brisk in his manner; impatient with folly. Would she call him argumentative? A little strong, perhaps, but she supposed she would. Did she have any idea of the sort of thing that encouraged him to argue—to annoy people?

"The Glastonbury Zodiac," said Miss Seeton, "and people who believe in it. He says—said—it isn't logical. Which," she added as she took her sketching block from her handbag, "may be so. Or not, of course, depending on one's viewpoint. But a most intriguing concept—and some very interesting books."

"Bedivere Books," said Faggus. Miss Seeton, twiddling a pencil between her fingers as she contemplated the photograph on the notice board, nodded. "Yes," murmured the chief inspector, watching her without seeming to, "we know he bought a lot of books there ..."

Wait for her to stop paying attention to her surroundings, Delphick had advised. She wouldn't like to think of herself as going into a trance, but that's how it will seem to you, once she focuses all her attention on that blank sheet of paper. And when she's done scribbling, get it away from her before she tears it up, because that's how it takes her—she never can believe it's what you wanted, and thinks it all a waste of time and effort. *Ashamed* isn't too strong a word, sometimes, for the way she feels about her work—but it's what we pay her for. Remind her of that if she fidgets too much. And if you can't make sense of what she's drawn—one, you're by no means unique, and two, send it down the wire to me and I'll think about it on your behalf.

Now Chief Inspector Faggus wondered how soon he could speak to the chief superintendent. It would take about ten minutes for the finished sketch to dot-and-dash its way down the telephone wires from the scanning machine in Glastonbury to its fellow in New Scotland Yard. Another ten to reach Delphick's desk; perhaps a further ten for thinking? If he himself had an hour—a day—a month—for thinking, it wouldn't be enough. Delphick had suggested that Miss Seeton, once retrieved by his Somerset colleagues, should be asked to study a photo of the murdered man and then sketch her impression of him. She might come up with something that would offer the police a different perspective; send the investigation in a direction they might not otherwise have considered.

Her perspective was different, all right. He'd never seen anything like it. High in the air, above a waving ground-cover of tall plants with sharp, spiky leaves, Hawley Bowyer's face wore a lively frown, and there was a spark of irritation in his eyes. His ... face. No body, no limbs, not even the man's neck. Just his face, floating in the air against a background of maps and open books, their pages flapping as if in a strong wind, criss-crossed by a jumble of parallel rules, several pencils, and with a compass rose ... upside down—back to front—off balance, anyway. It almost made him wish Delphick hadn't said he could ask for her help in the first place.

The artist herself had already left in an unmarked police car, accompanied by her luggage and a cheerful PC Birch, for Castle Cary railway station and the next train but one after her original choice. Mr. Delphick and the Scotland Yard computer, the chief inspector had told her as he said goodbye, would deal with the financial side of the sketch she had drawn; he understood that this was the normal procedure, and he thanked her very much.

And mopped a bewildered brow once she was safely on her way.

"How much did you tell her about the case?" The Scotland Yard man could guess at his Somerset colleague's bafflement.

"Didn't tell her anything beyond the fact he was dead," replied Faggus. "And she said she was sorry, and that she'd met him. And then she settled down with his photo and her sketchbook, and started scribbling."

"Hmm. You told me that the body had been moved. Are you sure you said nothing of this to Miss Seeton?"

"Told her as little as possible. That's the way you said to play it, so I did. All she said was, she'd run across the man last time she was here. A bit of a scrapper—verbal, at least, didn't know about physical—and I asked could she give me any idea of the sort of thing that might get him into an argument. She said, he didn't think much of the Glastonbury Zodiac because it was illogical."

"So illogical as to cause an argument? A somewhat comprehensive argument, it would seem from this picture—no arms, no legs, no body. I should say she feels that the corpse didn't really belong, as it were, where it was found—that he was killed elsewhere, as you already suspected. Do you have any thoughts as to why he was moved?"

"Best guess is he saw something he shouldn't when he arrived where he didn't mean to be, and they clobbered him to keep him quiet."

Delphick pounced. "Where he didn't mean to be? He was lost, then. Yes? Would I be correct in assuming that for some reason he had no map or guidebook to consult, and there was nothing but a faulty compass on which to rely?"

"Well ... yes," returned the chief inspector. "Yes!" He stared at the sketch, shaking his head. "How d'you make that out? His landlady told us he had plenty of maps, but that day it was pouring with rain. They'd have been unreadable pulp within minutes, if he'd tried to use them—and his haversack wasn't there when we found him. No thermos, no sandwiches—no maps—and no notes. Always took reams of notes, she said. And yes, his compass was

200

dodgy. We found it in his pocket, buried in a mess of soggy paper tissues. Whoever took away his maps and notes missed the compass—in too much of a hurry, at a guess."

"A reasonable guess that would suggest some degree of panic on the part of ... not necessarily the killer, but certainly the person who moved the body and, we must assume, also removed the other items. You've instituted a search, of course."

"Nothing found nearby, and no idea where else to look. That's why I had hopes of your Miss Seeton when you told me about her, right on my doorstep as she was—and when it turned out she'd even met the man, well ..."

"These plants she's drawn," Delphick ventured, "might possibly be a variety of hemp?"

"Ah," said Chief Inspector Faggus.

"News of your psychotic sheep has travelled as far as Scotland Yard," Delphick told him, a hint of amusement in his voice. "I would suggest that your investigation is in fact proceeding along the right lines. Find the spot where Bowyer was killed and you'll find the motive—which, again at a venture, I suggest may be not unconnected with the growing of illicit drugs. And," he warmed to his subject, "I offer a further suggestion that the place you seek will not be too far from where you found him."

"How d'you reckon that?"

"Everything is in focus, yet gives an impression of speed. When she blurs—draws out of focus—it makes you take a step back for a different perspective. This face—I take it the resemblance is accurate? Very well—this face, and the background of maps and books, might be said to represent what we can call the truth of the matter. The speed would be her idea of the panic reaction to the crime, at a guess."

"A lot of guesses," muttered the chief inspector.

"Interpretations, rather. With Miss Seeton, that's what we have to do. And you say she spoke of the man's interest in the Zodiac? There are no stars or constellations or mythical figures in this drawing. Had the Zodiac any bearing on your case, I believe she would have shown at least part of it."

"But the Zodiac was the only lead we had!" protested Tom Faggus. After the disappointment of the clueless search of Torry Salt's van, the chief inspector had directed his team to interview as many Zodiac believers as could be found, asking to see driving licences (if any) and vehicles (if appropriate); asking also for their movements and alibis at what the medical report gave as the likely time of death. "But if you think she thinks it's nothing to do with the Zodiac— well, I'd better take a closer look at your interpretations."

"Perhaps you had," Delphick said. "Consider the case from a different perspective."

"Just like Miss Seeton did," said Chief Inspector Faggus. A chuckle rumbled along the wires. "I'll bet she had some cock-eyed fun in that hot air balloon, too!"

Delphick was suddenly thoughtful as he ended the conversation.

Delphick was greeted by Miss Seeton with a smile, which he returned, complimenting her on how well she looked and how clearly her recent adventure had agreed with her.

"I envy you," he told his hostess as she busied herself with the tea things. "To have flown in a hot air balloon! I once rode in a police helicopter, but all I remember is the noise, and the distinct impression that my teeth must soon be shaken from my head. I certainly had neither the time nor the inclination to admire the view, and no particular reason to wish to repeat the experience beyond the call of duty which, I'm glad to say, has since that day remained silent."

"There is always the call of a brass bugle." Miss Seeton explained Vincent Weaver's preparations for aeronautical emergency, and spoke of the golden trumpet at Cadbury Castle, and the balloon flight in general. "Afterwards I had to purchase another sketchpad, for there were so very many new and remarkable impressions that I could not hope to capture them all at once."

Delphick nodded. "I'd be interested to see them," he said truthfully. He had given much thought to that throwaway remark made by the chief inspector. "But, before we settle to the purpose of today's visit, I mustn't forget to tell you that the Yard's computer has approved the drawing you did for Chief Inspector Faggus, and in due course the usual cheque will follow. He asks me to thank you again for your assistance—as he also thanked me." Miss Seeton looked surprised. "He sent me a copy," explained the Oracle, "and we discussed it together over the telephone. There were one or two hints I could offer, but the inspiration, shall we say, was entirely yours, and he was most grateful. It reassured him to know that in your opinion he had approached his murder investigation in more or less the right way all along, and apart from one false lead he could safely continue to do so."

"The poor man was lost in the wind and rain," she said. "That was all. Not Mr. Faggus, but the man who dropped his books when I bumped into him in the High Street, with my umbrella. As I thought I had explained when he first asked me for my impressions—Mr. Faggus, I mean, though it seems my explanation must have been somewhat confused over missing my train, except that thanks to kind Mr. Birch I caught it in the end. But he had no maps with him, you see, and his compass must have been damaged when he dropped it with the books." She blushed. "I did offer to buy some sticky tape, but he said there was no need because at the time it was not raining, and his hotel was close enough to carry them. He had climbed the Tor the previous afternoon, he said, and his muscles still ached and he had no particular wish to go up and down any more hills at present, or rather down and then back up, which it would have been to the stationer's."

After missing only a couple of beats, Delphick smiled. "That would have been on the occasion of your first visit to Somerset." Miss Seeton nodded. "May I see how the West Country appeared to you on your second visit? So short a time after your first there will have been few, if any, changes, but I am curious to know what you made of the same views when seen from the balloon. The different perspective, for instance."

"The views are indeed very different." Miss Seeton leafed through a selected sketchbook. "The Tor, for instance, from one angle on the ground stands out far more noticeably in the landscape than it does from the air, although so early in the morning the shadows are far more dramatic. Miss McConchie had to call me at half past four," she added. Delphick was duly impressed. "To be there in good time for the ascent," she told him, "because as the sun rises even a gentle warmth may cause turbulence, depending on how high one intends to fly, and in which direction."

Her original sketch of the Tor, embellished on her return to Plummergen, was no more than a picture postcard or a tourist photograph might show—a steep green hill shadowed round with earthworks, dotted with sheep, one side a shallower slope that was still steeper than many people would wish to climb, and with the ruined tower of St Michael pointing like a giant finger up into a cloudless sky.

Her second sketch, based (she explained) on what she had seen from the balloon, had early-morning shadows far blacker, sharper, longer than before. St Michael's tower pointed, not into a cloudless sky, but at a huge swirling mass of cloud, or possibly dark smoke, that dominated the heavens in the form of an enormous question mark.

"And what prompted this evident doubt?" enquired Delphick, pointing. "I am reminded of Kipling's six honest serving men."

"Ah, yes. Their names," Miss Seeton quoted happily, "are What and Why and When, and How and Where and Who. Except that I can't tell you, I'm afraid. Why, that is. Flying past, as it were, the withy beds we talked of the various uses to which willow can be put. I had no idea there were so many, but Mrs. Midney was most knowledgeable about eel traps, and sweet peas in the garden—as was Mr. Weaver, who makes his own baskets. Charcoal, too, for barbecues, and also, of course, for drawing. I bought some myself, though as yet I have not used it."

"Perhaps you might try it now." Delphick reached gently for the sketchbook. "As I said when we spoke yesterday, the kidnapping case has taken a rather more sinister turn." Miss Seeton sighed. Delphick, leafing through her sketches, smiled.

"At least we had no need to disturb your balloon flight. I'm relieved to see you were able to enjoy the experience before we needed to ask your advice again ... Do tell me—why the sword?" He had paused at a drawing of a long-robed woman, out of focus, brandishing an enormous blade that in contrast was as sharply defined as any sunrise shadow.

"The Three Swords of Arthur." Miss Seeton explained about Susan, "or Brenda, as she wishes to be called now."

"Good gracious. Why?"

Miss Seeton explained further. "I see," was all Delphick said.

"The young can be so very enthusiastic, Chief Superintendent, can they not? She is writing a book about it, her cousin told me when I visited her bookshop, as she herself told me—Brenda, that is—which is why she asked if Mr. Weaver might fly us over the landscape sword so that she could show me." She shook her head. "I fear that to me it was no more apparent than the Zodiac temple, and I looked for that as well, because I said I would."

Delphick hid a smile. "And here is your bookshop acquaintance again?" The new sketch showed Octavia Callender quite as long of robe and masked of face as before, but with a difference. Rather than the cat Graymalkin, she was accompanied by ... "A Dalmatian dog, surely," said Delphick. "So you see her now more as Cruella de Vil than Lady Macbeth—but why? Was she with you in the balloon? What did she do to upset you?"

"But there would hardly be room." She puzzled, then turned pink. "Oh. One could not help overhearing ... Her cousin and Mr. Weaver spoke of her, you see. I believe that at one time she and Mr. Weaver were close acquaintances, but he is a young man who enjoys the freedom of a quiet life. I suspect her personality may have been somewhat too forceful for him. And then he drove our little party back past a sign for a place called Catsgore."

She seemed to feel this was sufficient explanation, and Delphick, after a pause, realised that it was. "Rather than trying to wash her hands, she's saying 'Out, damned spot'? Miss Seeton, you have been dipping again into your ancestral riddle-book."

Miss Seeton assured him that Jack Crabbe, busy with the script for *Sir Gawain*, still had the borrowed riddle-book in his possession, and had told her as much only yesterday, when driving her home from the station.

"Good," said Delphick. "You were kind enough to spare us the worst, but it clearly contains some terrible jokes." Something flickered across his subconscious, but proved elusive. "Now, I fear, we must turn to matters more serious than Victorian riddles. I have two new photos to show you: the least unpleasant first."

Christy Garth held the newspaper in his bandaged hand, and Miss Seeton sighed, saying that he had never been very far from her thoughts. Even while she was enjoying the freedom of the skies he, poor young man, enjoyed no freedom at all. Delphick said quickly that it seemed she had been right to confirm the family's West Country supposition as a working hypothesis.

"The poor young man," she said again. "The young—so energetic, so full of life—but to be held captive ..."

"We have narrowed down the area where he's being held, but it is still a large one. Any suggestions you might make, having so recently visited one part of the west of England, could be invaluable in further narrowing."

Miss Seeton noted the strained expression on Christy's face, the sunken eyes, the grim set of his jaw. "One assumes he has been fighting—the bandage, the bruises ... Is there any significance in the date of the newspaper? Or of the headline? I seem to recall a film in which it was possible to narrow down the area of search by the time of the particular edition with, I believe, a message scribbled on it, left in a car. Or it may have been a train."

Delphick nodded. "One of the lesser headlines was indeed altered, which is another reason for our belief that the west is correct. As for the date, I'm not sure any of us gave the matter much thought. We assumed it was merely intended as proof that he was alive on the day." But now she'd put the idea in his head he began to wonder if they might have missed a trick. He'd have a word with Jasper Kebby, once he was back at the Yard.

Miss Seeton was grave. "Let us hope that he remains alive, Chief Superintendent. You said, after all, that the case had taken a sinister turn. You didn't mean—"

"Nothing like that," he broke in to reassure her. "So far as we know, he is alive. But I regret to tell you that he wears those bandages not because he has been in a fight—though I imagine he would have made some form of protest at the time—but because one of his fingers has been amputated."

Miss Seeton uttered one little gasp of dismay, then was silent.

"I'm sorry," said Delphick, passing her the photograph of the shoebox and its contents.

"At least your suspicions must now be allayed," she said at last. "It was not entirely certain that the kidnap was genuine, I believe, but after such wicked cruelty there can be no doubt, can there?"

"There can be *little* doubt," he amended. The early sketches had given the impression that the kidnap was not straightforward, and Delphick had faith in her impressions. Possibly it had started out the fake she'd hinted it was and then become, for some reason, the real thing. Maybe the reason was the Traffic Jam pick-up that had failed so dramatically near Evesham. In the west of England.

"Miss Seeton, there's a lot of countryside out there." He recalled that resolute urbanite, Jasper Kebby, on whose behalf he was here. "We simply must try to narrow down the area. The family can tell us nothing—the paper is one of the dailies on sale everywhere—the room, the furniture, the background are all anonymous. If you can suggest anything else ..." By this time, discretion might do more harm than good. "It may be of interest to you that the young man's name is Christy Garth."

"Garth?" Miss Seeton frowned, then slowly shook her head.

Delphick was disappointed, but hid his disappointment. Her newspaper was unlikely to chronicle Christy's wild exploits, he supposed; and, even if it had, she was unlikely to bother reading about them.

"Garth—a courtyard or garden, I believe," she said. "And 'Christy' has something to do with ski-ing, does it not? Which of course would be impossible at this time of year in the West Country, and even Wales in the middle of winter is unlikely."

Wales, to the west of England; Wales, famed for its sheep. Wales—not Worcestershire or Gloucestershire or Herefordshire in England. Not even Somerset. Had he misunderstood Miss Seeton's sketches from the very first? Wasted police time over ... "Red herrings," he said grimly, wondering what Chief Inspector Kebby would make of it all.

"Agatha Christie," said Miss Seeton promptly. "So very clever. An expert displaying his or her expertise is always a pleasure."

Delphick needed to think; had to interrupt. "Please, Miss Seeton, just take a look at the photos, would you? Consider what impression they give, while I clear the tea things away."

And think.

Chapter Twelve

In his office on the umpteenth floor of New Scotland Yard, Delphick contemplated the two sketchbooks borrowed, with official receipts and solemn promises for a speedy return, from Miss Seeton.

"Miss Seeton is perhaps not the only person on whose instincts we should rely. Oracles have feelings, too." Delphick smiled thinly. "From the start I doubted the wisdom of putting upon her the pressure applied to me by Superintendent Snowe when Kebby, or rather young Garth, had a prior claim. As for volunteering her help in the matter of the Somerset murder, that was to pile Pelion upon Ossa." He indicated the sketchbooks. "I am justly served."

Sergeant Ranger knew nothing of the Greek giants' mountain-moving attempt to storm the Odyssean heavens and destroy the gods, but he guessed the Oracle meant he'd added one problem to another. Which, Bob had to admit, was only the truth.

"The coincidence of her being already on the spot had its appeal, of course, but had I not allowed my professional sympathies to intrude, Chief Inspector Faggus would have done no more than ask her to call me here to arrange a convenient time for a consultation in the privacy of her own home. That was urgent; the rest was not. Sadly, there will always be drugs; sadly, there will always be murder. But things can move fast—sometimes too fast—in a case of kidnap. Christy Garth should always have been my first consideration. And likewise," he ended grimly, "that of the Yard's retained art consultant."

"She's never complained of being overworked! That's not like Aunt Em, sir. She's as conscientious as they come, and when she knows it's her duty she—well, she pulls out all the stops, and she never complains. Er ... does she?"

"Indeed not. She uttered no more than the exclamations of dismay proper to an English gentlewoman when she saw Garth with his bandaged hand, and then his severed finger. She studied both without a qualm." He opened the first sketchbook to a page marked by a slip of paper. His journey back from Kent had been a busy one; he was thankful that the travel allowance for an officer of his rank granted him the privacy of a first class compartment in the train.

Miss Seeton's response to the latest kidnap photos showed a tall, stooping man in a surgical mask above which eyes of deep blackness gazed down at his prospective victim, whose form was so heavily outlined in short, jagged stabs of the pencil that much of the shape was hidden, and the paper in places was torn. The masked man held in one hand a knife and in the other an instrument with a small, sharp blade. As he stooped from the shadows, he loomed over the shoulder of a waiting arm clamped sideways to a chest of drawers too heavy to overturn. The waiting fingers were outspread; the stabs of the pencil here were the most jagged of all.

"Phew!" said Bob. "The last time she saw a doctor it can't have been Dr. Knight—or I hope it wasn't. Talk about a

211

nightmare. If Gideon's grandfather really does turn into the Demon Barber like this, then it's no more babysitting for him!"

"Certainly not someone to whom I would care to trust my appendix. You, too, don't doubt that the knifeman is a professional, rather than a skilful amateur?"

Bob reconsidered. "It just feels like a real doctor, sir," was all he could say. "Would a kidnapper's henchman be so careful about wearing a mask?"

"If the object of the mask is to prevent the spread of infection, he might. After all, there is little monetary value in a victim dead from septicaemia."

"A live victim could recognise the face once it was all over," said Bob. "We can't be sure one way or the other, then."

"The scalpel has a distinctly medical appearance, which again suggests a professional, except that we know Miss Seeton was a studious observer of the dissection of numerous bodies in her art school days. The mask might thus be no more than instinctive memory." Delphick considered. "The mask does, however, serve another purpose. It renders the knifeman's expression hard, if not impossible, to fathom."

"Apart from his eyes," Bob pointed out.

"Yes, they have a distinctly hollow appearance. And the background shadows fill that quarter of the room. I wonder ... but at present nothing worthwhile comes to mind." He turned to another marker slip. "Glastonbury Tor," he announced.

Miss Seeton, understanding the Tor to be King Arthur's Isle of Avalon, had taken a number of different views of this distinctive landmark. Here was yet another sketch of the terraced hill steep on one side, steeper on the other, dotted with the forms of sheep that seemed to be cavorting on muffled hoofs in the fields that stretched all the way from the moorland base to the summit.

"But why," said Delphick, "has she drawn a willow tree in place of the church tower?"

Bob could give no answer. The Oracle flipped to and fro between the various slips of paper he had used as markers. "This particular sketch seems to have been drawn after her flight in the balloon, but before my arrival at the cottage. It was therefore not drawn in response to anything I may have said. She knew that she would be seeing me the following day. More dancing sheep, and a willow tree ..."

"Something she saw from the balloon, sir? Or something somebody else has said?" Bob was eager to assist. He never properly understood his adopted aunt's swift sketches, but it seemed that the Oracle, who generally could, was for once finding interpretation hard. That's what came of dealing with three cases at the same time. Everyone got muddled, and if Delphick blamed himself for the muddle, you couldn't argue with that. But you had to help, if you could. The sergeant pulled the sketchbook towards him across the desk, turning the pages one at a time, with or without markers. He laughed. "Here's someone striking a blow for Women's Lib, sir!" It was white-robed Susan Callender, with her sword.

"The Three Swords of Arthur." Delphick emerged from his thoughts to contemplate again the sketch Miss Seeton had explained resulted from her meeting with Susan, now Brenda, the reincarnated Lady of the Lake with an interest in Arthurian myth and "a perhaps excessively romantic nature, Chief Superintendent."

"I never knew he had more than one," returned Bob. "Excalibur, wasn't it? Pulled out of a stone so he could claim the throne and build the Round Table."

"Something along those lines. This young woman, according to Miss Seeton, discovered a hitherto unknown depiction of Excalibur in the Somerset landscape—" Bob allowed a bemused *What?* to escape him—"and in the course of their shared balloon flight pointed it out to Miss Seeton, or rather attempted so to do. It would appear that her enthusiasm made more of an impression on her audience than did the landscape sword."

Delphick explained, as far as he could understand it from Miss Seeton's somewhat incoherent explanation, the concept of the Glastonbury Zodiac and the use by its devotees of maps, photographs, and inspiration.

"Wishful thinking, sounds more like to me." Bob turned to another sketch. "Someone else waving swords about ... I think." A knight in armour full a-gleam stood on a bridge, holding above his head a sword, out of focus. It seemed he had the intention of directing this indistinct weapon towards a ripple of water in the middle of a willow-fringed pool.

"Sir Bedivere, one assumes," said Delphick, "with the Arm In White Samite about to rise from the waters of the mere."

"Bedivere." Bob tried to recall what he could of the stories he'd read to his sister's children, making up for what he hadn't much bothered with when himself a child, being more interested in outdoor rather than indoor pursuits. "Oh, yes, the bloke who took three tries and was yelled at by Arthur before he could bring himself to chuck the sword away."

Delphick smiled at his sport-loving sidekick's throwaway reference to rugby football, and agreed that the sergeant had once again demonstrated a firm grasp of the essentials. As to whether Sir Bedivere, or the Lady of the Lake, or indeed the imminent Arm had any importance beyond reminding Miss Seeton of what she had learned during her two visits to Somerset, he could do no more than guess.

"There is a considerable body of Arthurian literature," he went on, "and a number of variations between individual versions of the stories." The office encyclopaedia, which the Yard's new broom had attempted to banish, now lurked, volume upon volume, in a tactful corner rather than continuing blatant upon the shelves. Fortunately for Delphick, the "A" volume was on top, and he had refreshed his memory to good effect. The new broom's efforts to remove from its pride of place on the office wall the display case containing the wreck of Miss Seeton's long-ago umbrella had been coldly, and firmly, ignored.

"I am justly served," said the Oracle again, after prolonged perusal of both sketchbooks yielded no helpful clues, only more confusion. "These must be photocopied in their entirety, and returned to their owner while copies are distributed to Superintendent Kebby and Superintendent Snowe. They may spot something you and I have missed."

"U and I." Bob chuckled. "Aunt Em and her daft riddles, sir. Remember?"

Delphick sat very still. "I do. The centre of gravity—and there was something else ... Perhaps a third visit to Plummergen is indicated, Bob. Once the photocopying is complete. Jump to it, Sergeant Ranger!"

In Glastonbury, the Closed sign was being hung on the door of Bedivere Books as a shadow loomed. A thump and a rattle made Octavia pause. Through the glass half-window she saw her elder brother scowling at her.

She sighed, and let him. "Hello, Bill." It was not the most hearty of welcomes.

"You've been to see Janner in hospital again."

"Yes, I have, but it's for the last time—"

"You've never done something to him!"

"—because they're letting him go home later today, once Jan can spare the time to fetch him. And of course I haven't. Why do you think I would?"

"Because he's a stubborn old cuss and you're as sick of the whole affair as I am," said Bill. "This is ending up with you and me against Cris and Val. I don't like it one bit. The four of us have always got on pretty well, considering, but all because of Janner being so bloody-minded we're taking sides and wasting time with arguing when we should be concentrating on the business."

"I am." Octavia waved a hand around the crowded bookshelves. "Concentrating on my business, I mean. And so is Val on hers."

"And on Jan, seems to me," grumbled Bill. "Fleeces! That's not all he's got in mind to give her, I don't doubt."

"She might be trying to sweet-talk him into seeing reason," suggested Octavia. "Better yet, she'll be trying to apologise for the fight you two had the other night. There was no call for you to let it go that far. We should be talking him and his father round before that Act becomes law, not making them so angry they won't speak to any of us about anything and we miss our chance."

"That why you've been visiting Janner?"

Octavia shrugged. "Two visits, four days apart. Someone had to try. But you're the very last of us four he'd talk to; Cris and Val don't seem as bothered now as you and me; it seemed too good a chance to miss. A captive audience. With that drip attached, he wasn't going anywhere in a hurry."

"But it didn't work," said Bill, "or you'd have let me—us—know."

"No, it didn't. The first time he was still too groggy to stop me being there, which I'm sure he'd have tried if he'd been himself, but I told the nurse I was his niece, and waved a bunch of flowers under her nose to prove my good intentions. He couldn't argue with that, but he couldn't really take much in of what I said, either. So I stopped saying it and turned the conversation to the weather, and what a serious accident it had been and how he'd had a lucky escape, and hoped he'd be better soon."

"Usual bedside chat," said Bill. "In your place I'd have been tempted—but then, I'd not have gone hospital visiting the awkward old basket for fear I'd be tempted to shake a bit of sense into him. Or worse."

Octavia understood her brother's hasty temper, and had to smile. "The drip was gone the second time, and he guessed what I might be up to the moment he clapped eyes on me. Or perhaps he remembered the first visit. Talk about language! A whole shopful of flowers wouldn't have worked. He as good as told the nurses to throw me out."

"So you left before you were thrown. Don't blame you. But for all your fine education, you did no better with him than me losing my temper." Once more he scowled at her. "Which is what I've said all along—none of that side of the family can ever be made to see sense. So what do we do now?"

"Perhaps," said Octavia, "there might be another accident. Janner's not old, but he's no spring chicken and he'll be none too sure of himself after being shaken about the way he was. They'll advise him not to drive—those drips take a while to work their way out of your system—but he's stubborn, as you said. That tractor ... some of the local hills are steep ..."

"So they are," agreed her brother.

There was a long, thoughtful silence.

It was one of Martha Bloomer's days at Sweetbriars. Miss Seeton's recent break had meant an alteration in the schedule of Plummergen's domestic goddess, and there was much noise in the little kitchen as the breakfast crockery, which her employer had been about to wash for herself, was subjected by Martha to her most thorough bout of cleansing in weeks. Martha was in one of her Grand Slams—and it was mostly the fault of Miss Seeton.

With her final mouthful of toast it had dawned on Miss Seeton that, now Delphick had returned to London with her sketchbooks, there were no Arthurian records from which to design the scenery for *Sir Gawain*. Her memory must therefore be her guide. She cleared the table, opened the bureau drawer in which her artist's materials were kept ... and the rattle disturbed a large spider that had been enjoying the peace of an almost undisturbed slumber since the owner of the bureau had taken herself off to Somerset.

Miss Seeton rose from her knees, darted into the kitchen and snatched her breakfast cup and saucer from the draining board. Holding the cup, the saucer, and her breath, she hurried back to the sitting room. Good. The spider sat still where she had left it.

The manoeuvring was delicate. The legs of spiders are all too easily damaged. The huntress wondered if she should have fetched a soft cloth duster instead, but thought that Mrs. Bloomer might not approve, and would besides have meant opening another drawer, taking time she could not spare: Martha could arrive at any minute. Miss Seeton had no fear of spiders, and understood the benefits of their webs in the catching and despatching of unwelcome insect life; but she didn't want and couldn't risk webs inside her cottage. If Martha Bloomer, Plummergen's acknowledged

Queen of Cleanliness, suspected even one arachnid of trying to take up permanent retiary residence in her kingdom, she would be much more than affronted: she would be forever shamed.

Miss Seeton lost track of time as she pursued the spider at last into a corner from which it could not escape, popping over it the upturned cup, sliding the saucer carefully underneath, and preparing to make for the kitchen, the door, and liberty for the spider to spin as many webs under the eaves, or round the gutters and downpipes, as it chose.

She was too late. Martha, like her husband Stan, had a key to the door that opened from the garden to the narrow side lane.

"Oh, dear." A guilty blush tinged Miss Seeton's cheeks as Martha stared at her.

"Miss Emily, your second-best china! What have you got in there?"

"I thought I would release it out of doors, Martha dear, as the weather is not too cold and it will have ample time to prepare for hibernation—if in fact they do," she added. When Nigel Colveden had told her so much of interest about sheep and their teeth, pigs and their pillows, and spiders with their makeshift balloons, he hadn't enlarged on the winter habits of any of them.

"It's never a mouse!" The shocked Martha was as pale as her employer was pink.

"Oh, no." Miss Seeton presented the cup and saucer for Martha's inspection. "They can creep through the smallest of cracks, can they not? Under the door, perhaps, or down the chimney. But it has done no harm, that I can see," she added hastily as Martha took the saucer, removed the cup, clicked her tongue and shook the intruder to the ground.

"I'll start with the dishes." Martha was brisk as she followed Miss Seeton indoors. "But there, I might have known something of the sort would happen. It was in the paper."

Miss Seeton read *The Times*; Martha preferred *Anyone's*. "In the paper?" echoed Miss Seeton.

"In my stars." Martha began rinsing the cup and saucer vigorously under the cold tap. "Look for an unwelcome visitor, it said. Well, when I looked up The Street as I was coming across here I thought it might be Miss Nuttel and Mrs. Blaine, because they were heading this way, only they went right on past down towards the canal—and anyway there's two of them. I heard them say something about wool caught in the hedge, and arguing how with so many sheep grazing there ought to be enough to stuff a whole cushion." Martha sniffed. "If they come knocking at your door, dear, asking what you do with your chicken feathers, you tell them Stan wants them all for his compost."

In the half-dozen years she had lived in Plummergen Miss Seeton had never thought to enquire what happened to the feathers produced by the Sweetbriars hens. Stan kept the henhouse clean, the hens fed and watered, and the eggs ranged in order of lay: he would never permit an elderly egg to find its way to her table, or to his own. The garden and the hens were Stan's private kingdom as his wife reigned supreme in the kitchen.

"Compost?" Had the mischievous influence of Nigel Colveden been spreading? He had known the Bloomers for most of his life ... But no. The Bloomers had known Nigel and his sense of humour far longer than had Miss Seeton. Martha enjoyed a laugh and a joke, but it was unlikely she'd be fooled by one of Nigel's extravagant stories.

"Compost?" said Miss Seeton again. "I had no idea you could." The idea had received no attention in *Greenfinger*

Points the Way, but Stan took no notice of Greenfinger's words of what she supposed to be wisdom, and Stan suggested was no more than making it all up as the man went along, born and bred in some town or other as he obviously was.

"Give them a good soak overnight," said Martha, splashing busily, "and make sure the wind's not blowing when you put them on the heap. They rot down lovely, Stan says, and it don't really smell beyond a whiff on the breeze, and even then you have to stand close."

This reminded Miss Seeton of her balloon ride, and Somerset, and King Arthur, and Sir Gawain. With a quick word she left Martha to rinse the spider-cup for a third time, and went back to her interrupted sketching.

The next interruption came when Martha, the crockery finally scoured to her satisfaction, the house energetically swept, mopped, and dusted, came in with a fresh pot of tea and two cups. "You've been working that hard, dear, you never noticed when Bert brought your letters. I didn't like to disturb you even when I realised there was another from the police. I expect it's a cheque from that computer of theirs. Didn't you say you'd been doing some more pictures?"

Miss Seeton confirmed that she had, while in Somerset, been asked for one or two IdentiKit drawings; and only yesterday Mr. Delphick had borrowed her latest sketchbooks. "That is to say, I hope he understood they were merely a loan. Dear Mr. Jessyp would be so disappointed if I were to let him down and, although my memory as a rule is most reliable, somehow I cannot seem to recall the scenery exactly as I would have wished, and will be glad once they are returned."

It took little prompting on Martha's part for the memory sketches to be displayed. Miss Seeton, concerned for the accuracy of the *Sir Gawain* backdrops, believed that by having to explain them to her friend she would remember what was not quite right about them, and would be able to correct it.

"I am sure, you see, that there is no such willow tree on the summit of Glastonbury Tor." Miss Seeton produced as proof the guide book sold to her by Octavia Callender. "In the photograph there is clearly a ruined church tower, just as I remember it—and yet this is not the first time it has happened. And why there should be such an unusual cloud, I cannot imagine. It was a glorious sunny day when I climbed the Tor. It didn't rain until the next day, when I went on the bus to Wells."

"Why?" chuckled Martha.

"Because the book said the cathedral was one of the most interesting and beautiful in the country, and the west front one of the most impressive." Miss Seeton turned back through the pages. "So many statues, including, I believe, Thomas à Becket ..."

Martha glanced at the tiers of stone figures, and shook her head. "I didn't mean why go to Wells, I meant that's what that cloud looks like. A great question mark in the sky, asking everyone Why?"

"Nigel attended Wye Agricultural College, did he not?" Miss Seeton, turning another page, saw yet another Hereford bull, mighty and white-faced where she was almost sure she remembered the shaggy-coated Highland cattle as being of solid colour, and boasting huge upswept horns rather than almost demure stumps.

"And as for the Zodiac, I couldn't even see the sword." Miss Seeton indicated her third sketch of a woman still masked, still wearing robes, but this time with a rampant lion as her companion rather than a cat, or a Dalmatian dog. "Her cousin did her very best to point it out, but I fear it made no impression. You said, Martha dear, that you had been reading your horoscope, and I believe that Leo is the appropriate sign, her birthday being the eighth of August, which is why she is called Octavia." Mrs. Bloomer was unable to see why, and said so. Miss Seeton explained the explanation at greater length.

"Oh," said Martha. "So that's why, is it?"

"That," Miss Seeton assured her, "is why."

And again she looked at the clouded question mark in the sky, and puzzled.

The photocopying finished, Delphick telephoned Sweetbriars to ask when and how most efficiently he should return Miss Seeton's property. Would she be content with the registered post, or would she prefer a personal delivery, possibly tomorrow? Miss Seeton, wrestling with wayward memories of the Somerset countryside, said that of course whichever method suited the chief superintendent would likewise suit herself, but perhaps, for the sake of Mr. Jessyp and the Padders, if he did not mind too much she would be glad if it could be as soon as convenient.

There was a note in her voice that Delphick recognised. He sat up straight. "You've been sketching again, Miss Seeton." Miss Seeton confessed that she had, but that try as she might it still wasn't coming out quite as she had hoped. Which is why the sketchbooks would help, she felt sure, although he must not go to any trouble over the matter.

Delphick looked towards his sergeant, who as was his custom had been listening on the extension. "First thing tomorrow, Bob!"

"Yes, sir," said Bob, grinning widely. "I'll go and sort out a car, shall I?"

"Do, please." Delphick readdressed the telephone, which was uttering little chirrups of pleasure at the thought of visitors—protests that she was putting everyone to a great deal of bother—and some relief that her sketches would soon be back and she could try, yet again, to capture something of the atmosphere of that enchanted landscape.

There was gingerbread, there was rich fruit cake, there was a sponge and there were plain chocolate biscuits, to all of which Bob brought his usual hearty appetite while Delphick, declining more than a welcome cup of tea, discussed with Miss Seeton her latest sketches as well as her earlier efforts.

"This young woman has made quite an impression on you." Octavia Callender's third likeness, to which the artist had added some dashes of colour—green for her robe, tawny gold for her companion—intrigued him. Apart from Glastonbury Tor, Miss Seeton both during and after her visits to Somerset had drawn nothing, and nobody, else in triplicate. Even the Three Swords of Arthur were commemorated but once, in the form of Susan dressed as the Lady of the Lake. Yet Octavia, always masked, nevertheless dominated the pages whether her familiar was a tabby cat, a spotted dog or, as now, a lion rampant. Leo the Zodiac sign, who had a later page to himself in full star-spangled splendour, Delphick understood, but as king of the jungle a lion did not yield his place to another living creature. Miss Seeton's original lion ramped realistically at Octavia's side but, on closer inspection, its eyes were wary. Delphick hunted for the two previous drawings. The cat Miss Seeton had called Graymalkin looked no more than smug and self-assured, in the way of cats. The Dalmatian dog, however, flinched away from the wringing hands in her second portrayal.

The first time he saw this sketch Delphick had supposed the hands to be spraying drops of water in the dog's direction, even though the water itself was no more than a few swift dots and darts of the pencil to indicate something that, on the stage, is not there at all. But this third likeness of Miss Callender ... Or—was it? Behind that mask, who could tell? Her Lady of the Lake cousin was of a similar build, and Miss Seeton had evidently liked, or at least found some sympathy with, her. But this masked face ...

"I'm right, am I, that this is the same person in each drawing, Miss Seeton?"

"I believe so, although I cannot think why she has made so strong an impression, except that she is an excellent actress, as well as a good businesswoman. Her cousin told me she obtained a first class degree at university, too." Miss Seeton sighed for the brilliance of another when she, herself, had so mediocre a talent. "It is always a pleasure to watch an expert performing with expertise, is it not? I confess to being somewhat apprehensive about returning to her shop, in case she talked me into buying even more books that I probably did not need."

Delphick knew Miss Seeton, in some ways, perhaps better than she knew herself. She was not one to be tricked or coerced into doing something she did not wish to do; politeness alone would make her buy the unwanted books, not pressure, no matter how skilful the sales talk—even if on first acquaintance she had seen the saleswoman as ...

"Lady Macbeth again," said Delphick.

Miss Seeton nodded. "A difficult part to play, or rather to cast." She smiled. "There was much discussion when Mrs. Benn suggested *Macbeth* as a welcome change for the end of term play from what many might regard as the more normal fare for an all-girls school. I helped with the scenery then, too. The vexed question of how many Macbeth children there were, or were not, was settled by treating him as the lady's second husband, and herself as an older woman, which also of course explains the ease with which she persuades him to the murder." She smiled again, ruefully. "Many of our actresses were reluctant to portray a bossy older woman, no matter the strength and depth of the character. Indeed, it was only by allowing a degree of extravagance in the sleep-walking scene—strange lighting effects, and so forth—that anyone could be persuaded to do it. They preferred, you see, to dress in chain mail and fight battles rather than wring their hands and go mad in long green robes—that is, white, of course—or cackle and prophesy as hideous witches."

"The clang of sword on sword," agreed Delphick, contemplating Sir Bedivere's grasp of a misty Excalibur, "does have a more satisfying sound than the wails of nightmare terrors. Would you say that Miss Callender was the sort to experience nightmares?"

"I would think it unlikely. She seems to have a most practical outlook on life, as her cousin and her former boyfriend both agreed. Indeed, I understood him to suggest that for him she was somewhat too practical." Vincent Weaver, cocking his cheerful snook at authority, taking whenever he could to the freedom of the skies, must have felt constrained by Octavia Callender's more energetic style. "I believe," said Miss Seeton, "that the phrase to describe him would be 'laid back', which I would not apply to Miss Callender."

"Then I wonder what prompted you to this third sketch, Miss Seeton. Has someone said something to make you revisit the subject?"

Miss Seeton did her best to give an accurate reply. "Martha spoke of her horoscope," she offered. "It said she must expect an unwelcome visitor, and she found me putting a spider outside. After Glastonbury I know that many people take such matters seriously, though in Martha's case I believe it is no more than harmless amusement—the horoscope, not the spider, which some people dislike, and some even fear. Spiders, not star signs. I do not, of course, read my own, but I happen to know my sign is Virgo—" could it be anything else, Delphick mused—"and as a child one learned that clever little rhyme, so I knew that the previous sign, with her birthday on the eighth of August, must be Leo."

She saw Delphick's look of interested ignorance, and began to recite. "The Ram, the Bull, the Heavenly Twins / After the Crab, the Lion shines / The Virgin, and the Scales / The Scorpion, Archer, and Sea-Goat / The Man who bears the Watering Pot / The Fish, with glittering tails."

Delphick thanked her. She smiled. "So clever, all twelve in just six lines, even if the idea of a sea-goat is puzzling, but then so can the rest of them be. While I was in the shop someone came in to complain about the Zodiac books he had bought, and how there were only eleven signs and one had to be divided to make twelve. Most puzzling. And she sold him more books, which is why I see her as a clever actress because I strongly suspect that she doesn't believe a word of it. She has such a sound business brain."

Delphick was silent; Bob, who had finished his snack and begun jotting the occasional shorthand note, read through the little Zodiac rhyme and thought it might make a bedtime chant for Gideon as he grew older. Children, Anne had said, enjoyed routine. The same toys in the bath, the same book each night, the same little joke as the covers were pulled up. The Ram, the Bull, the Heavenly Twins ...

Delphick frowned. He pondered. He coughed, braced himself, and said:

"Miss Seeton, might I use your telephone?"

Five minutes later, with the sitting room door firmly closed against laughing incredulity, Delphick was asking Glastonbury's police station sergeant to run Chief Inspector Faggus, if he was on the premises, to earth. "He's in the middle of a murder investigation," he was told. "And I may be able to help him," said Delphick. "I may be," he repeated, stressing *may* because he was starting to lose his nerve. Before, however, he could break the connection the rumbling tones of Tom Faggus came along the line to ask what he wanted.

"It's a very long shot," the chief superintendent warned him.

"And you're an oracle," said the chief inspector. "Specialise in ambiguity and guesswork, don't they? And looking at life in a cock-eyed way, same as your lady-friend who draws the pretty pictures. She bin up to her tricks again?"

Delphick hesitated. Faggus laughed. "Well, that's *my* long shot, certain sure. Come on now, fair exchange being no robbery, why not tell me yours?"

"The laws of slander," began the chief superintendent, "prevent my saying too much without proof, and I stress again that it is an extremely long shot—but if there should be a young woman in town who owns a bookshop and wears long dresses, the date of whose birthday has a decidedly octagonal feel to it ..."

"Ah," said Tom Faggus, after working it out. "Yes. And if there is?"

"If there is, she and her associates might—just might—be worth a closer look than any of them may so far have received in your investigations."

"None," said Faggus promptly. "No obvious reason. What put you on to her?"

Delphick hesitated. If he was wrong, talk of the Sir Bedivere sketch—the emphasis on the knight himself, the apparent unimportance of the sword—might be too slanderous a hint. "Miss Seeton has drawn her likeness three times, always in a mask and remarking, when asked about this peculiarity, that the lady in question is a consummate actress as well as a good businesswoman. Those who excel in the business world often have something of a ruthless streak. From your knowledge of the young woman, would you agree?"

"Thinking about it, perhaps I would."

"Miss Seeton," said Delphick, "sees her not as a bookseller, but as Lady Macbeth."

"Does she, now." Delphick said nothing. Let Faggus work it out again.

"I see," said the chief inspector at last. "Bit of a bossyboots, right? Told her husband to kill the king and he did, poor sap."

"I understand," offered Delphick, "that a previous male associate of the bookshop lady experienced some relief when she chose to break off their association, as he preferred a quiet life."

"Ah, yes." Tom Faggus could almost always see the lighter side. "A quiet life for a bit of a real high flyer, would you say?"

The smile in his voice was echoed by Delphick. "Thinking about it, perhaps I would."

"We'll ask around," said the chief inspector. "And ... thanks."

Chapter Thirteen

Miss Seeton had asked if she might attend the first public run-through of Mr. Jessyp's script so that she could put final touches to her scenery designs. Though her Somerset sketchbooks had been returned, a little more inspiration would not hurt. Mr. Jessyp said it was to be a principals-only performance, with everyone but Daniel Eggleden in plain clothes. Dan would wear the high-collared green cloak essential for the decapitation scene, but chain mail (dishcloths knitted in grey wool) and armour (cardboard shapes cut out and painted by the Junior Mixed Infants, supervised by Miss Maynard) would be absent, as also the gorgeous gowns and gauze-draped hennins the ladies of the court were to wear.

Emmy Putts, who had realised far too late that Queen Guinevere was not the female lead, was in an even deeper sulk than might have been expected because her dark and luxuriant wig was at this early stage thought unnecessary. In that case, she wanted to know, what were they doing with the long green cloak and the papier mâché head?

"Practice," said Mr. Jessyp. "We must be sure the illusion will work as intended. The head has to be concealed until the proper moment, and then dropped exactly right in case it bounces."

"Then oughtn't they to be practising with the axe, too?" retorted Emmy.

Blacksmith Daniel was a man of great stature; Nigel Colveden, though tall and well-made, a rather less substantial Sir Gawain. It had been a challenge to design an axe that both could comfortably use: the balance best suited to the strength, shoulders, and reach of one did not suit the other so well. Martin C. Jessyp, pedagogue, had been studying log tables and Euclid, and experimenting with bits of twig on his kitchen scales. Nigel's proposal that it was only cardboard, and if it didn't work properly then having two different axes would, had not been well received. Mr. Jessyp prided himself on his ability to solve all problems, large and small; his dignity was affronted.

"Next time," snapped Mr. Jessyp.

Miss Seeton tut-tutted to herself. It was unlike Mr. Jessyp to be so tetchy, though she could understand why he was. Teachers must cultivate patience, and the headmaster was an excellent teacher; but Emmy, not so many years ago one of his pupils, was in an irritable mood, and of course irritability could often be catching. Emmy had remembered to bring her new wig, and been told there was no need for it. Mr. Jessyp had forgotten the axe, and was naturally blaming himself.

"Perhaps they could use my umbrella, for the moment," she offered. Mr. Jessyp winced, thanked her, and accepted the offer. Emmy tittered, tossed her head, and put on her wig. Mr. Jessyp, in clipped accents, announced that the rehearsal would begin.

At her fireside, where she sat now with a cup of tea and her sketchbook, Miss Seeton sighed. Things had begun so well. Even Emmy Putts had appeared to settle to the business of the evening. Admiral Leighton was in the wings as Prompt and Non-Principal Extra. The Christmas festivities began. Speeches of goodwill were delivered. Actors and audience shook their heads and groaned at the jokes inserted by Jack Crabbe into Mr. Jessyp's more dignified script based on the mediaeval original. Rather like the axe, the balance wasn't yet quite right, but of course it would be all right on the night. It always was.

Then the Green Knight, his high-collared cloak billowing about him to conceal the papier mâché head, had made his entrance, Miss Seeton's umbrella over his shoulder in place of the missing axe. Dan Eggleden boldly greeted the court, announced that he came in peace to learn if the fame of Arthur's Round Table was justified, issued his challenge, and then scorned the knights for their silent response. Where was their thirst for adventure? Where their sense of fair play? One blow of his axe—he swept the umbrella magnificently through the air—to be exchanged for another, in twelve months' time—was it so much to ask? Had he heard wrong? Was there in fact nobody in the whole of Camelot with sufficient valour? Was the Round Table a lie?

King Arthur jumped to his feet to accept the challenge on behalf of his knights, but Sir Gawain raised his voice in protest that his uncle's life should be thus put at risk. Let King Arthur's nephew take his place!

And then ... Despite everything, Miss Seeton had to smile at the memory of how Daniel the Green, with another grand gesture, handed the umbrella axe to Sir Gawain and knelt to receive the blow. Which had been when the papier mâché head caught in the fabric folds of his cloak, slipped from its pocket, and rolled into view rather sooner than it should. There was laughter among the audience of waiting actors and backstage crew; a snigger from Emmy

Putts. Mr. Jessyp frowned. Nigel and Dan automatically bent. By a hairsbreadth they missed cracking their skulls. Dan reversed the umbrella to hook back his head.

"We'd better try that again," said Mr. Jessyp.

And again.

But it had not been third time lucky. The Green Knight's head simply would not behave. "And 'twill be a sight more okkard to hook with the proper axe than it is with this ole brolly," remarked Dan, nodding to the brolly's owner before reminding Mr. Jessyp that when he was in full costume there would be the spikes of his golden spurs, and a branch of holly with prickles, to add to his difficulties. He could wear the cloak and run the risk, or his head could be hidden somewhere else. What did Mr. Jessyp think?

Mr. Jessyp sighed. "We'll skip to after the beheading," he said ...

Miss Seeton recalled the impertinence of Emmy Putts, who had giggled in a very silly way and asked how much blood there was likely to be, and how much of it would be real, what with using a proper axe like Mr. Eggleden said. Miss Seeton thought back to her teaching days, and the cheekiness of some children that was rather more than ordinary high spirits. These could be suppressed by making the child in question sit on its hands, or put them on top of its head, or over its mouth. Rather like the Three Wise Monkeys—monkeys were mischievous—children were sometimes little monkeys—Emmy Putts was old enough to know better than to laugh at Mr. Jessyp—Mr. Jessyp had struggled to keep his temper ...

Without realising she did so, Miss Seeton turned to a clean page and dashed off Emmy's face in triplicate monkey posture. Emmy's hands over her mouth; Emmy with a criss-cross of sticky tape over her mouth; Emmy with a massive bandage wrapped round and round to silence her.

Miss Seeton was shocked; dismayed. This was not the behaviour one should expect from a teacher, even in thought. Blushing, she tore off the sketch, crumpled it, and tossed it in the bin. She leafed hurriedly back through her notes, and began a painstaking design for the entrance hall that could with a few embellishments double, as Mr. Jessyp had asked, for the Green Chapel where Sir Gawain was destined to meet the Green Knight in a year and a day to receive the return blow of the axe.

Delphick was working his way, yet again, through the photocopies of Miss Seeton's sketches when the telephone rang. Bob answered on his extension.

"Two birds with one stone!" cried the telephone. "Oracle, that MissEss of yours is a blooming marvel!" Bob had never known Superintendent Snowe so animated. "The drugs and the murder solved at the same time!"

It was hard to interrupt the babbling flow of congratulation, but when Snowe had to pause for breath Bob managed it. "I believe you want Chief Superintendent Delphick, sir, not me." The Oracle glanced up. Bob indicated the other telephone and, as Miss Seeton was involved, stayed listening as Snowe began to congratulate himself, the chief superintendent, the Somerset police—*I wanted to get in before Tom Faggus, but he won't be far behind*—and most of all Miss Seeton, all over again at far greater length.

"But what happened?" demanded Delphick, at last stemming the flow, pleased the two cases had been resolved but, as ever, more concerned with the kidnap of Christy Garth.

"Well, it's a shame to steal Faggus's thunder," said Snowe, "but it's my case too ..."

Chief Inspector Faggus had thought carefully over the suggestion from Scotland Yard. He talked the matter through with Sergeant Bloxham, inviting DC Hannaford to join the conference. "Associates," he explained to the detective constable. "You were at school with her, I'm told. Kept in touch, have you?"

"Not my type, sir," said Jem Hannaford quickly. "I like a quiet life."

"Ah," said Tom Faggus. "But some folk like to live dangerously. Any ideas?"

"There's a lot I hear," said Sergeant Bloxham, who prided himself on missing very little, "but it's your generation, my son. She going out with anyone these days?"

Jem concentrated. Backalong there'd been rumours—Vince Weaver had dumped Octavia, or she'd dumped him, nobody really knew—she'd been in an odd mood for a bit, then they said she'd took up with ...

"Bloke called Simon, sir." He frowned. "College friend, they say. Dunno where he lives, or much about him, but he turned up here a while since. He's around off and on, but seems the sort to keep himself to himself. One of the campervan types as don't much come into town, at a guess. Except for shopping."

"You'd recognise him? You know where he hangs out?"

"Yes, sir." Jem smothered a grin. "No, sir."

The chief inspector, to Jem's relief, grinned back. "Three bags full. Yes, daft of me. Sorry. Well, we can't hang around until he runs short of baked beans or joss sticks. Any other ideas?"

"Family, friends, acquaintances, casuals, random," chanted Sergeant Bloxham. The priority list was generally applied to murderers and their victims, but it was as good a start as any. "She went visiting her uncle in hospital the other day.

Not like our Tavy. That field of theirs hasn't been sorted yet, and the two sides of the family ain't really speaking."

"Except Val and Jan," put in DC Hannaford, "having the wool in common, like."

"Has anyone heard of Valentine Callender visiting her uncle in hospital?" Nobody had. "Or her brothers?" added the chief inspector. Further shakes of the head. "Just Octavia, then. And out of character, seemingly. So, maybe they had some urgent business that couldn't wait until he was safely home again?"

"He's home now, I heard," put in Sergeant Bloxham. "But if their urgent business was dodgy—well, I'd say that's out of character for Janner."

"It could've bin a nasty accident," said Faggus slowly. "Do no harm to check up on him, now he's home. To make sure he's got everything he needs, we could say, with that Susan being soft in the head and Jan so busy on the farm."

"Pretty thin," said Bloxham.

"You got anything better? Right, then. And you come too, young Jem."

DC Hannaford was gratified, but puzzled. "We might need a decoy," explained the chief inspector. "We'll try to talk to Janner on his own, but if it chances the Lady of the Lake's in the house with him rather than wandering about Pomparles Bridge, or if Jan should come in from the fields for a cup of tea, it'll be your job to catch 'em and stop 'em if the sergeant and I've not finished our chat."

The car bumped its way up the rutted drive to the farmhouse. In the near distance the three policemen could see a busy figure working from a pick-up truck and trailer. It must be Jan Callender, supervised by an older man leaning heavily on a stick and, with rather more energy, by a black and white collie that trotted between the two men and from time to time, bored with waiting, jumped up and snapped at the air. Jan's father had evidently set his son to checking the sheep-run fences to see which rails and hurdles must be replaced: Janner's spell in hospital would have interrupted the farming timetable, and the Callenders hadn't finished dipping all their sheep. Or perhaps hadn't even started yet.

At the approach of the police car both Callenders stopped what they were doing, waved a quick greeting, and settled back to work. The collie uttered one quick bark, but as neither master spoke, ignored the newcomers to resume his or her supervisory trot-and-snap.

A distant movement among the farm buildings caught Hannaford's eye as he turned the car towards the house. The others noticed it, too.

"Is that Susan, Brenda, whatever she calls herself?"

"If it is, she's not wearing that long white nightie. Almost looks like she's hiding."

"They got any casuals working here? The sort as might not welcome a visit from us."

"Shouldn't think so, knowing Janner." Sergeant Bloxham considered. "Jan, now, he's a bit more on the hasty side. I suppose he might chance it—but then his dad'd be sure to find out, and there'd be trouble right enough. Keeps a close rein, does Janner."

"Trespasser?" Chief Inspector Faggus climbed out of the car. "Not come back in sight, anyhow, whoever he is. Wonder if they know?"

"Wonder if they even know he's here," added Sergeant Bloxham as all three scanned the buildings for another glance of the unknown, and saw nothing.

"Eyes peeled," said Chief Inspector Faggus, making a megaphone from his hands.

His bellowed "Oy!" startled both the Callenders. The dog's head went up, but only the chief inspector noticed. Eyes peeled as instructed, the other two policemen watched the farm buildings. A swift flurry of ... something in retreat; then again, nothing.

"Oy yourself!" roared back Jan Callender, as his father waved his stick and made it plain he wasn't hurrying anywhere at anyone's beck and call.

"Keep watching," said Faggus. Through the megaphone he bellowed once more. "Just the two of you here today?"

"You got eyes in your head," yelled Jan, though after a quick word with Janner he was moving down towards the visitors, the collie in close attendance. "Can't 'ee count, then? And can't 'ee tell we're busy?"

"I saw something, sir!"

Sergeant Bloxham's fist smacked Hannaford's rising arm. "Don't point, my son. No sense letting him know he's spotted. But he's right, sir. Definitely not Susan. Youngish bloke, longish hair, beard, pale face."

"Indoors type, then," said the chief inspector, as Jan came closer.

"So what's all this?" he demanded. "If it's t'other night's dustup between me and Bill Callender you're way out of line unless that cousin of mine's sworn a complaint against me, and if he has you can tell him I'll punch even harder next time."

These words must have been audible to the shadowed skulker among the farm buildings. Faggus nodded. "We'll catch him off guard yet," he said. "Eyes peeled, remember." He raised his voice. "You going to plead guilty, then?"

Jan's face turned red, and not just from the burst of speed he now put on. "There ain't one of them Callenders—" he began, in a tone that had the collie's ears flattening; but he was now within speaking distance and Faggus was able to tell him, without raising his voice, to be quiet.

"Shut you up, Jan, we're setting a trap and doing you a favour. Unless you got lodgers you've a prowler about the place—*don't look!* But he heard us coming and did his best to hide, so we're trying to smoke him out and find why he's got a guilty conscience. Anything stolen recently? Damage to outbuildings, animals harmed, general mischief?"

"No more'n usual," said Jan, with a shrug. "Kids, at a guess."

"This one's older. Druggie of some sort, perhaps, looking for what he can pinch to sell."

"From a sheep farm?" Jan Callender was scornful. "Only stuff here worth pinching'd need wheels to carry it away, and apart from you lot we've heard no other vehicle today. And Ben's not raised the alarm." He pulled gently on the collie's ears. "Course, we've bin some way from the house, but ... You sure you ain't imagining things?"

"No," said Bloxham, whose gaze had not for an instant left the outbuildings. "Long hair, beard, pale face."

"Tried to hide when he saw us coming," said Faggus, "and hasn't made a dash for it, so he's still around. Mind if we go and find him?"

"We'll come with 'ee," said Jan. "Ben's as good as any police dog, unless it's a bloodhound, but if 'ee dunno who it is you've no scent to give a bloodhound, have 'ee?"

"Four men and a dog between 'em did ought to find anyone where he ain't meant to be," said Faggus as the five set off towards the farm buildings. "Get a bit closer and we'll spread out. Jan, you and Ben work to the left—Jem, circle to the right—the sergeant and I'll take the two middle routes on account of being not so nimble these days."

In the end, to his surprise, the chief inspector himself found the intruder, who had in his haste left clear tracks on the rungs of a ladder leading up to an unused loft space where old sacks and rusty containers had for years been stored just in case they might come in handy.

There was one small metal drum container in the general clutter that was neither rusty, nor coated with dust ...

"Something the long-hair brought with him," Delphick deduced at the end of the recital. "What was in it?"

"You'll never guess," gloated Superintendent Snowe, making the most of it. You didn't often catch the Oracle at a loss. "Go on—best of three."

Delphick looked at the photocopies of Miss Seeton's sketches, recalling the originals. "If it was an aerosol can," he began, "gas of some sort." A hot air balloon uses gas.

"Not an aerosol, more a jerry-can. Try again."

"Paint."

"Why would he want to hide a can of paint? Last go."

His idle stab at "paint" as the answer to a game Delphick, humouring Snowe, had never expected to win set up a train of oracular thought that rushed now to a wild, yet plausible, solution. Miss Seeton was involved with *Sir Gawain and the Green Knight*. Could that be the reason for the rich greens she had lavished on her study of Glastonbury Tor—the green robe in which she had depicted Octavia Callender?

Or ... "Arsenic?"

There was a stunned silence on the line. Bob, his jaw dropping, gazed in wonder at his superior. Delphick forced himself to say nothing for a moment, though his lips twitched.

"How the hell did you know?" demanded Superintendent Snowe at last.

"But you told me so yourself. 'That MissEss of yours,' you said, 'is a blooming marvel'. I certainly would not dream of contradicting you."

When Superintendent Snowe found his voice he was forcefully vocal, and the ears of his audience rang with expostulation and incredulity. Once he had grown more coherent, and Delphick had explained about Napoleon's poisonous wallpaper, famously green from its arsenic dye, he delivered the rest of the tale, to the pleasure of both Delphick and of Bob, on behalf of his adopted aunt. The conversation ended with Delphick's promise to pass on to Miss Seeton the compliments and gratitude of Chief Inspector Faggus as well as those of Superintendent Snowe.

"First, however," he decided, "I will mark on these drawings the various elements of the case, or rather cases, that no longer apply. Further study of what remains may just point us in the right direction towards finding the unfortunate Garth ..."

Miss Seeton answered the telephone in her usual manner, with a smile in her voice. "Plummergen 35. Oh. Good morning, Chief Superintendent."

Delphick was sufficiently pleased with the news he had to impart that he did not at first notice the slight constraint once she had recognised her caller. "Miss Seeton, I am delighted to advise that there will soon be another cheque in the post, and I have been instructed to pass on sincere thanks for all your help from Chief Inspector Faggus in Glastonbury, and from Superintendent Snowe who heads the Yard's drug investigations."

Miss Seeton forgot, for a moment, her unease, and thanked him before venturing to ask if she might know why, for she could think of nothing in particular she had done ...

"Except a few sketches, remember." Delphick chuckled. "As ever, Miss Seeton, you and your impressions were spot on. I regret to tell you that your bookshop acquaintance was indeed of the Lady Macbeth persuasion." Miss Seeton was shocked. "Not herself a killer," went on Delphick, "but certainly a manipulator of weaker-minded males. You said yourself that she had an excellent mind." Miss Seeton had certainly suspected as much.

"She took a first at university, and could have stayed on for a doctorate, but she was impatient. Biological science doesn't give quick results, so she opened the shop intending it as the foundation of her customer base, once she'd persuaded Simon Carfax, a college friend, to continue the drugs research she began after moving into her own premises and conducting some very private experiments. She had the idea that cannabis, which requires heat in order to flourish, might be crossed with willow, of which Somerset has an abundance. The resultant hybrid would have the best, as it were, of both species—a robust approach to the British climate plus the chemicals, including aspirin, that when combined would blow an addict's mind."

"A disgraceful waste of her education and qualifications," said the retired teacher.

"And of his. But his character was by no means as strong as hers. She was also far brighter than he, with an excellent brain, particularly for business, and an ability to prioritise and to make quick decisions. Had Octavia Callender rather than her henchman been there when Hawley Bowyer turned up unexpectedly in the course of his Zodiac hunt, she would have found it easy to fob him off with a plausible story when he entered the laboratory to get away from the rain and consult his maps and notes." Miss Seeton, recalling the dead man's purchase of several books he had not wanted, was unable to disagree with this. "Carfax, however, panicked at the sight of an intruder, and accidentally killed the poor chap. Then in further panic he had to dispose of both the body and the experimental plants, for neither of which tasks he was adequately prepared."

Miss Seeton supposed that very few people could adequately prepare themselves for such tasks, especially if they were inclined to panic under stress.

Another oracular chuckle. "You think a course of yoga might have made things easier for him? Fortunately he never undertook similar studies to your own, Miss Seeton. He was in yet another state of panic once he'd been spotted by Chief Inspector Faggus at the farm where, acting again on the orders of his lady-friend—she applied the moral force of blackmail over the murder—he was preparing to lace the sheep-dip with a dose of arsenic far greater than generally used."

"Arsenic in sheep-dip?" Once more Miss Seeton was shocked. "Surely not!"

"Oh, it's been banned now, but it was in general use for a couple of hundred years. Farmers up and down the country still have tins of the stuff in odd corners, I'm told." Delphick coughed. "I find it quite as hard as anyone must, to suppose that a deadly poison would be left just lying about, but having telephoned Rytham Hall—the Colvedens are the only sheep farmers of my acquaintance—and spoken to Sir George, I must accept it. Had I asked Nigel," he conceded, "my doubts might have continued, but Sir George was open about the fact that even he, as a magistrate, had been slower than intended in disposing of the tins, or rather drums, of banned sheep-dip. A matter of time, I understand, coupled with uncertainty as to how exactly to go about it." *Can't pour the stuff down the drain*, Sir George had said. *Kill all the fish for miles. Can't bury the drums—rust, sooner or later, and leakage. Wondered about leaving it to evaporate, but then what would happen to the powder?*

Miss Seeton agreed that she, too, would be puzzled if asked to dispose of quantities of arsenic; and farmers, of course, were always busy.

"A fact Octavia Callender used to her advantage. She visited her uncle in hospital after his accident—it was a genuine accident, but it gave her the idea—and told him he should be taking things a little easier, at his age. This, naturally, infuriated him as she intended, and he told her if she came near him again he'd chuck her in the dip along with the sheep when, as he later explained to me, if she had said nothing at all he would have asked his son to take over this year while he recuperated. I believe," he added, "she originally thought of sabotaging the tractor, but the sheep-dip was worth trying first—less effort, and less noisy, to unscrew a lid and pour in a liquid, as opposed to clattering with spanners and so forth, running the risk of being heard."

A gentlewoman is not inquisitive. Delphick knew Miss Seeton well. "As to why Octavia wanted her uncle dead," he began; and told her of the family's long-running feud, the current squabble over the field, and the approaching change in the law. Guy Callender's younger half-brother and his heirs might well (Guy's children feared) decide out of cussedness to run their sheep permanently on the field that could otherwise have been used to build a new factory ...

"It is to be regretted when families quarrel," observed Miss Seeton, whose closest relative had for many years been her mother's cousin Flora. She herself was content in her solitude, for it was not loneliness: she had friends, she had a home, she had a place in the world. But when one thought of the Colvedens, so happy together; of Martha with her brood of cockney siblings, cousins, nephews and nieces who had taken Martha's Stan to their warm hearts ... "Such a waste," mourned Miss Seeton.

"Let us hope the shock of all this will bring the Callenders to their senses, although as to the resolution of the field problem I confess myself at a loss. There was talk of arbitration and the National Farmers' Union, I believe."

"One can but hope," agreed Miss Seeton. "The loss of good farming land, of course, is likewise to be regretted."

"Nigel Colveden wouldn't approve, certainly. And wasn't it Nigel's stories about sheep that prompted some of the drawings that helped to solve the case?"

"Nigel? Oh. Those foolish pictures." The note of constraint was back. This time, Delphick heard it. In other circumstances he might have taken it for her habitual modesty about the worth of her "little scribbles" as she sometimes called them, but now he could tell there was something more than a flock of dancing sheep, or a gumbooted bishop with a bottle of Worcester sauce and a halo of sevens round his head, to embarrass her.

"Miss Seeton, what have you thrown away today?"

A little gasp. "Why, nothing, Chief Superintendent."

Miss Seeton's scrupulous honesty was almost a byword. "And yesterday?"

A little pause.

"Miss Seeton, please."

"A foolish scribble, nothing more, after last night's rehearsal when Emmy Putts was so snappish about her wig and began teasing Mr. Jessyp. Emmy is not a child, and ought to know better, but Mr. Jessyp ignored her and in the end all was well, apart from the head."

"You drew the head of Emmy Putts wearing a wig?"

"It was really Daniel Eggleden's head, but ..." A further pause. "The Three Wise Monkeys," said Miss Seeton at last. "Only instead of the three different poses it was her mouth, each time. Her hands—a criss-cross of sticking plaster—and bandages right round her head, although not to cover her eyes or her nose," she finished hastily.

"She was really a touch impertinent," she added, as Delphick said nothing. He was turning the photocopies to and fro, and thinking.

"It was Daniel Eggleden's head," she repeated. "He did his very best, and tried three times, which is, I suppose, why I saw Emmy three times, too ..."

"Miss Seeton, would you please retrieve your sketch from the bin and put it in the post? If I'm right, we may have to alter that cheque before we send it. And—thank you."

He cradled the receiver and turned to Bob. "The atlas, Sergeant Ranger. The Hereford and Worcester area, in the largest scale that fits them on one page."

Together the two pored over the area in question. "She as good as told us when we went to see her," said Delphick. "That rivers riddle—Exe, Wye, Dee. Hereford stands on the Wye. She drew a Hereford bull. And a lion—two lions, in fact—Leo-minster, even if that's not how it's pronounced. All those sevens in the bishop's halo—Worcester stands on the River Severn, and the bottle of sauce should have told us far sooner. Let us attempt a little triangulation, Bob."

"Never heard of the place." Superintendent Kebby, summoned urgently to the Oracle's office, scowled at the open atlas. "Munderfield Bishop? Talk about in the sticks. That's wild country, all right."

"Exactly. Remember what Sherlock Holmes said about the greater possibilities for evil-doing in the country, Jasper. In and around Munderfield Bishop there will be a considerable number of isolated houses and farms ideal for holding a kidnap victim prisoner."

"You said it yourself, Oracle—a considerable number. How the blazes would we know where to start looking? Even if she's right. Or you are, about what she means."

"She was right about the cannabis and the Glastonbury murder, or, if you prefer, I was right in my interpretation of her sketches. Miss Seeton has been unwontedly confused, as have I, by being asked to think about three cases at the same time; but, to quote Holmes again, when you have eliminated the impossible whatever remains, however improbable, must be the truth." Delphick brandished the photocopies. "I have eliminated from these drawings as many indications as possible towards drugs and murder, and believe I have been left with enough probable pointers to this small village, Munderfield Bishop, to suggest that closer investigation would be worthwhile."

Kebby stared at the seven-haloed bishop with his bottle of sauce, and shook his head. "Last time we asked out-of-town cops for a house-by-house search they ended up with an abandoned cannabis factory, a flock of psychotic sheep, and a murder. If I'm expected to make a fool of myself asking anybody anything that risks stirring things up like that, I need more to go on than the name of some village in the middle of nowhere."

"In the middle of a triangle formed by Hereford, Worcester, and Leominster. Moreover, Miss Seeton has developed an interest in bandages, Superintendent Kebby. The amputated finger was neatly removed, I understand; the bandaging, to judge by the photograph, is of professional standard. The indication is that someone with medical knowledge but of shaky reputation should be looked for."

"Hmph." Kebby scowled again at the atlas, then leafed once more through the sketches. Then he gave a resigned nod. "I'll phone the police in Worcester and ask 'em if they can suggest anyone. Unless you'd care to talk to 'em? After all, you're the one who started this."

"You started this, Superintendent. You asked me to ask Miss Seeton for her help."

Kebby grunted again. "All right, all right—but I'm still not convinced. I certainly won't risk telling 'em where the idea comes from, and make a blasted fool of myself when you turn out to be wrong."

"I may indeed be wrong, but I suspect Miss Seeton is not. Come now, Jasper. There's no need to say more than 'acting on information received'. You don't have to go into details. Begin with the caveat that it's a very long shot, but should the target be successfully hit there will be feathers in caps all round. My sergeant and I will, on our arrival in Worcester, add our own encouragement if required."

Bob blinked; Kebby stared.

Delphick nodded. "By the time you have talked them into consulting every local bobby for the relevant information, and that information has been obtained, we can be there to urge them on to the interviewing of likely prospects. Sergeant Ranger, you have fifteen minutes to telephone your wife, tidy your desk, and indent for a car."

Chapter Fourteen

Many city dwellers underestimate the worth of local knowledge. Delphick did not. He was confident that in three or four hours' time, depending on the traffic between Scotland Yard and Worcester, he and Bob would be presented with a comprehensive list of medical, and possibly including veterinary, practitioners of dubious repute, or upon whom some form of outside pressure could be imposed by persons of sufficient ruthlessness.

It spoke volumes for the west-of-England character that the list was so short.

"Only two?"

Superintendent Smith nodded. "Within the specified area, yes—and one of them's doubtful, depending on your exact time-frame. Kebby said the last fortnight, but this one—" he pointed with a bony finger—"was away for the first week. Spending her ill-gotten gains, at a guess." He sniffed as Delphick looked a question. "We've never been able to prove it, but for a general practitioner she seems to have more than the average number of weaklings on her books. Dodgy sick-notes at the drop of a hat, and my word they make a wonderful alibi when the chummies want to be off doing something they know we wouldn't like. You can't argue with a bad back or a sore throat. Not easy to disprove, for the likes of us, and it's never more than a few days—just long enough to rob the bank or hold up the jeweller's or steal the classy car and have it resprayed and sold on."

"And Dr. Muxworthy?"

Smith noticeably brightened. "His daughter. Seems she could be the pressure point. Betty, she was when they first arrived in the village, but she pined for the bright lights the way so many of 'em do, and off she went to London and called herself Bettina."

Delphick thought of Susan-now-Brenda Callender, and remarked that there was no law against changing one's name unless for some illegal purpose.

"Prostitution's not illegal," agreed Superintendent Smith. "But what it can lead to can be something else altogether. She started in a very small way, but like her dad she's good at her job and was, you might say, promoted. Nightclub hostessing, drink, drugs—the people she now hangs out with have some very unpleasant habits, and do their best to encourage others to share 'em."

Delphick stiffened at the mention of nightclubs and drugs. "An easy way to approach a playboy and set him up for kidnap."

Smith nodded again. "Bettina was spotted in the village a week or so back, trying not to be spotted, in a swanky car driven by a big bloke who tried even harder. All our local lad could see was dark glasses, which is why he paid attention because it was raining. Only, when the car parked at Dr. Muxworthy's and the pair of 'em went inside, he took it Betty was taking her boyfriend to ask her dad's consent, or something such."

"She might have been. Even these days it's not unknown."

"Maybe." Smith understood that it was Delphick's job to play Devil's Advocate, but he had hopes of his argument and pressed on. "Our lad saw all three of 'em drive away a bit later. Thought no more about it until we started asking. Then he remembered he'd not seen Betty or her boyfriend since that day, and the doc's been a bit quiet, which our lad put down to him not caring too much for the boyfriend, and blaming himself for the way his girl'd gone off the rails after her mother died and he couldn't face staying in Evesham and found himself a nice, quiet practice in the country."

Again Delphick had stiffened. Evesham. The Traffic Jam. Local knowledge—the girl could have recommended the ransom pick-up point ... "Perhaps we might talk to the father."

"Our lad told us the surgery hours. You could go along now, with no fear of being interrupted unless it's an emergency. You on?"

"We're on," said Delphick.

Our Lad, on discreet watch, shook with amusement at sight of the enormous Sergeant Ranger emerging from the unmarked car he'd been warned to expect. "Pity you weren't here a week or so back," he told Bob. "I thought young Betty's chap was a fair size, but you'd've scared him off without even trying, if he'd turned nasty—not that I really thought at the time there was anything wrong."

"And now you do?" Delphick hoped that hindsight wasn't reading too much into what might still have been a chance encounter.

"Wouldn't care to say one way or t'other, sir. Best thing'd be to ask the doc, I reckon."

"A good man," observed the chief superintendent as, directions obtained, they drove to the doctor's house. "Prepared to admit he might be wrong."

"Not many do," agreed his sergeant.

"Over-confident certainty," proclaimed the Oracle, "too often breeds confusion."

Bob, at the wheel, had time to spare for neither philosophy nor a neatly-turned phrase. "Yes, sir," was all he said, as he found the right house and pulled on to the empty drive.

Delphick glanced around. "Garage open, car inside—he's ready to rush off to an emergency, but currently taking the time to relax. Let us interrupt him."

Dr. Muxworthy's door was opened by a small woman with a head of dainty white curls, and quick dark eyes that looked from one man to the other, evidently trying to assess which was in search of medical attention as both appeared to be in such excellent health.

"Good afternoon," began Delphick, his open wallet in his hand. "We are—"

"If it's religion," her Scottish accent cut him short, "or encyclopaedias—"

Delphick held his warrant card more clearly under her nose. The brows above the quick dark eyes lifted in surprise, but at first she said nothing, looking past him to the unmarked police car in the drive. Her eyes widened; her shoulders drooped.

She braced herself. "Is it me or the doctor you're wanting?" she enquired, without any great conviction that she was the one they wanted.

"We'd like to see Dr. Muxworthy, please."

She sighed. "Come away in, then. I'll take you through."

As Bob wiped his feet, floorboards rattled along the hall. A latch clicked at the end of the passage and a voice called: "Is it for me, Janet?"

"Aye, Doctor. It's the police."

There was a pause that seemed to everyone too long to be mere natural curiosity. "Oh," said Dr. Muxworthy.

He was tall, thin and pale, with a hangdog expression that grew still more depressed as the giant Sergeant Ranger was introduced by Chief Superintendent Delphick and pulled out his notebook. "Oh," said the doctor again. "You'd better sit down. Thank you, Janet."

Janet closed the door firmly as she retreated.

"Dr. Muxworthy, we are from Scotland Yard and would like to ask you a few questions." Delphick's tone indicated that questions would be asked—and answers would be expected. While first impressions could, he knew, mislead, this time he was confident Miss Seeton's impressions had not. The real-life doctor of her shadowed knife-man sketch was a worried man, and had been under strain for some days, to judge by the lines on his face and the puffiness around his eyes.

"About what?" brought out Dr. Muxworthy, after another lengthy pause during which the chief superintendent allowed him to think things through.

"You might care to hazard a guess," Delphick said. "It would certainly save time."

Dr. Muxworthy's gaze shifted under the oracular stare. "Why the hurry? About what?"

"Fingers, Dr. Muxworthy."

The doctor, already pale, turned almost white, but brought out with a gasp: "Would this be a—a London pickpocket to whom you refer?"

"I think you know it wouldn't, sir. Indeed, I'm sure you know it."

Suddenly the doctor dropped his head in his hands. "Yes," he groaned. "I knew just as soon as I heard the car, and your footsteps on the gravel. I knew it must be either the police, or ... or that terrible man, returning to ask me—force me—again ..."

"To do what, sir?"

The doctor sat up and licked dry lips, tugging at a collar that seemed suddenly too small. "To—to amputate another finger from the young man being held captive in a place I don't know, and could never find again—they took very good care of that. If I didn't do as they asked, they ... They have my daughter, you see. Elizabeth. She—they had apparently employed her to lure him into the trap and then ..."

"Used your natural affection for her to force you to break your Hippocratic Oath."

Dr. Muxworthy shuddered. He looked sick. "They—he pulled her hair. He slapped her. Shook her. She screamed. It wasn't play-acting. There was a—a ferocity ... He enjoyed ill-treating my daughter, Chief Superintendent, and threatened far worse if ..."

Delphick nodded. "For the moment we will take the rest as read. A metaphorical gun was held to your head, and under duress you amputated the kidnap victim's finger."

The doctor swallowed, nodded, and whispered a guilty *Yes* before again burying his face in his hands.

"You wouldn't recognise the place where the operation was carried out, yet you weren't taken there in the dark," as Our Lad had explained, "so did they hold you somewhere until the evening, or were you blindfolded?"

"He had a real gun, Chief Superintendent. He made Betty drive the car to a quiet spot, and took off my watch. He smashed it and slipped it in my pocket. He told her to tie my hands—my thumbs—I was helpless—and then my ears were stuffed with cotton wool. A bandage was tied over my eyes. He forced me to lie down on the back seat. I have no idea how long we waited before setting off again, or how long it was before we reached ..."

There was a considerate pause, broken only by Bob's shorthand scribbling. Delphick asked at last: "You bandaged the injured hand very neatly, sir, and probably saved the young man's life by preventing his bleeding to death."

The doctor shuddered. "I treated him for shock, and gave an anti-tetanus injection. There was little else I could do apart from leave a course of penicillin, having ascertained that he was not allergic."

"He spoke to you? What else did he manage to say?"

Muxworthy shook his head. "I spoke to him. I had to, though the—though his captors were very much against it, but I had to be sure the antibiotics would be safe for him to take. They warned me to speak on nothing but medical matters, and told him to say nothing at all. He could shake his head or nod in reply to my questions. Only that."

Delphick reflected that the Sherlock Holmes analogy had returned: this was becoming a cross between *The Greek Interpreter* and *The Engineer's Thumb*. "You saw nothing of your route," he mused aloud. "You had no idea of how long, or in which direction, you travelled. You could see nothing of the place beyond, I gather, the one room in which you performed the operation." Dr. Muxworthy confirmed this supposition with a weary nod.

"They must have removed the ear-plugs to give you your instructions. What could you hear, when they did? Were you on a farm, in a town, close to a railway or a busy road?"

"They had a cassette recorder playing rock and roll very loudly, just by the door."

"You could make out no other sounds at all?"

The doctor sighed. "They took very good care I should know nothing. Cotton wool doesn't make a totally efficient seal, but it muffles and distorts whatever you hear, as well as disturbing the sense of balance. It was difficult to think of much beyond walking without tumbling down."

"They couldn't stop you breathing. What could you smell? Petrol fumes, agricultural deposits, unusual chemicals, rotting fruit—yes?" as Muxworthy frowned.

"Aftershave," he said. "They sprayed it on my clothes, my face—they even soaked my surgical mask in the stuff."

"Yet something about fruit caught your attention just now."

"Did it? Yes, I remember now ... It was wasps. Wasps or bees. As I left the car, before I was taken into the house, there was a great deal of buzzing in the air, uncomfortably close to me—I felt the vibration of their wings as they passed—and an outbreak of hand-flapping on the part of my guards—I was pulled about, and almost fell—quite the wrong thing to do if you don't want to be stung, but a natural instinct, of course. If anyone was stung I can't say. I heard no outcry, but the—the swarming behaviour seems to have taken my ... captors by surprise. They did not realise, perhaps, that the aftershave might attract unwelcome visitors as well as blocking my sense of smell."

Delphick thought carefully. "Have you heard anything from your daughter since then?"

"One photograph."

"With a newspaper headline and date clearly visible, and a warning that if you discuss the matter with the authorities she will suffer?"

"Yes," said the doctor, too exhausted to ask how he knew.

"You are discussing the matter now with a senior police officer," Delphick pointed out.

"I've hardly slept and barely eaten since it happened, Chief Superintendent. I'm too tired to think up convincing lies to cover ... what I did to that poor young man. My daughter is dear to me as all that remains to me of my late wife, but Betty ... made her choices. The young man ... did not choose to be a prisoner. My first duty, as a doctor, is to my patient. If I can, in any way, help you to find him ... then it might compensate in some small manner for my previous regrettable lapse in the matter of the Hippocratic Oath."

"You can bring him in for a detailed chat any time you wish," Delphick told Superintendent Smith. "He won't put up a fight."

"Our lad can keep an eye on him in case he does a bunk," said Smith. "Or in case he has any more visitors."

"Unlikely, I suspect." Delphick unfolded the Ordnance Survey map showing Munderfield Bishop and surrounding areas. "He's not a professional crook. They would guess he'd find it hard to keep quiet if we tracked him down, which after the amputation would logically be our next step. We must hope they consider the precautions taken to disorient him will hinder if not prevent our working out where Christy Garth is being held—with, or without, Betty Muxworthy, whose involvement would appear to be of an ambiguous nature."

"She seems to have lured the poor bloke into a trap easily enough," said Smith. "Then she gets bashed about, and her dad thinks the basher really meant it—a trap that backfired, you reckon?"

"A fake kidnapping turned into reality," agreed the man from Scotland Yard, hiding a quiet smile. "As was suggested by a reliable source very early in this case." He heard Bob, adopted nephew to the reliable source, smother a cough. "But her father, sadly for Miss Bettina, has the right of it. Our first duty is to find and rescue Garth: if in the process we can also rescue the young woman, we must consider that a bonus."

"Cold-blooded blighter," said Smith.

"Practical," amended the Oracle, studying the map. "We have more clues to Christy's whereabouts than to hers. How many dog handlers are there in this district?"

It was an unexpected change of subject. Superintendent Smith had to think. "Two here in Worcester, if you mean police dogs," he said. "There are guard dogs at various commercial properties—scrap yards, that kind of thing— but you don't mean them, I think."

"I don't," Delphick agreed. "Does anyone in these parts sell honey?" The Traffic Jam: that unexpected jar in Miss Seeton's lively cartoon ...

Smith was a local man, and this time did not need to think. "Any number of people. This area is noted for its fruit farms and hops. Every other housewife has a hive or two in the garden and a notice on the gate."

"Larger scale than that, and for preference within an easy drive of Dr. Muxworthy."

The superintendent frowned. "I seem to remember ... Yes, they made local news a bit back—oh, not in our line," he enlarged as Delphick regarded him with interest. "A family squabble over the family farm. Soft fruit, a few flowers, apples. They tried cider but couldn't make a go of it. They moved into honey and changed the name of the place to Melissa Products—odd, when the wife's called Deborah. Second wife, which was why they hit the headlines. Father died unexpectedly, the widow and children argued over the inheritance because she claimed the honey was all her idea. Then it turned out there were tax problems he'd kept quiet about during the divorce. First wife reappeared to spill some financial beans, things got messy and they ended up having to sell. The place is rented out now while the legal bods try to tidy things up."

"The land is rented out," said Delphick. "Does the same apply to the house?"

"I'd have to check, but so far as I know the place is empty."

"Or," said Delphick, studying the map, "is it?"

At Delphick's request, Christy Garth's finger was briefly removed from cold storage for a sample of blood to be dabbed on a piece of cotton wool taken, using forceps, from a fresh packet, and immediately sealed in plastic to avoid contamination.

Only one police dog was available that day: Sancho, an enthusiastic cross-breed almost as large as his handler. PC Markham had cheated official height regulations by wearing insoles and standing on tiptoe at the appropriate

259

moment during his recruitment interview. He was obviously keen, and the police doctor on duty had a kind heart. Panza, the senior dog, with his handler and a selection of uniformed officers was waiting outside a bank into which a posse of armed men in stocking masks had stampeded two hours earlier. It was market day; the streets were busy; the operation was likely to take some time.

"So you pair will have to do," said Superintendent Smith. Fergus Markham beamed. It would be his first solo outing. Sancho had twice been put back in his training. The dog had qualified at last; the new partnership's chance had finally come.

A small party set out from Worcester for Munderfield Bishop and the former premises of Melissa Products. Delphick explained, as they went, that "Melissa" was the Latin word for "bee" just as "Deborah" was the Hebrew equivalent. Superintendent Smith remarked that it was no wonder the deceased farmer's children had found their stepmother a hard nut to crack. "If she's clever enough to go in for that sort of wordplay she's clever enough to find the best lawyers. It could drag on for years."

Checks with lawyers on each side of the dispute confirmed that officially the property was empty. No caretaker was employed: the place was too far off the beaten track for any but the most determined burglar to break in. The family thought that a burglar so determined would break in whether or not a caretaker was present. It was the one point on which every litigant seemed to agree.

"Saving their money to pay the legal bods," said Smith, leading the way with Delphick and Ranger. PC Markham, Sancho, and three uniformed officers were in the car behind.

"And perhaps a false economy," said Delphick absently. He was thinking back through Miss Seeton's sketches, applying the most relevant to his mental map of the area to which the party was heading, and finding as yet nothing amiss with his deductions.

He hoped.

"At the T junction," the superintendent reminded driver Ranger, "we go left, they go right." He gesticulated over his shoulder as Bob flicked the indicator. The driver behind waved acknowledgement, indicated in his turn, and the two vehicles set off in what for several hundred yards were two totally opposite directions, before further turns and twists would bring them, by a circular route, to the distant outskirts of Munderfield Bishop.

A cautious pincer movement had been decided upon. The sealed plastic bag of blood-stained cotton wool was in PC Markham's pocket as, licking his finger, he made sure of the wind direction and began working his steady way towards the house in which—its curtains closed, its doors shut, its chimneys smokeless—it seemed not a soul was in residence.

But there were fresh tyre tracks at the entrance to the long, winding drive where a five-barred gate sagged open on its hinges. "Not just someone lost and reversing to turn round," murmured Superintendent Smith, pulling the walkie-talkie from his pocket.

"Gone up and not recently come back." Delphick likewise murmured, though the farmhouse was well out of earshot. He and Bob studied the ground. Two vehicles, both saloon or estate cars rather than anything larger.

"I don't think they'd see us from the house if we shut the gate, sir," offered Bob.

Delphick looked at Superintendent Smith. "If they're there," said Smith, "then probably they couldn't. But they might hear the noise. Those hinges look dodgy."

Bob flexed willing muscles. He knew he could lift the battered gate easily without letting it scrape along the ground, but Delphick held up a warning hand.

"Count the tyre marks again, Sergeant Ranger." The Oracle was as ever scrupulous about addressing Bob in public. "Can we be absolutely sure one of them hasn't gone out to buy groceries? He might return, spot the ambush, and make a bolt for it." The police car, unmarked as it was, had been left concealed behind a hedge in a nearby field.

As Superintendent Smith again muttered into his radio, Delphick kept watch while Bob did as instructed. "I'd say they're both in there," he said at last. The Oracle nodded.

"I would agree, but we can't be too careful. What do you say, Smith?"

"It wouldn't do the cars any good to smash through a farm gate, but they might still get away. If they're in there, I'd rather try the old potato trick to stop 'em before they start."

"Ah," said Delphick with relish.

Bob's eyes gleamed. "Haven't thought of that in years, sir. Good idea."

Smith grinned. "Born and bred in these parts, me. Not one of your city slickers. The tricks we played as kids ..."

"How perverse of this farm to grow fruit rather than vegetables," said Delphick.

Smith was determined to show these Scotland Yarders he was no country bumpkin. "A large apple would do, but they might spot us from the house if we go apple-picking. A stick and some cloth, or a thick wodge of grass, will do just as well."

Once more he addressed the walkie-talkie, while Delphick continued to keep watch and Bob scanned the hedgerows for a likely stick and grass of sufficient length to muffle the car exhaust, when the time came.

"Markham's in position," announced Superintendent Smith. "Start moving in," he told the walkie-talkie, and led the way, listening, reporting what was needful to know. "He says, still no signs of life, but now he's letting Sancho take the scent ... The dog seems excited ... Nose to ground, tracking ... Heading for the front door—says he'll wait until—"

A loud bark. Frantic shushing. The twitch of an upstairs curtain.

"Damn!" said Superintendent Smith. "Okay, everyone—go, *go*, GO!"

They ran: Delphick, Bob and Smith up the drive, the trio of uniformed support closing from the back of the house. The superintendent thumped on the front door as someone else thumped at the back. "Police! Open up!" came simultaneous cries. Delphick checked the windows, wary of curtain-twitchers who might be armed. Bob, gauging the strength of the door, found he still clutched the stick and the wodge of grass. He threw away the stick and looked at Delphick.

"Window, sir?" he said, and without waiting strode to the nearest casement, thrust the grass against it, and drove an elbow through. Splinters caught in curtains as cries of alarm arose from further inside the house. Bob's arm swept in a mighty arc to push back the curtains along the rail, then he flung himself over the window sill.

Delphick and Smith were quick to follow; Sancho was quicker still. PC Markham, as the action began, had let his dog off the leash and Sancho, the abandoned stick in his jaws, now leaped between the two policemen straight into the room and landed, tail wagging, on all four paws. He raised his head, sniffed, and charged, nails clattering on bare boards, out of the room, into the hall, and up the stairs.

There came further cries, angry shouts, screams for help and shrieks as the confusion spread. Fergus Markham forgot rank and pushed aside his superiors to follow his dog, who was bouncing up and down uttering muffled barks outside a bedroom door that otherwise looked identical to the other half-dozen on the landing.

"Police!" cried PC Markham, as Sancho bounced faster. "Open up!"

Other doors opened, figures emerged, fists flew—*not armed, thank heaven* thought Delphick—and a general commotion ended with Bob Ranger banging heads together as the three uniformed men scooped up the fallen and made sure they fell again, to be set in an untidy row along the wall while Delphick (who had stuck out a helpfully tripping foot as required) and Smith (who swung a powerful and efficient fist) joined PC Markham in breaking down Sancho's door.

Inside they found a figure handcuffed to the bed. Sancho, bursting with pride, jumped on the bed, landed on the figure's stomach, and dropped the stick on his chest.

For what he later told the authorities was the first time in days, Christy Garth smiled.

"Miss Seeton?" The telephone was apologetic, and embarrassed. "Martin Jessyp here." The schoolmaster coughed. "You've heard nothing from Lady Colveden? Or from anyone else on the Padders committee?"

Miss Seeton was likewise embarrassed. She had heard from nobody; she was sorry she had been unable to deliver the scenery sketches, but she had been rather delayed by her sketches for the police, which, as she believed Mr. Jessyp knew, she was duty bound to make her priority. "But I heard from Chief Superintendent Delphick today, and he tells me everything is happily resolved, so it will not be long now," she promised.

A gentlewoman does not discuss matters involving money. There was no need to tell Mr. Jessyp that Mr. Delphick had assured her there would soon be a fresh cheque from the Scotland Yard computer; of how the chief superintendent had teased her by saying that perhaps she might also have another win on her Premium Bonds, and take yet another holiday somewhere else, with a flight in another hot air balloon, in search of other invisible landscape figures ...

"I'm pleased to hear that," said Mr. Jessyp, "and I regret having to dampen the mood, but I, ah, bring bad news, Miss Seeton. It's Daniel Eggleden's head."

"Has the poor man met with an accident?" Miss Seeton well remembered the time an alcohol-fuelled carthorse had kicked the blacksmith and injured his bowling arm, just before Plummergen's needle match against Murreystone's cricket team.

"No, no." Mr. Jessyp was flustered. "I should have said, the Green Knight's head. Try as we might, we cannot make the illusion work as intended. The difference, I fear, between theory and practice. But as the whole point is for Sir Gawain to cut off the knight's head with one blow, and to receive a blow in return ..." He took a deep breath. "The Padders have reconsidered the Christmas play," he confessed. "With a large green man and his castle already arranged—the costume, the scenery, the axe—they have decided to unearth an old production of *Jack and the Beanstalk* instead."

"Oh," said Miss Seeton. No wonder Mr. Jessyp was upset: so much of his hard work gone to waste. And yet one should always try to make the best of things ...

"*Jack and the Beanstalk* will be far more in the pantomime spirit than King Arthur," she said. "I feel sure Jack Crabbe, so very clever, will add most suitable jokes and riddles to your script."

"He's already hard at work," said Martin Jessyp, much relieved at the way she was taking it. So much of her own hard work gone to waste ... "As we know that you yourself have been, Miss Seeton, on behalf of the Green Knight and King Arthur's court. We don't really like asking you to put yourself out again, but ..."

"Anything I can do to help, Mr. Jessyp, I assure you I will happily do."

"Miss Armitage and her team have repaired the costume as well as they can, but Nigel Colveden and Len Hosigg are to play the front and back legs of Daisy the Cow. They are both young men of great energy and enthusiasm—and after last night's scratch rehearsal, Nigel needs a new head. The children will of course build it in Miss Maynard's handicraft class, but would you be able—willing—to design it for us?"

Miss Seeton's first drawing showed a wide-horned Highland cow bearing a sword in its mighty mouth, supervised by a large tabby cat in a mask. She attributed her confusion to memories of Glastonbury prompted by Mr. Delphick's talk of a second balloon flight.

Her Friesian cow, however, was perfect.

Preview

Watch the Wall, Miss Seeton

Lucky Miss Seeton! A modest Premium Bond win means a whole week in legendary Glastonbury. She can draw and drink in the surroundings, just what she needs for her scene-painting role in the village production of 'Camelot'.

By coincidence, the kidnapped Heir to an industrial family may be hidden around there and Chief Superintendent Delphick has asked the ex-art teacher to create some of her famous, insightful sketches. Even he is nonplussed by the resulting images of capering sheep in straitjackets, flashing false teeth!

But the Heir is in danger, a murderer is lurking, and the first victim may not be the last. Then fortune favours Miss S again, her raffle ticket winning her a hot air balloon flight, and well, it's just amazing what you can see from above . . .

The new Miss Seeton mystery

COMING SOON!

About the Miss Seeton series

Retired art teacher Miss Seeton steps in where Scotland Yard
stumbles. Armed with only her sketch pad and umbrella, she is
every inch an eccentric English spinster and at every turn the
most lovable and unlikely master of detection.

Further titles in the series—

Picture Miss Seeton
A night at the opera strikes a chord of danger
when Miss Seeton witnesses a murder . . . and paints
a portrait of the killer.

Miss Seeton Draws the Line
Miss Seeton is enlisted by Scotland Yard when her
paintings of a little girl turn the young subject into a
model for murder.

Witch Miss Seeton
Double, double, toil and trouble sweep through
the village when Miss Seeton goes undercover . . .
to investigate a local witches' coven!

Miss Seeton Sings
Miss Seeton boards the wrong plane and lands
amidst a gang of European counterfeiters. One
false note, and her new destination
is deadly indeed.

Odds on Miss Seeton
Miss Seeton in diamonds and furs at the roulette table?
It's all a clever disguise for the high-rolling spinster . . . but
the game of money and murder is all too real.

Miss Seeton, By Appointment
Miss Seeton is off to Buckingham Palace on a secret
mission—but to foil a jewel heist, she must risk losing the
Queen's head . . . and her own neck!

Advantage, Miss Seeton
Miss Seeton's summer outing to a tennis match serves up more than expected when Britain's up-and-coming female tennis star is hounded by mysterious death threats.

Miss Seeton at the Helm
Miss Seeton takes a whirlwind cruise to the Mediterranean—bound for disaster. A murder on board leads the seafaring sleuth into some very stormy waters.

Miss Seeton Cracks the Case
It's highway robbery for the innocent passengers of a motor coach tour. When Miss Seeton sketches the roadside bandits, she becomes a moving target herself.

Miss Seeton Paints the Town
The Best Kept Village Competition inspires Miss Seeton's most unusual artwork—a burning cottage—and clears the smoke of suspicion in a series of local fires.

Hands Up, Miss Seeton
The gentle Miss Seeton? A thief? A preposterous notion—until she's accused of helping a pickpocket . . . and stumbles into a nest of crime.

Miss Seeton by Moonlight
Scotland Yard borrows one of Miss Seeton's paintings to bait an art thief . . . when suddenly *a second* thief strikes.

Miss Seeton Rocks the Cradle
It takes all of Miss Seeton's best instincts—maternal and otherwise—to solve a crime that's hardly child's play.

Miss Seeton Goes to Bat
Miss Seeton's in on the action when a cricket game leads to mayhem in the village of Plummergen . . . and gives her a shot at smashing Britain's most baffling burglary ring.

Miss Seeton Plants Suspicion
Miss Seeton was tending her garden when a local youth was arrested for murder. Now she has to find out who's really at the root of the crime.

Starring Miss Seeton
Miss Seeton's playing a backstage role in the village's annual Christmas pantomime. But the real drama is behind the scenes . . . when the next act turns out to be murder!

Miss Seeton Undercover
The village is abuzz, as a TV crew searches for a rare apple, the Plummergen Peculier—while police hunt a murderous thief . . . and with Miss Seeton at the centre of it all.

Miss Seeton Rules
Royalty comes to Plummergen, and the villagers are plotting a grand impression. But when Princess Georgina goes missing, Miss Seeton herself has questions to answer.

Sold to Miss Seeton
Miss Seeton accidentally buys a mysterious antique box at auction . . . and finds herself crossing paths with some very dangerous characters!

Sweet Miss Seeton
Miss Seeton is stalked by a confectionary sculptor, just as a spate of suspicious deaths among the village's elderly residents calls for her attention.

Bonjour, Miss Seeton
After a trip to explore the French countryside, a case of murder awaits Miss Seeton back in the village . . . and a shocking revelation.

Miss Seeton's Finest Hour
War-time England, and a young Miss Emily Seeton's suspicious sketches call her loyalty into question—until she is recruited to uncover a case of sabotage.

Miss Seeton Quilts the Village
Miss Seeton lends her talents to the village scheme to create a giant quilted tapestry. But her intuitive sketches reveal a startlingly different perspective, involving murder.

About Heron Carvic
and Hamilton Crane

The Miss Seeton series was created by Heron Carvic; and continued after his death first by Peter Martin writing as Hampton Charles, and later by Sarah J. Mason under the pseudonym Hamilton Crane.

Heron Carvic was an actor and writer, most recognisable today for his voice portrayal of the character Gandalf in the first BBC Radio broadcast version of *The Hobbit,* and appearances in several television productions, including early series of *The Avengers* and *Dr Who.*

Born Geoffrey Richard William Harris in 1913, he held several early jobs including as an interior designer and florist, before developing a successful dramatic career and his public persona of Heron Carvic. He only started writing the Miss Seeton novels in the 1960s, after using her in a short story. Heron Carvic died in a car accident in Kent in 1980.

Hamilton Crane is the pseudonym used by Sarah J. Mason when writing 15 sequels and one prequel to the Miss Seeton series. She has also written detective fiction under her own name, but should not be confused with the Sarah Mason (no middle initial) who writes a rather different kind of book.

After half a century in Hertfordshire (if we ignore four years in Scotland and one in New Zealand), Sarah J. Mason now lives in Somerset—within easy reach of the beautiful city of Wells, and just far enough from Glastonbury to avoid the annual traffic jams.

Note from the Publisher

While he was alive, series creator Heron Carvic had tremendous fun imagining Emily Seeton and the supporting cast of characters.

In an enjoyable 1977 essay Carvic recalled how, after having first used her in three short stories, "Miss Seeton upped and demanded a book"—and that if "she wanted to satirize detective novels in general and elderly lady detectives in particular, he would let her have her head …"

You can now **read one of those first Miss Seeton short stories** and **Heron Carvic's essay in full**, as well as receive updates on further releases in the series, by signing up at farragobooks.com/miss-seeton-signup

Printed in Great Britain
by Amazon